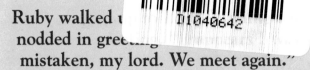

Ruby walked ... nodded in gree... mistaken, my lord. We meet again."

He pulled himself out of his reverie and bowed. "Miss Hollingsford. A pleasure to see you again, particularly as you are not a dead body."

Ruby couldn't help chuckling. "I suppose I deserved that after my remark by the bridge. You may have noticed that I have a temper. I also tend to speak my mind."

"Really?" he said, though she could see the twinkle in those purple-blue eyes.

"Surprising, isn't it? And given that tendency, allow me to make something clear." She leaned forward and met him gaze for gaze. "I meant what I said at the river. I'm not here for a proposal."

"Excellent," he replied, unflinching. "Neither am I."

Ruby frowned as she leaned back, but her father came out of his room just then, and the earl excused himself to start down the stairs ahead of them.

There had to be a reason she and her father had been included in the earl's invitation. But for the life of her, she couldn't understand why.

Books by Regina Scott

Love Inspired Historical

The Irresistible Earl
An Honorable Gentleman
The Rogue's Reform
The Captain's Courtship
The Rake's Redemption
The Heiress's Homecoming
†*The Courting Campaign*
†*The Wife Campaign*

*The Everard Legacy
†The Master Matchmakers

REGINA SCOTT

started writing novels in the third grade. Thankfully for literature as we know it, she didn't actually sell her first novel until she learned a bit more about writing. Since her first book was published in 1998, her stories have traveled the globe, with translations in many languages, including Dutch, German, Italian and Portuguese.

She and her husband of over twenty-five years reside in southeast Washington State with their overactive Irish terrier. Regina Scott is a decent fencer, owns a historical costume collection that takes up over a third of her large closet, and she is an active member of the Church of the Nazarene. You can find her online blogging at www.nineteenteen.blogspot.com. Learn more about her at www.reginascott.com, or connect with her on Facebook at www.facebook.com/authorreginascott.

The Wife Campaign

REGINA SCOTT

HARLEQUIN® LOVE INSPIRED® HISTORICAL

Recycling programs
for this product may
not exist in your area.

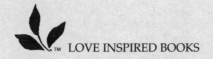 LOVE INSPIRED BOOKS

ISBN-13: 978-0-373-82992-7

THE WIFE CAMPAIGN

Copyright © 2013 by Regina Lundgren

www.Harlequin.com

Printed in U.S.A.

For faith is being sure of what we hope for
and certain of what we do not see.
—*Hebrews* 11:1

To my own Earl, for all your advice about fishing.
May you one day catch the King of Trout.
And to my King, for opening his arms to catch me.

Chapter One

Fern Lodge, Peak District, Derbyshire, England
July 1815

Ruby Hollingsford threw herself out of a moving coach.

There was little danger—it hadn't been moving very fast, the carriage slowing to take the gracefully arching bridge over the River Bell. And her father should have expected it. How else was she to react to his cork-brained, ninnyhammer of an idea?

I know I told you we were going to Castleton for business, her father, Mortimer Hollingsford, had said. *But the truth is, the Earl of Danning has taken a fancy to you.*

Ruby's temper had flared like a match to oil. *Not another aristocrat! I told you I'd have none of them!*

He'd pulled a gilded invitation from the travel desk on the leather-upholstered seat beside him and held it out to her with a commiserating smile. *Oh, he's a fine fellow. I asked about him. He's never invited a lady to his Lodge before. You behave for once, and your future will be secure.*

If she had taken that note, she'd have torn it to shreds her hands had been shaking so hard. *My future? Why would my future need to be titled? If you want a title so much, you marry one.*

And then she'd bunched her skirts with one hand, wrenched open the door with the other and jumped.

She landed on the verge of the road, her ankles protesting, then gathered herself to stand. Behind her, she could hear Davis calling to the horses as he reined them in.

"Ruby!" her father shouted after her. "Oh, come now!"

In answer, she ran down the grassy embankment for the river's pebbled edge.

Really, what else was she to do after such an announcement? She'd thought her father couldn't shock her any further after she'd discovered an elderly viscount— an utter stranger to her—lounging in her withdrawing room, waiting to propose. After that, she had learned to be on her guard from her father's future attempts, which thus far had been many and varied. What wastrel aristocrat in the vicinity of London didn't leap to do her father's bidding when he dangled her sizeable dowry? But to drag her all the way out to the wilds of Derbyshire, to make up a Banbury tale of business up north? That was the outside of enough.

Her father must have signaled Davis to continue, for their coachman gave the horses their heads, taking the carriage farther along the road. Very likely he was looking for a place wide enough to turn the coach and team and come back for her.

But she wasn't ready to face her father, not when she was in such a temper. He'd always said there was a reason she'd inherited her mother's sleek red hair and catlike green eyes. They were a warning to beware. A shame her father didn't heed them.

Shaking out the folds of her wine-colored pelisse, she marched down the riverbank, gaze on the speckled stones to keep from tripping. But despite her efforts to calm herself, the anger bubbling up inside her found its way out of her mouth.

"Doesn't bother to tell the truth, oh, no, not him." She detoured around a leafy shrub overhanging the shore. "'Think of it as a holiday, Ruby,' he says. 'A chance to see the sights.' I'll give him a sight—my back as I head for London!"

Someone coughed.

Ruby's head jerked up, heart ramming against her ribs. She pulled herself to a stop to avoid colliding with a tall man who stood on the riverbank, blocking her way forward. "Oh!"

Her first thought was to run. Even in skirts and on a rocky shore she ought to be able to beat him to the road. But what help would she find there? All that remained of her coach was the dust lingering in the summer air.

As if he knew her fears, the man before her held up his hands to prove he meant no harm. Indeed, now that she looked closer, he didn't appear particularly dangerous. His thick hair was not quite as bright gold as a guinea and neatly combed about his head despite the breeze that followed the stream down the dale. And his eyes were perfect for Derby: they matched the swirling combination of purple and blue found in the fabled Blue John stones native to the area that her father sold in his jewelry shop. His clean-shaven face was firmly molded like the alabaster statues her father imported, body tall and strong.

In fact, the only things about him that weren't first-rate were his clothes, which consisted of scuffed, water-stained boots, corduroy breeches and a wool waistcoat over a linen shirt. He probably wasn't even a second son, much less a selfish, self-absorbed aristocrat like she was sure to find in the Earl of Danning, who thought he could summon a gentlewoman he'd never met to Derby with a perfunctory note. With his head cocked and that smile on his handsome face, he looked as if he wanted nothing more than to help her.

However, looks could be deceiving, as she knew to her sorrow.

"Forgive me for intruding," he said. "May I be of assistance?"

Nice voice—warm, earnest. Nice manners. She still didn't trust him.

"I don't need assistance," she said, using a tone that brooked no argument. "My carriage will return for me any moment." As her boxing instructor had taught her, she positioned her feet in a preparatory stance, one forward, one back, and held her arms loosely at her sides. She was tall for a woman, and she was fairly sure that if the situation called for it, she could hit that perfectly formed nose of his with sufficient force to make him think twice about pursuit.

He glanced at the road as if considering how quickly the coach would return. "I'm glad to hear you have an escort." His voice betrayed his doubts.

She could only wish for an escort, but she'd failed to even snatch up her reticule and the pistol it contained when she'd jumped, worse luck!

Perhaps if she explained her circumstances, this fellow would be less likely to think her easy prey. She waved a hand to the north, where the coach had been heading, and hoped there truly was a lodge somewhere about, close enough that someone might hear her if she had to scream. "Oh, they'll all be looking for me. I'm to attend a fortnight's house party in the area."

He frowned. "I didn't realize His Grace had returned, much less begun entertaining."

His Grace! Her temper thrust past her logic once more, and she threw up her hands. "Oh! My father said he was an earl! Another lie!"

A shadow flickered past his face, and he bent as if to keep her from seeing it. For the first time, Ruby noticed a long wooden rod lying at his booted feet. His fingers closed around it and tugged it up before the lapping water pulled it in. "I'm sorry, madam, but the only earl in this area is the Earl of Danning, and he isn't entertaining."

Ruby made a face as he straightened. "That bad, is he?"

He chuckled, one hand on the rod, which rose even above his considerable height. "Not really. I've even heard him called affable. What I meant is that he doesn't come here to entertain." He nodded toward the river. "He comes to fish."

"Really?" She gazed at the swirling green waters as they leaped over stones, chattered past mossy boulders. Hard to imagine a puffed-up aristocrat willingly standing by a stream, angling for his dinner. Could there be more to this earl than the other nobs she'd met? Her look swung back to him. "How well do you know him?"

He hesitated, then shrugged. "Reasonably well."

Such a cautious response. Was he a servant of his lordship and feared retribution if he gossiped? Was the Earl of Danning a vengeful man? She had no wish to put this kind man at risk, but she had to use the opportunity to learn more about the earl who had somehow taken a shine to her. She stepped closer. "Is it true he's looking for a wife?"

He recoiled, eyes widening. "What?"

She smiled sweetly and repeated her question, enunciating each word with care. "Is. He. Looking. For a wife?"

He frowned at her, and it struck her that he probably thought she was bent on pursuing a title. Ruby shuddered at the idea.

"Forgive me for speaking so plainly," she said. "Please understand, I'm not after him. I'd like nothing better than for you to assure me that he is old and fat and quite set in his ways, sworn never to wed."

A muscle worked in his cheek as if he were fighting a smile. "He just reached his thirtieth year, and I believe some would consider him reasonably fit. However, I can promise you he is not actively seeking a bride."

Relief coursed through her. All that worry, for nothing! But then, who'd sent the invitation? Oh! Not another prank! Far too many aristocrats of her acquaintance found juvenile amusement in reminding her and her father of their "place" in Society. She had learned to ignore their petty jokes, but her father still hoped for the best in them. When would he learn that interaction with the upper class led to nothing but heartache?

Her would-be rescuer was still regarding her as if not quite sure what to do with her. Ruby smiled at him.

"How rude of me," she said, sticking out her hand. "Ruby Hollingsford. And you are?"

"Whitfield Calder," he supplied, taking her hand and inclining his head over it as if he were honoring her. She liked that he was taller than she was. She was growing decidedly weary of looking down onto balding crowns when she danced.

Ruby beamed at him as he released her hand. "And apparently you and the earl have something in common. You like to fish, too. I'm very sorry to have interrupted you."

He smiled. For some reason, she thought he was rusty at smiling. Perhaps it was how slowly his lips lifted. Perhaps it was the way his golden lashes veiled his eyes. Had he seen tragedy then?

"It was no trouble," he assured her, bending to retrieve a tweed coat and shrugging in his broad shoulders. "Allow me to escort you back to the bridge. A lady should not be left alone."

Ruby started to protest. For one, she wasn't considered a lady by the standards of the upper class. She was merely the daughter of a cit, a merchant, if a happily wealthy one. For another, if she could protect herself on the streets of London as she'd been forced to do as a child, surely she could take care of herself on a remote road in Derby.

Yet he seemed so sincere, and so charming, as he offered her his arm, that she decided to let him think he was taking care of her. "How kind," she said, linking her arm with his.

But as he walked slowly, carefully, putting his hand on her elbow and helping her over every little bump in the uneven ground, Ruby felt her charity with him slipping. Did he think her so frail that she couldn't keep up if he walked his normal pace, or so clumsy that she'd trip over a stone? She might have been wearing a velvet pelisse with lace dripping at the cuffs, but her boots were sturdy black leather. Hadn't he noticed that she'd already crossed the distance, at a run part of the way, with no need to lean on his manly arm?

As the ground rose sharply to the road, she broke

away from him and lifted her skirts with both hands
to complete the climb. Still, she felt him hovering, as
if he expected her to take a tumble any second. When
they reached the top, he positioned himself beside her,
keeping her safely between him and the stone column
of the bridge head. His deep blue gaze flickered from
the road winding up the hill to the copse of trees across
from them to the bridge, as if he expected a highway-
man to leap from hiding. Concern radiated out of him
like heat from a hearth.

What sort of man took such responsibility for a
woman he'd known less than a quarter hour? What
would he say if he knew she'd taken boxing lessons
and could shoot the heart from an ace at fifty paces?

"Do you have sisters or a wife," she asked, bemused,
"that you're so mindful of a lady's safety?"

Again something crossed behind his watchful gaze.
"Alas, no. I'm not married, and I'm an only child. My
parents died many years ago now."

An orphan. Instantly her heart went out to him.

The crunch of gravel and the jingle of tack told her a
coach was approaching, and she could only hope it was
her father's. Sure enough, Davis brought the carriage
around the bend and pulled the horses to a stop beside
her and her handsome stranger, wrapping them in dust.

Her father lowered the window and scowled at them.
"Leave you alone for ten minutes and look what you
drag up," he complained. "Are we hiring him or pay-
ing him off?"

Ruby's cheeks heated as she waved her hand to clear
the air. Though her father's long face and sharp nose
gave him a stern appearance, he was more bark than
bite. The man beside her didn't know that, of course,

but he stepped closer to her instead of backing away in dismay.

"This man was very kind to wait with me," Ruby explained. She turned to find her hero frowning as if he wasn't sure he was leaving her in reliable hands. She could understand his concern. The coach was more serviceable than elegant, the team of horses unmatched except in strength. Even the two servants sitting behind looked common in their travel dirt. Nothing said that the master was one of the richest merchants in London. Her father was careful where he spent his money.

He was equally careful of her. "Well, wasn't that nice of him?" he said. "And what did you expect in return, fellow?"

Mr. Calder inclined his head. "Merely the opportunity to be of service to a lady. If you have no further need of me, Miss Hollingsford, I wish you good day."

"I'll be fine, Mr. Calder," Ruby replied, suddenly loath to see the last of him. "Know that I appreciate your kindness."

He took her hand and bowed over it, and Ruby was surprised to find herself a bit unsteady as he released her.

Her father must have noticed a change in her, for he leaned out the window. "Calder, did you say? And your first name?"

"Whitfield, sir," he said with a polite nod.

Her father's narrow face broke into a grin. "Whitfield, eh? Very good to meet you, my lord."

"My lord?" Ruby stared at him, heart sinking.

Mr. Calder, who had seemed so nice until that moment, inclined his golden head again. "Forgive me. I neglected to offer my title. I'm Whitfield Calder, Earl of Danning."

* * *

In Whit's experience, when a marriageable young lady was introduced to an eligible member of the aristocracy, she simpered or fawned or blushed in a ridiculously cloying fashion. Miss Hollingsford did none of those things. Her green eyes, tilted up at the corners, sparked fire, and her rosy lips tightened into a determined line. If anything, she looked thoroughly annoyed.

"*Lord* Danning?" she demanded as if certain he was teasing.

He spread his hands. "To my sorrow, some days."

She turned her glare on her father. "Did you arrange this encounter?"

Her father raised his craggy gray brows. "Not me, my girl. Seems the good Lord has other plans for you."

She did not look comforted by the fact.

Whit offered her a bow. "Forgive me for not being more forthcoming, Miss Hollingsford. I enjoy my privacy while I'm at Fern Lodge. I hope we'll meet again under more congenial circumstances."

"Over my dead body." She yanked on the handle of the door. Whit offered her his arm to help her. She ignored him, gathering her skirts and nimbly climbing into the carriage. She slammed the door behind her.

"Many thanks, my lord," her father called. "Looking forward to an interesting fortnight."

"Drive, Davis!" Whit heard her order, and the coachman called to his team. Whit stepped away as the coach sped off back across the bridge.

Interesting woman. When he'd first seen her jump from the coach, he'd wondered whether she was in some sort of trouble. Her clothes had said she was a lady; her attitude said she was intelligent, capable and ready to defend herself if needed. The women he seemed to meet in Society were either retiring creatures so delicate that the least wrong word set them to tearing up or bold misses who angled for an offer of marriage. Miss Hollingsford's open friendliness, without a hint of flirtation, made for a charming contrast.

But much as the intrepid Miss Hollingsford intrigued him, her father's parting words seemed stuck in Whit's head. *An interesting fortnight,* he'd said, as if he intended to spend that time with Whit. And his coach had originally been heading in the general direction of the Lodge, Whit's private fishing retreat, shared only with his cousin Charles. Then again, Miss Hollingsford had said she was attending a house party. Could Charles have planned one?

Not if Whit had any say!

He ran back to the shore, snatched up his fishing gear and strode up the slope for the house. The road, he knew, wound around the hill to come at the Lodge from the front. The path he followed led to the back veranda and his private entrance.

His father had introduced him to Fern Lodge for the first time the summer after his mother had died attempting to bring his little sister into the world. Both were buried in the churchyard in Suffolk. Life had seemed darker and bleaker then, until the carriage had drawn up to this haven. Even now, the rough stone walls, the thatched roof, looked more like a boy's dream of a wilderness cottage than a retreat of the wealthy. The humble exterior of the cottage orné masked its elegant interiors and sweeping passages. It had been his true home from the moment he'd entered.

These days, it was all he could manage to come here for a fortnight each summer. This was his time, his retreat, the only place he felt free to be himself.

I know You expect me to do my duty, Lord, but I'm heartily tired of duty!

He came in through his fishing closet, a space his father had designed, and hung up his rod on a hook. He shucked off his boots and breeches and pulled on trousers. He traded his worn leather boots for tasseled Hessians. The coat, waistcoat and cravat he'd have to change upstairs. Then he walked down the corridor for the entryway.

He found it crowded, with footmen in strange livery bumping into each other as they carried in bags and trunks while maids wandered past with jewel cases. His stomach sank.

His butler, Mr. Hennessy, who cared for the Lodge when Whit was not in residence, was directing traffic. A tall, muscular man who'd once been a famed pugilist before rising through the servant ranks to his current position, he had little patience with a job poorly done.

"No, the rear bedchamber," he was insisting to one of the footmen, who was carrying an oversize case from which waved a series of ostrich plumes. "She is sharing with Lady Amelia."

"Lady Amelia." Whit seized on the name as the footman hurried off. "Lady Amelia Jacoby, by any chance?"

"Ah, my lord." Hennessy inclined his head in greeting. "Yes, her ladyship and her mother are expected downstairs shortly, Mr. Hollingsford's coach is just pulling up to the door, I believe your cousin Mr. Calder is to arrive before dinner, and the Stokely-Trents are awaiting you in the withdrawing room."

"Are they indeed?"

His butler must have noticed the chill in his tone, for he frowned. "Forgive me, my lord. I understood from Mr. Quimby that that was your desire. Was I mistaken?"

Quimby. Peter Quimby had been his valet since Whit's father had passed on. A slight man Whit's age, his practical outlook and attention to detail had never failed. He knew what this quiet time at the Lodge meant to Whit. Why would he threaten it with strangers?

"No, Mr. Hennessy, you were doing your duty, as usual," Whit assured him, heading for the stairs. "It was Mr. Quimby who was mistaken, greatly mistaken." And he would tell the fellow that this very instant. He started up the stairs, and the footmen and maids scattered before him like leaves in a driving wind.

On the chamber story, Whit spun around the newel and into the room at the top of the stairs. He'd been given this bedchamber as a boy, and though it was the smallest of the seven, he still found it the most comfortable. He stopped in the center, the great bed before him, the hearth at his back, and thundered, "Quimby!"

His valet entered from the dressing room, a coat in either hand. As always, a pleasant smile sat on his lean face. Though his straw-colored hair tended to stick out in odd directions, his clothes, and the ones he kept for Whit, were impeccable.

"Good," he said. "You're back. Which do you prefer for dinner, the blue superfine or the black wool with the velvet lapels?"

"What I prefer," Whit gritted out, "is to know why I have guests."

"Ah." Quimby lowered the coats but never so much that they touched the polished wood floor. "I believe each of the three invitations read that you are desirous to put an end to your bachelor state and would like to determine whether you and the lady suit."

Feeling as if every bone in his body had instantly

shattered, Whit sank onto the end of the bed. "You didn't."

"I did." With total disregard for the severity of his crime or his master's distress, Quimby draped the coats over the chair near the hearth. "You aren't getting any younger, my lad. And we none of us are looking forward to serving your cousin should you shuffle off this mortal coil prematurely." He glanced at Whit and frowned. "You look rather pale. May I get you a glass of water? Perhaps some tea?"

"You can get these people out of my house," Whit said, gathering himself and rising. "Or, failing that, find me other accommodations."

Quimby tsked. "Now, then, how would that look? You have three lovely ladies here to learn more about. I chose them with great care. I thought you rather liked Lady Amelia Jacoby."

It was true that the statuesque blonde had caught Whit's eye at a recent ball, but he'd never had any intentions of moving beyond admiration. "If I liked her," Whit said, advancing toward his valet, "I was fully capable of pursuing her without your interference."

"Of course," Quimby agreed. He came around behind Whit and tugged at the shoulders of his tweed coat to remove it. "Yet you did not pursue her. I also invited Miss Henrietta Stokely-Trent. You did mention you thought she had a fine grasp of politics."

He'd had several interesting conversations with the determined bluestocking last Season. "She's brilliant. But perhaps I want more in a wife."

"And perhaps you've been too preoccupied to realize what you want," Quimby countered, taking the coat to the dressing room.

"Rather say occupied," Whit corrected him, unbuttoning the waistcoat himself. "Parliament, estate business, the orphan asylum…"

"The sailor's home, the new organ for the church," Quimby added, returning. "I am well aware of the list, my lord. You are renowned for solving other people's problems. That's why I took the liberty of solving this problem for you." He unwound the cravat from Whit's throat in one fluid motion.

"Dash it all, Quimby, it wasn't a problem!" Whit pulled the soiled shirt over his head. "I'd have gotten around to marrying eventually."

"Of course." Quimby took the shirt off to the dressing room for cleaning.

Whit shook his head. "And why invite Miss Hollingsford? I don't even recall meeting her."

Quimby returned with a fresh shirt and drew it over Whit's head. "I don't believe you have met, sir. I simply liked her. I thought you would, too."

He had liked her immediately. All that fire and determination demanded respect, at the least. That wasn't the issue.

Whit closed his eyes and puffed out a sigh as his valet slipped the gold-shot evening waistcoat up his arms. "Have you any inkling of what you've done?"

He opened his eyes to find Quimby brushing a stray hair off the shoulder. "I've brought you three beautiful women," he replied, completely unrepentant. "All you need do is choose."

Whit stepped back from him. "And if I don't?"

"Then I fear the next batch will be less satisfactory."

Whit drew himself up. "I should sack you."

"Very likely," Quimby agreed. "If that is your choice, please do it now. I understand Sir Nicholas Rotherford is seeking a valet, and as he recently married, I should have less concern for my future with him."

Whit shook his head again. If Quimby had been anyone else, Whit would have had no trouble firing him for such an infraction. But he'd known Quimby since they were boys. The two had been good friends at Eton, where Peter Quimby, the orphaned son of a distinguished military man, had been taken in on charity. When Whit became an orphan, and the new Earl of Danning at fifteen, he'd offered his friend a position as steward.

"Who's going to take orders from a fifteen-year-old?" Quimby had pointed out. "Make me your valet. They get to go everywhere their masters do. We'll have some fun, count on it."

At times over the past fifteen years, Whit thought Quimby was the only reason Whit had had some fun, even when duty dogged his steps. He couldn't see sacking his friend now.

"Rotherford can find another valet," Whit told him.

Quimby smiled as he reached for the coats.

"But don't take that to mean I approve of this business," Whit insisted. "I'll do my best to clean up the mess you've made. I will be polite to our guests but expect nothing more. You can campaign all you like, Quimby, but you cannot make a fellow choose a wife."

"As you say, my lord," Quimby agreed, though Whit somehow felt he was disagreeing. "Now, which will you have tonight, the black coat or the blue?"

"Does it matter?" Whit asked as his valet held out the two coats once more. "By the time this fortnight is over, I'm the one most likely to be both black *and* blue, from trying to explain to three women that I don't intend to propose."

Chapter Two

Ruby was equally certain she would do no more than survive the fortnight as she and her maid were escorted to a lovely room overlooking the river. She'd tried to convince her father to return to London, but he'd refused, having Davis turn the coach once more and take them back to the Lodge, a quaint stone building tucked between the river and the rising hills.

Her father seemed even more certain than before that Lord Danning was part of some plan God had for her. After all, the earl had been waiting for her when she'd jumped from the coach. She didn't believe God worked that way. God's plans involved momentous things—war and peace, sun and rain and stars falling. Surely He wouldn't intervene in the life of one Ruby Hollingsford.

Besides, she could take care of herself. She had her future all planned—good works, good books, a drive through the park and the opera on occasion. She didn't need the unreliable companionship of a husband.

Hadn't she managed in London alone when she'd been a child and her father had worked as a mudlark, scouring the banks of the Thames for treasure? After their wealth was established, hadn't she endured the

four years of tutelage at the Barnsley School for Young
Ladies, where half the students shunned her because
of her past? Wasn't she spearheading the creation of a
school in poverty-stricken Wapping? Hadn't she sur-
vived when the one man she thought she might love
turned out to be a scoundrel? The Earl of Danning
would find her made of stronger stuff than the dewy-
eyed Society damsels he probably courted.

But it did seem odd that, when she exited her room
to try to persuade her father once more, the very first
person she saw was the earl standing by the stairs.

He'd changed into evening clothes. Had he been
dressed like that when they'd met, she would have had
no doubt he was a member of the aristocracy. The black
coat and trousers emphasized his height; the tailoring
called attention to his shoulders. Though he did not
seem to know he was being observed, he held himself
poised, as if posing for a portrait.

She hadn't noticed him on the riverbank at first, she'd
been so angry at her father's betrayal. This time she
didn't think he saw her, and for a similar reason. His
hands were clasped behind his back in tight fists, and
he was gazing down the stairs as if he simply couldn't
force himself to descend.

She shared the feeling. But why was he so loath to
start the house party he'd instigated? And why had
he organized the house party at all? He'd said he only
wanted to fish. She'd seen the other carriages being
unloaded at the door. More people were attending this
party than just her and her father. How would having
a house full of people allow him time to fish? How
would fishing allow him time to court a lady? Was he
as big a liar as the other aristocrats she'd had the misfortune to know?

She considered tiptoeing behind him for the room her father had been given across the corridor, but she thought Lord Danning would probably notice. She wasn't exactly inconspicuous. She disdained the white muslin gowns young ladies were expected to wear because they made her dark red hair look like some sort of fire beacon. Instead, her evening dress was a smoky gray, with long sleeves wrapped in white lace and a band of the same lace around her neckline and hem. The gown tended to rustle as she moved. So he would either see her or hear her, and she'd be stuck making polite conversation anyway.

So she decided to start the conversation herself. She walked up to him and nodded in greeting. "It appears I was mistaken, my lord. We meet again."

He pulled himself out of his reverie and bowed. "Miss Hollingsford. A pleasure to see you again, particularly as you are not a dead body."

Ruby couldn't help chuckling. "I suppose I deserved that after my remark by the bridge. You may have noticed that I have a temper. I also tend to speak my mind."

"Really?" he said, though she could see the twinkle in those purple-blue eyes.

"Surprising, isn't it? And given that tendency, allow me to make something clear." She leaned forward and met him gaze for gaze. "I meant what I said at the river. I'm not here for a proposal."

"Excellent," he replied, unflinching. "Neither am I."

Ruby frowned as she leaned back, but her father came out of his room just then, and the earl excused himself to start down the stairs ahead of them.

"Ah, getting to know the fellow already," her father said, rubbing his white-gloved hands together. Now that he was dressed for the evening, anyone looking at him,

Ruby thought, would see a prosperous gentleman. His blue coat and knee breeches were of an older style but of fine material, his linen was a dazzling white and a sapphire winked from the fold of his cravat. They wouldn't know where he'd come from, how hard he'd worked to rise to the enviable position of jeweler to the *ton*.

The earl must know. An aristocrat would certainly want to be sure of the family he was considering uniting with his own. Yet why would he invite the daughter of a jeweler to stay? Was he pockets to let, like the viscount her father had offered up?

Either way, Ruby could not encourage her father's tendency to matchmaking. "I have no reason to get to know our host further," she told him. "I have little interest in the Earl of Danning."

He grinned. "A little is at least a start. Come on, my girl. Let's show them how it's done."

With a shake of her head, Ruby accepted his arm, and they descended the stairs.

So her father would not change his mind. She considered appealing to the earl about her enforced stay at his lodge instead. If he was sincere in not wanting to propose, perhaps she could convince him to rescind his invitation. Whatever his reasons for inviting her, surely now that they'd met, he'd seen that they would not suit. She was far from being the sort of exquisite beauty whose genteel manners and biddable nature might make her low birth forgivable. They could have little in common, nothing on which to base a true marriage. But when she and her father entered the withdrawing room, she found the earl missing. Instead, others were waiting, five in all, arranged in two groupings.

Indeed, two groupings was about all the manly space would afford. The withdrawing room at Fern Lodge

seemed designed to dominate. The warm wood paneling was set in precise squares. Each painting celebrated
capture, from grouse to fish to bear. The polished brass
wall sconces ended in spikes like spears. The stags in
the relief over the massive gray stone fireplace at one
end of the room looked ready to leap from the wall and
dash away to safety.

So did at least one of the women in the room. Two
had claimed the sofa before the fire, and by the simi-
larities in the lines of the patrician faces, Ruby guessed
that they were mother and daughter. The daughter had
hair the color of platinum, perfectly coiled in a bun at
the nape of her neck, and a figure just as perfect, as if
carved from marble. The drape of her silk gown said it
cost as much as one of Ruby's father's Blue John orna-
ments. Every angle of nose and cheek shouted aristocrat—just as every facet of her expression showed her
wish to flee.

The other group, positioned on chairs by the glass-
paned doors overlooking the veranda, appeared to com-
prise a mother and father in staid but costly evening
wear. The young woman standing beside them was
likely their daughter, though she didn't resemble them
with her dark hair worn back from an alabaster face.
She had an enviable figure in a lustring gown the color
of amethysts. Her movements were sharp and precise,
as if each was calculated for effect.

Why were they here? If the earl truly meant to propose to Ruby as the invitation implied, could these be
his relatives or close friends? But if they were family,
surely they'd stand closer, perhaps reminisce? If friends,
why were they mostly women?

"Evening, all!" her father announced, strolling into

the room and pulling Ruby with him. "Let's call the ceiling our host and get to know each other better."

As Ruby dropped his arm in embarrassment, he went to the ladies on the sofa and stuck out his hand. "Mortimer Hollingsford and my daughter, Ruby."

The mother eyed his hand as if he had thrust out a dagger. "Lady Wesworth," she said without physically acknowledging his gesture. "And my daughter Lady Amelia."

Wesworth? Ruby knew the name and fervently wished her father wouldn't reveal the connection. Somehow she didn't think the Marchioness of Wesworth would want the rest of the guests to know that her husband had recently exchanged the diamonds at her throat with paste copies.

But her father was too much the businessman to ever betray a client. "Your ladyship," he said with a bow. "News of your daughter's beauty and charm has spread far, but I see that the gossips neglected to mention how much she takes after you."

The marchioness visibly thawed, her double chins relaxing, her impressive chest settling. "I'm afraid I haven't heard any stories of you, Mr. Hollingsford," she said in a voice that managed to be polished and commanding at the same time. "Are you related to Lord Danning?"

If she asked the question, she couldn't be related either. Ruby wandered closer to hear the conversation. The matter apparently interested the others, for they rose and joined the group by the sofa, as well.

"Not me," her father promised. "Not at the moment, leastwise." He winked broadly at Ruby.

The other man held out his hand to her father. "Winston Stokely-Trent," he intoned as if the name should have meaning for all present. "My wife and my daughter. Did I understand you to say you hope to soon be related to the Earl of Danning?"

"You did not," Ruby said, threading her arm through her father's and giving it a squeeze in warning.

"Certainly not," Lady Wesworth said, nose in the air. "I understand he has set his sights elsewhere."

Her daughter blushed.

Mrs. Stokely-Trent smiled at her own daughter. "So I understand, as well."

Ruby glanced from Lady Amelia, who had bowed her head in humility, to Miss Stokely-Trent, who had raised hers in pride. Had the earl really implied marriage in his invitations to the two of them as well as Ruby? How arrogant and how like an aristocrat!

Well, she wouldn't stand for it. As soon as Ruby could, she drew her father away from the others, leading him to the doors overlooking the veranda. Twilight was falling, and a mist seemed to be rising from the river. But she could not afford to appreciate the view.

"This is a farce," she whispered, mindful of the other guests. "Let's make our regrets and go."

"Now, then, you can't be cowed by these girls," her father insisted with a glance at the other two candidates for the earl's hand. "Lady Amelia is a stunner, but she obviously lacks backbone. And I've heard Miss Henrietta Stokely-Trent is too clever for her own good. No, my girl, I'd cheer for you any day."

"Then you'd be disappointed," Ruby said. "I'll have no part in this business. You know how I feel about these nobs."

"Once a nob, always a snob," her father agreed. "But they're not all so bad."

"Most of the ones I've met have been," Ruby countered.

Just then another man strolled into the room. Like their host the earl, he was tall, blond and handsome. But his features were softer, as if he were the resin mold rather than the finished statue. His clothes were of cheaper material, lesser cut. Ruby recognized the signs immediately. So did her father.

"The poor relation," he murmured as the man came forward.

Poor relation or fortune hunter, Ruby amended silently as he fawned over Lady Amelia and Henrietta Stokely-Trent. The others appeared to recognize the signs, as well. Lady Amelia's shy smile was effectively countered by her mother's curt stare. Miss Stokely-Trent quizzed him unmercifully. Ruby told herself not to feel sorry for him.

When at last he made his way to their sides, his charming smile was a little frayed.

"Hollingsford," he said with a nod.

"Mr. Calder, good to see you again," her father replied. "You may remember my daughter, Ruby."

Why would he remember Ruby? She certainly didn't remember him, though apparently he knew her father. Before Ruby could question either of them, the other man bowed to her. "A pleasure, Miss Hollingsford."

Ruby inclined her head as he straightened. "And how do you know my father, Mr. Calder?"

He paled, but her father clapped him on one broad shoulder. "Business," her father said and by his refusal to say more, Ruby knew that Mr. Calder had likely had to sell some jewel of great personal value to pay his bills.

Mr. Calder managed a smile. "I am in your father's

debt, and I will be forever in my cousin's debt for inviting me to bask in the glory of three such lovely creatures."

He said it as if he knew he had no hope of attracting any of them. Ruby couldn't help trying to raise his spirits. "Oh, did your cousin catch so many fish today?" she teased.

He chuckled. "Ah, a wit, as well. I can see I shall have to be on my toes. But tell me, how do you know my cousin?"

Ruby glanced at her father, brow raised.

"Never met him until today," her father proclaimed. "But he must have seen my Ruby at some social function else he wouldn't have invited her."

Ruby wasn't convinced. She'd never seen the earl or his cousin at any event. But then, she ran in different circles. Her literary club comprised women who had either inherited money from trade or were independent, like her friend Miss Eugenia Welch. When she went out of an evening, it was most often with her father and his acquaintances.

Still, because she'd attended the prestigious Barnsley School for Young Ladies in Somerset, she knew any number of women currently on the *ton*. Unfortunately, some of her former classmates still snubbed her. They certainly had never mentioned her to the earl.

As if summoned by her thoughts, Lord Danning appeared in the doorway. His golden hair mirrored the candlelight. The diamond stickpin in his cravat sparkled. His smile of welcome included everyone in the room as he glanced about. She found herself wondering when the portrait painter would arrive.

Then his gaze met hers, and his smile deepened.

Ruby felt her face heating and raised her chin. Oh, no. He would not find her as easy to catch as his fish.

"Ladies, gentlemen," he said, strolling into the room, "welcome to Fern Lodge. You were kind to accept the invitation. Join me for dinner, and we can discuss plans for the fortnight." He held out his arm. "Lady Wesworth, if I may?"

Funny. Ruby wouldn't have thought the earl such a stickler for propriety, not having met him in rough clothing on the riverbank. By the looks that crossed Lady Amelia's and Henrietta Stokely-Trent's faces, they'd also expected him to offer for someone other than the highest-ranking woman in the room. Had he meant what he'd said earlier, when he'd claimed he was truly not seeking a wife? If so, perhaps it wasn't so much good manners as self-preservation that made him escort Lady Wesworth rather than any of the young ladies he'd invited to court. But if he was not seeking a bride, why invite them all in the first place? Just to amuse himself with their reactions?

The other pairings were nearly as interesting. Mr. Calder eyed Ruby, but she anchored herself to her father, and he excused himself to offer Lady Amelia his arm. Henrietta Stokely-Trent looked even more annoyed because she had to walk with her father and mother. The posturing for position at the table was nearly as laughable, with parents and offspring colliding and glowering at each other. Ruby wasn't sure whether to be concerned or amused when Henrietta Stokely-Trent seated herself next to Ruby near the end of the table.

Of course, none of them had much choice. The Lodge, while decorated in sumptuous materials, was clearly meant for a retreat, not to host so many people. The mahogany table had been extended its full length to accommodate them all, and the high back on the earl's chair said it belonged elsewhere in the house. Still the polished wood of the table mirrored the shine of the pristine china plates, silver service and porcelain platters of the dozen dishes the chef had produced for their delight.

One nice thing about Ruby's vantage point near the end of the table, however, was that it gave her a good view of the earl. He seemed pleasant, answering Mr. Stokely-Trent's imperious question about a bill coming up in Parliament as easily as Lady Wesworth's lament that there were no pickled beets to accompany the meal.

Indeed, he chatted easily with Lady Amelia and her mother on either side, making sure they were given choice portions of the salmon and duck, smiling at their sallies. But she saw no spark, no furtive glance, no touch of hands as he passed the platters, to indicate that he had any feelings for the lady.

"An interesting gentleman," Henrietta Stokely-Trent said as if she'd noticed the direction of Ruby's gaze.

Ruby offered her a smile. "Have you known him long, then?"

"We've met several times this Season." She lifted a forkful of the duck. "He's reasonably intelligent, well read, with opinions of his own on any number of topics. Where did you meet?"

"On the riverbank this afternoon," Ruby supplied, "on my way to the Lodge. But he sent the invitation earlier."

Miss Stokely-Trent frowned. "Why would he invite you if you'd never met? Is he a friend of your father's?"

"Not that I'm aware," Ruby replied, looking across the table to where her father was regaling Mrs. Stokely-Trent with one of his tales. By the way the lady's mouth was pursed in an *O,* Ruby would likely need to apologize at some point.

"Surely I can be of assistance, Miss Stokely-Trent," said Mr. Calder on her other side, smiling winsomely. "Perhaps some more of the duck?" Henrietta turned her attention to him.

Ruby was just as glad to be left alone with her thoughts. There had to be a reason she and her father had been included in the earl's invitation. But for the life of her, she couldn't understand why.

Whit was also feeling the dining room a bit crowded as the visiting footmen brought in the second course. When he was in residence, he generally made use of Mr. Hennessy's skills to serve rather than bothering with footmen. And he only ate a single course. If he'd been fortunate, it was of the fish he'd caught. But with a house full of guests, his chef had obviously determined that something more substantial was needed. And Whit had never been one to argue with strawberry trifle.

"So what do you plan for us, my lord?" Mr. Stokely-Trent asked from midtable, leaning back in his seat to rest his hands over the paunch of his stomach.

They all regarded Whit with interest. For some reason, he found his gaze centered on Miss Hollingsford near the end of the table. He hadn't been sure of the color of her hair inside her bonnet as they'd stood by the river that afternoon, but when they'd met on the stairs earlier, he hadn't been surprised to find it a deep red, like the fading glow of the coals at night.

Now it was sleeked back in a bun at the top of her head, and little tendrils like sparks framed her face. One corner of her mouth was drawn up, as if she expected his answer to be amusing. He would have been more amused if Quimby had given this house party some thought. Whit wasn't about to sit around the Lodge conversing for a fortnight, and he hardly wanted all their company fishing. But his wants would have to give way to his duty, as usual—and duty dictated that he be an accommodating host, even to guests he had never intended to invite.

"Dovecote Dale is renowned for its sights," he said. "Perhaps a walk into the hills. There's a cascade about a mile up the side stream."

Lady Wesworth fanned herself as if even the thought was tiring. "So long as we can take the carriage. I wouldn't want Amelia to be exposed to the elements."

By the pallor of the young lady's creamy skin, Whit thought a little exposure to sunshine might not be remiss. Miss Hollingsford had been wearing a fetching ostrich-plumed bonnet to protect her skin this afternoon, and she positively glowed. She also looked less than impressed that a lady wouldn't be able to make so short a jaunt.

"A visit to Lord Hascot's horse farm might be entertaining," Whit tried. "We can take the carriages there."

"Does he raise draft horses, Thoroughbreds or common stock?" Henrietta Stokely-Trent asked.

"Are you a horse enthusiast?" Charles asked, leaning closer to her as if her answer meant the world to him.

She regarded him with a frown. "No," she replied. "Just curious."

Whit thought he heard a smothered laugh from Miss Hollingsford. She was enjoying his predicament entirely too much. "And what would you like to do, Miss Hollingsford?" he challenged.

All gazes swung her way. She dimpled at the other

guests. "Return to London as soon as possible?" she suggested.

"What a tease," her father said with a laugh. "I'm sure whatever interests you will interest us, my lord."

"You could take us all fishing," Miss Hollingsford added, with particular spite, he thought.

Mr. Stokely-Trent brightened, but Lady Amelia shuddered.

"Do you fish, Miss Hollingsford?" Charles asked, aiming his charming smile her way. Whit could only bless his cousin for intervening.

"Very likely for something larger than trout," Lady Wesworth murmured. Unfortunately, in the small room, her voice was all too audible. Her daughter squirmed in embarrassment, but Mrs. Stokely-Trent nodded archly, and Mr. Stokely-Trent traded knowing looks with his daughter.

Whit frowned. Did they think Ruby Hollingsford a title hunter? From what he'd seen, nothing was further from the truth. In fact, given her questions at the river and the statement on the stairs, she had no interest in courting. It sounded as if she'd only accepted Quimby's invitation at the insistence of her father.

"I've never had the pleasure of fishing," she replied to Charles, and only the height of her chin said she'd heard the marchioness's unkind remark. "What about you, Mr. Calder? Do you join the earl in his delight at capturing smelly creatures?"

Whit couldn't help a laugh at her description of fishing.

"I do indeed, Miss Hollingsford," Charles answered with a similar smile. "And I'd be pleased to teach any of you lovely young ladies the fine art. It takes patience, skill and daring, not unlike a courtship."

Henrietta Stokely-Trent beamed at him. "I may accept that offer, Mr. Calder. I always like learning new things from a practiced teacher."

"Then Charles would be perfect," Whit teased. "He requires a great deal of practice."

"Ho, a palpable hit!" Charles declared, fainting back in his chair as if wounded. "Miss Stokely-Trent, I will trade my services as an angler for yours as a nurse. Promise me you will never leave my side."

"That might be difficult if you intend to fish," Miss Hollingsford pointed out, but Whit noticed that the bluestocking was studying his cousin as if seeing his potential for the first time.

Now, there was a thought. What if he could pair up the ladies with someone else? That might take them off his trail. Charles was forever in need of funds, but he had a good heart and a sound mind. Henrietta Stokely-Trent could do far worse. Now who could Whit find for Lady Amelia?

As if her mother suspected the direction of his thoughts, she rose from her seat. "I believe the ladies are finished. Shall we wait for you gentlemen in the withdrawing room, my lord?"

Rather presumptuous of her to think he expected her to act as his hostess, but then he had escorted her in to dinner. Whit rose, as well. "If you'd be so kind."

The other ladies stood and followed the marchioness from the room. Mr. Stokely-Trent eyed his wife, hands braced on the linen, but she cast him an imploring look and he excused himself, as well. Ruby Hollingsford offered Whit a grin as she sashayed past, but he was certain it had more to do with amusement than from any flirtation. Indeed, he rather thought he'd find greater enjoyment in the dining room in the company of Mr.

Hollingsford and Charles than the ladies would have in the withdrawing room waiting for them.

How will I withstand two weeks of this, Lord?

As the footmen came forward to offer another drink, Charles and Mr. Hollingsford took the opportunity to move closer to Whit at the table. Neither of them seemed the least concerned with the turn of events. Charles had a smile playing about his mouth, as if he were genuinely pleased with the glimmer of a response from Henrietta Stokely-Trent. Hollingsford belched and covered the noise with his hand.

"Excellent dinner, my lord," he said. "You've a talented cook."

"I'll be sure to pass your compliments to Monsieur Depavre," Whit promised.

Hollingsford wrinkled his long, pointy nose. "Frenchie, eh? Normally, I prefer good English cooking, but he did very well."

Whit hid his smile, knowing his chef's opinion of so-called good English cooking.

"Better than usual," Charles agreed, leaning back in his chair. "But I am surprised to be surrounded by so many guests, Danning. I thought it was to be just the two of us as usual."

Whit could hardly tell his cousin the truth in front of Hollingsford. He still found it difficult to believe Quimby's audacity. "It was a last-minute decision."

"Well, I'm grateful." Charles lifted his glass. "To the fairest ladies in England, all here at Fern Lodge."

"Hear, hear," Hollingsford agreed, and raised his glass, as well.

Whit joined them in a sip. They were lovely women. By the snippets of conversation he'd caught, they were intelligent, as well. Discounting the unkind attitude toward Ruby Hollingsford, any man would be lucky to court one of them. Yet none of them stirred his heart the way he had imagined a man should feel for his intended wife.

What was wrong with him? Had fifteen years of duty sucked the romance from his very soul?

Charles pushed back his chair. "Give a fellow a chance, eh, Danning? Wait ten minutes before joining us in the withdrawing room. That ought to give me sufficient time to steal a march on you."

"If you can win a lady's heart in ten minutes, you're a better man than I am," Whit said with a chuckle.

"You'll find out shortly," Charles promised, and he strode from the room.

Hollingsford chuckled, as well. "I like a chap with confidence." He studied his glass, turning the stem this way and that with fingers as pointy as his nose. "If I may, my lord, I thought you had similar fire when we met this afternoon. But somewhere along the way you lost your spark. Is something troubling you?"

Whit regarded him. His head was cocked so that the candlelight gleamed on his balding pate, and his craggy brows were drawn down. He seemed sincerely perplexed and ready to offer support and guidance.

It had been a long time since Whit had seen such a look, not since his father had called him to his bedside fifteen years ago to tell Whit he'd soon be the earl. What would his father have said about this mess Whit found himself in?

What would Hollingsford say?

"I have a house full of guests to entertain," Whit replied. "You heard them. They have little interest in seeing the sights, visiting the neighbors. I find myself wondering what I should do with them."

Hollingsford grinned. "It's not the sights or the neighbors they came for, my lord. I think you know that. They came here for you."

The very idea made him want to stalk from the room, dive into the river and let it wash him out to sea. "I am unused to being the sole entertainment."

"Now, then, it's not so bad," Hollingsford said, hitching himself higher in his seat as if he intended to deliver a speech. "You have three lovely ladies before you. It shouldn't be so difficult to determine which you like best."

Why had he even considered having this conversation? "I wasn't prepared to begin serious courting," he tried. "I haven't given the matter much thought until recently."

"No need to think," Hollingsford insisted. "You take this lady for a drive, that one for a walk. You talk to them, ask them what they like, sound out their opinions, see how they relate to their Maker. Then, when you find one you like, you let her know and arrange for the banns to be read."

Whit laughed. "You make it sound easy."

"It is easy," Hollingsford declared, reaching for the decanter the footman had left to pour himself another glass. "Courting is supposed to be fun. It's the marriage part that takes work."

Perhaps that was what concerned him. Surrounded by requirements, was he now to add the responsibility for a wife? He knew his duty to his family to marry and have an heir. It was a duty he took far too seriously to rush into a hasty marriage, especially now when he already had enough on his hands!

Besides, he couldn't help remembering his father, sitting at this very table, staring at a painting of Whit's mother that had then hung on the paneled wall. His gaze had never strayed to the food, as if she alone sustained him. He'd never even attempted to court again after her death. That, Whit couldn't help thinking, was true love, that unbridled devotion, that all-consuming emotion. Having seen such a love, how could he settle for anything less?

"It's not so bad, you know," Hollingsford said, offering him the decanter. Whit waved it away. "Marriage can be a blessing. Someone to care about you, to encourage you. I still miss my Janey, and she's been dead a good fifteen years now." He took a deep draught from his glass, and Whit saw that his hand shook.

It seemed even Hollingsford had been touched by the tender feelings of love. Was it possible Whit might find it here at the Lodge, with one of these women?

Chapter Three

Whit wasn't sure what to expect when he and Ruby's father entered the withdrawing room a short while later. He had rather hoped Charles would prove true to his word and wrap Henrietta Stokely-Trent, at least, around his little finger. Whit had seen any number of ladies succumb to his cousin's charm. Charles found it easy to converse, easy to smile. He found duty harder to swallow. Sometimes Whit thought they were exact opposites.

However, Charles had focused on Ruby Hollingsford, the two of them in close conversation as they sat across from each other in armchairs by the doors to the veranda. The candlelight from the brass sconce glowed in his cousin's hair; his gaze was aimed directly at the feisty redhead.

But Miss Hollingsford seemed barely to notice. Her attention had wandered toward the door to the withdrawing room, and when her gaze lit on Whit, her lips curved.

For some reason, Whit wanted to stand a little taller.

"Looks as if you have a clear field, my lord," Mortimer Hollingsford chortled as he passed Whit to stroll into the room. Whit blinked and quickly tallied his other guests. Instead of hanging on his cousin, Miss Stokely-Trent had discovered the ancient spinet he'd forgotten rested on the far wall and was tapping at the keys while her parents looked on and Lady Amelia sat expectantly on the sofa with her mother.

"How kind of you to join us," Lady Wesworth said as if Whit had kept them all waiting. She glowered at her daughter. "Amelia was just saying how much she wanted to sing for you."

Lady Amelia's elegant brows shot up, and she visibly swallowed. If she had wished to sing, she now very likely wished herself elsewhere. Even though he could see her shyness, duty required that he encourage her, and the other gentlemen followed suit. But it was Ruby Hollingsford's voice that won the day.

"I imagine you have a lovely voice, Lady Amelia," she said, her own voice warm and kind. "I hope you'll share it with us."

Lady Amelia rose with a becoming blush. "Well, perhaps a short tune. I wouldn't want to inconvenience Miss Stokely-Trent."

The other woman eyed her as she approached the spinet. "I didn't realize you'd require accompaniment. Don't you play, Lady Amelia?"

The blonde's blush deepened. "Not as well as you do, I fear."

"Nonsense," Lady Wesworth declared, but Henrietta Stokely-Trent appeared mollified enough that she agreed to accompany Lady Amelia. While they put their heads together to confer about the music, Whit drifted toward to his cousin and Ruby Hollingsford.

"I must say," Charles was murmuring, leaning closer to the redhead as if to catch the scent of her hair, "that though your father may be a jeweler of some renown, he surely had his greatest gem in you, my dear Ruby."

Whit couldn't help frowning. How had Charles managed to gain the right to use her first name so soon? And what was this about a jeweler? Was that the source of his other guests' disapproval? Were they so arrogant they looked down on a lady for having a father in trade?

Ruby Hollingsford shook her head at his cousin's praise, hair catching the light. "You'll have to do better than that, sir, if you hope to win one of these women."

So she'd taken his cousin's measure already. Whit tried not to smile as his cousin promised her his utmost devotion. Ruby just laughed, soft and low, a sound that met an answering laugh inside Whit.

Just then, Henrietta Stokely-Trent played a chord, and Lady Amelia began to sing. Whit was surprised to find she had a beautiful voice, clear as a bell and equally as pure. Ruby beamed as if she'd known it all the time. When Lady Amelia finished, the applause from all his guests was spirited.

Not to be outdone, Henrietta Stokely-Trent launched into a complicated sonata with precision and skill and earned a similar round of applause as well as a smug smile from her father.

Charles put his hand on Ruby's, where it lay on the arm of her chair. "I would very much like to hear you play, Miss Hollingsford. I warrant you have some skill."

Whit, too, wondered how Ruby would play. He'd have guessed with a great deal more emotion than Henrietta Stokely-Trent, but Ruby didn't take advantage of the opportunity Charles had given her to preen.

She pulled her hand out from under his cousin's. "I have little skill at the spinet," she replied cheerfully. "And I'm not much of a singer either."

"It is difficult for those outside Society to excel in the graces," Lady Wesworth commiserated with a look to her daughter, who had returned to her side.

"Music, literature, poetry," Mrs. Stokely-Trent agreed with a sigh. "Those are, indeed, the elevated arts."

Ruby Hollingsford's look darkened. "Oh, I learned to appreciate poetry. Shall I declaim for you?" She rose, head high, gaze narrowed on the two mothers.

"There once was a baker named Brewer, whose home always smelled like a—"

"Miss Hollingsford," Whit interrupted, thrusting out his arm. "Will you take a stroll with me on the veranda?"

Everyone else in the room was staring at him. Ruby Hollingsford, the minx, turned her glare on him, yet managed a tight smile. "Surely I shouldn't deprive your other guests of the pleasure of your company, my lord. Or isn't that done in polite society? I know so little about it, after all."

"Your knowledge is quite sufficient for me," Whit said. "But I fear I must insist."

He thought for a moment she would refuse, her face was so tight. But she slapped her hand down on his arm, and he opened one of the glass doors out onto the veranda and led her through. Behind him, he heard Charles inviting the others to play whist. Whit shut the door on their answers.

She drew away immediately, going to the edge of the veranda and putting a hand against one of the square wooden pillars that supported the roof. Night had crept over the dale. Above the trees beyond her, a thousand stars pricked out fanciful shapes in the sky. In the darkness, the River Bell called, eager to reach its joining with the Dove a few miles to the west. The cool air touched Whit's cheek tenderly, leaving behind the vanilla scent of the fragrant orchids that crowded the meadow nearby.

Miss Hollingsford did not seem to appreciate the cool air or the scent. "If you intend to offer a scold," she said, turning to gaze at him and crossing her arms over the chest of her gray evening gown, "get it over with or save your breath."

The golden light spilling from the windows behind him outlined her figure, the tense lines and stiff posture. As he had suspected, the careless words a few moments ago had hurt.

"What I intended," Whit replied, "was to apologize for my other guests. They diminish themselves in my estimation by their behavior."

She took a deep breath and trained her gaze toward the meadow. "I should be used to it by now."

She had obviously heard such slurs before. Why was it people felt so compelled to pick at each other? "You should not have to accustom yourself to abuse," Whit told her.

She snorted. "Try telling that to Lady Wesworth. I'm sure she thinks she's being edifying."

"I intend to tell her. I thought it more prudent to speak to you first. One should not reward bad behavior."

"Yet you rewarded mine." She dropped her arms. "Forgive my fit of pique, my lord. I'll try to keep my temper in check. Unless, of course, you'd like me to leave."

She glanced back at him, brows raised. Even her tone sounded hopeful. She wanted him to send her packing. Having her leave would certainly solve part of his problem—one less woman to placate, two fewer guests to entertain. Yet she seemed the most practical person of the group, and he could not help feeling that, by losing her, he would lose one of his only allies.

"Please stay, Miss Hollingsford," he said. "At least with you, I can speak plainly with no fear of losing my heart."

Ruby ought to take umbrage. Was she such a hag that he could never admire her? So lacking in the social graces she embarrassed him? So beneath him that marriage was unthinkable?

But though she couldn't see his face with the light shining behind him, she could hear the smile in his voice, feel his pleasure in her company, and she couldn't be angry. Besides, he was right. It felt as if they were in this together.

"Very well," she said. "I'll stay. But you must answer a question for me."

"Anything," he assured her, taking a step closer.

Anything. She couldn't imagine an aristocrat actually meaning that. What if she asked which lady he preferred? What if she asked whether an influx of cash from a dowry such as hers would be welcome in his finances? Somehow, she didn't think he would answer those questions so easily.

She wasn't even sure he'd answer the one that plagued her, but she tried anyway. "Why did you invite me? We've never met."

"Likely not," he agreed. "I'd remember otherwise."

His tone was warm, admiring. Ruby smiled despite herself. "Well, it appears you know how to compliment a lady, my lord."

He inclined his head, and she caught a glimpse of his grin. "It takes little imagination to find praise for beauty, Miss Hollingsford."

She could feel heat creeping up her cheeks as he gazed at her. Did he think her beautiful? She'd had women enough complain about her red hair, as if she'd had any choice in the color. Then there were the men who ogled it, as if it somehow signaled her heart was as fiery. Some of them had learned it was a closer match for her temper.

And what was she doing wondering whether he found her winsome? She had no intention of competing for his hand, and she'd had a purpose in asking him that question.

"The other two ladies will appreciate your compliments even more, I'm sure," she said, putting a hand back on the solid wood of the pillar to steady her thoughts. "I'd simply like to know why I'm among their number."

He shook his head, gaze going out to the night as if it held the answer. "Believe me when I say that this house party was not my idea. Someone arranged it with the best of intentions, and I will honor those intentions to the extent I can."

He was obviously shielding someone. Who would be so audacious as to sign an earl's name to an invitation that could cause him to choose a bride? A parent came immediately to mind. Certainly her father would not be above such an action. Look at the way he'd manipulated her into coming to Derbyshire!

But Lord Danning had said he was an orphan. The only relative at the house party was Charles Calder. Had he arranged this? After conversing with him, she was even more certain they'd never met, despite her father's remark. Now Ruby shook her head. Always it came back to her father. Very likely he'd encouraged Charles Calder to invite her. She could hear him now.

She's a great girl, my daughter. You put in a good word with his lordship, and I'll give you an excellent price on this diamond. She shuddered.

"Forgive me for keeping you, Miss Hollingsford," the earl said, clearly thinking she'd shivered from the cool air. "I merely wanted you to know that I appreciate your presence here, and I'll do all I can to make your time in Derbyshire enjoyable. Establishing a friendship with you and your father might be the best thing that could come of all this."

A friendship with an earl? Surely such a thing was impossible. Oh, he seemed kind and considerate, his lean body relaxed as he stood there, rimmed in gold. By the tilt of his head, she thought those purple-blue eyes were watching her with kind regard. She steeled herself against them. She'd had warmer looks trained her way, and they'd promised lies. A shame the angler she'd met by the river this afternoon had turned out to be an aristocrat.

"Thank you for the explanation, my lord," she said, pushing off the pillar and lifting her skirts to start for the door. "We should return to your other guests."

He did not argue but merely opened the door for her and bowed her in ahead of him.

She thought she might be greeted by a fresh barrage of insults, but the other guests did not seem overly distressed by her and Lord Danning's absence. Her father, Lady Wesworth and the Stokely-Trent parents had begun playing whist at a table brought in for the purpose, further crowding the withdrawing room. Mr. Calder was seated on the sofa between the other two ladies, and by the blush on Lady Amelia's fair cheek and the smile on Henrietta Stokely-Trent's pretty face, he was at least holding his own.

"You have a choice, Miss Hollingsford," Lord Danning murmured beside her as they paused by the doorway. "Would you prefer to make the fourth in another game of whist, or would you like an excuse to escape?"

Ruby glanced up at him. His look held no censure. He truly was giving her the option to leave all these people behind. The very thought sent such relief through her that she knew her answer.

"You play whist," she said. "I'll run. And thank you."

No one said a word as she slipped from the room.

The air in the corridor was still perfumed with the lingering scent of roast duck as she took the stairs to her room. Peace, blessed peace. No one to impress, no one to start an argument or berate her for simply being born without a silver spoon in her mouth. She filled her lungs and smiled.

And nearly collided with another man at the top of the stairs.

He caught her arms to steady her, then stepped back and lowered his gaze. He was not as tall as Lord Danning, and more slightly built, with hair like the straw that cushioned her father's larger shipments and movements as quick as a bird's. His dark jacket and trousers were of the finest material, the best cut. She couldn't help the feeling that she'd met him before.

"Forgive me, sir," she said. "I didn't realize Lord Danning had another guest."

Keeping his gaze on her slippers, he inclined his head. "I'm no guest, Miss Hollingsford. I'm Quimby, his lordship's valet. I do hope you enjoy your time at Fern Lodge. I'm certain if you look about, you'll find something of interest." With a nod that didn't raise his gaze to hers, he turned and hurried toward the front bedchamber, shutting the door with a very final click.

Odd fellow. She couldn't recall meeting a valet before, unless she counted the manservant who assisted her father. But somehow she wouldn't have thought them quite so subservient. Was Lord Danning such a harsh master? Perhaps she should do as Mr. Quimby suggested and keep her eyes open.

Unfortunately, it was her ears that troubled her that night.

The room she had been given was lovely to look upon, plastered in white with a cream carpet on the dark wood floor and golden hangings on the bed. A shame the designer had not taken similar care in the soundness of the structure. Ruby had just settled beneath the thick covers when she heard voices coming through the wall. Lady Amelia and her mother were evidently situated next door, and by the sound of it, Lady Wesworth was much put out about the fact.

"I have never slept two in a bed in my life," she complained, so ringingly that the gilt-edged porcelain rattled in the walnut wash stand against Ruby's wall. "Why can't one of the others share?"

Lady Amelia must have answered, because there was silence for a moment before Lady Wesworth continued. "And why is she here at all? You cannot tell me Danning covets her fortune. With his seat in Suffolk and the leasehold here in Derby, he has quite enough to suffice."

Interesting. At least she could cross fortune hunter off the list of potential concerns about Lord Danning. If she had been willing to consider him as a husband, of course.

"Well, I suppose she is pretty," Lady Wesworth acknowledged to something her daughter had said, "but I doubt she came by that magnificent red naturally."

Oh! Small wonder the minister preached against listening to gossip. She fingered a strand of her red hair, knowing that she came by it quite naturally.

"Oh, cease your sniveling, young lady," Lady Wesworth scolded her daughter. "You can still have him. You must exert yourself tomorrow. Find ways to be close to him, and don't let that Hollingsford chit get in your way."

That Hollingsford chit reached for one of the feather pillows, thinking to block her ears before she heard any more.

"And he had the affront to advise me to be civil to her. Me! As if I needed to be reminded how to go about in polite society!"

Ruby paused in the act of covering her head. So Lord Danning had kept his promise and spoken to Lady Wesworth about her. His advice didn't seem to have been taken to heart, but at least he'd tried. Remembering her own manners, she stuffed the pillow over her head and attempted to get some sleep.

In the morning, Ruby was swift to finish dressing in a green striped walking dress and disappear downstairs before she heard another word from her neighbors. She truly felt for Lady Amelia to live with such a termagant.

Ruby's mother had died when Ruby was a child; she didn't remember a great deal about her. She'd seen to her own needs until she'd gone to school, where a maid had been provided for her. Since graduating, she'd hired a maid in London, an older woman with an eye for fashion who sadly seemed to care more fervently for Ruby's wardrobe than her well-being. So she'd never had a woman to fulfill what she'd always thought to be a mother's role—fussing over her, encouraging her to reach her dreams. Somehow she'd always imagined such a person would be more uplifting than censorious.

If the other guests had heard anything of Lady Wesworth's complaints, they did not show it. Ruby passed Mr. and Mrs. Stokely-Trent in the corridor, and both nodded civilly to her, making her wonder whether Lord Danning had spoken to them, as well. Charles Calder called to her from the withdrawing room, raising a silver teapot to indicate he had sustenance ready should she wish it. Very likely she'd need it; she could barely make out the lawn beyond the veranda it was raining so hard. But she had no wish to encourage him, so she waved him good-morning and hurried on.

She finally reached the dining room and stayed only long enough to grab an apple from the sideboard, then retreated to a room she'd spotted the previous day—the library. If ever any morning warranted curling up with a good book, it was this morning. Unfortunately, that room, too, was occupied.

Henrietta Stokely-Trent paused in her survey of the crowded walnut bookshelf on the opposite wall. The soft lace at the throat and hem of her white muslin gown was all frivolity. But the arched look she cast Ruby made it seem as if the floor-to-ceiling bookcases, which paneled two of the four walls, and the sturdy leather-bound chairs in the center of the carpet were hers alone.

"Good morning, Miss Hollingsford," she said, inclining her dark head. "Looking for a novel?"

A novel, according to Miss Pritchett, the literature teacher at the Barnsley School, was considered by some the lowest form of literature. That hadn't stopped her from sharing tales of the Scottish Highlands with her students, each book full of romance and adventure. But not all women were as open-minded as Miss Pritchett, and Ruby knew the offer of a novel was this young lady's way of implying Ruby lacked the intelligence to read anything more challenging.

"Perhaps a novel," Ruby replied, refusing to encourage her. She trailed a finger of her free hand along the edge of the spines nearest the door. "Or a Shakespearean play and some of Wordsworth's poetry."

"So you do know more than common rhymes," the bluestocking surmised, watching her.

Ruby smiled. "I pick the poem to suit the audience."

"Then you very likely chose well," she said, to Ruby's surprise. She moved to join Ruby. "I must apologize for the behavior of my family, Miss Hollingsford. Between our social connections and financial blessing, we tend to overestimate our own worth."

Her gray eyes were serious, so Ruby decided to give her the benefit of the doubt. "The actual estimate, I suspect, is impressive enough."

"But lording it over others is hardly fitting," Henrietta countered. Then she leaned closer and lowered her voice, as if suspecting someone might come upon them at any moment. "Still, I must know. What do you make of all this?"

Ruby glanced around the library, thinking it only polite to pretend to misunderstand. "It seems a fine space to me, although if it often rains so hard here a bit more light would be warranted."

The bluestocking's lips twitched, but whether from annoyance or amusement, Ruby wasn't certain. Unlike her calculated movements, her face was soft, pampered.

"I suspect you know I was looking for a different sort of enlightenment," she said. "You were the only one to manage a private word with the earl last night. Is he truly intent on courting?"

Ruby refused to lie, but neither did she feel comfortable confiding last night's conversation with Lord Danning. He had intimated she was the only one he truly trusted, if for no other reason than because she had made it plain she did not plan to participate in this business of choosing a bride.

"You would have to ask him," she replied, edging away from the woman, gaze on the line of shelves.

"And what of you?" the bluestocking pressed, following her. "You do not seem to be trying to impress him. By your own admission, you are not well-known to him. Exactly why are you here, Miss Hollingsford?"

Ruby set her apple on a shelf, yanked out a book and flipped to a random page. Better that than to tell the woman to mind her own affairs. "I was invited to a house party," she said, gaze on the precise lettering going down the page, more design than words. "I have no interest in courting."

"That seems odd for a lady our ages," Henrietta replied. "Are we not told that marriage is the sum of which we might attain?"

Was Ruby mad to hear bitterness behind the words? "Marriage is often needed for money or prestige. I have plenty of the former and have no interest in the latter."

"And love?" Henrietta pressed. "Have you no use for it either?"

Ruby closed the book and set it back on the shelf. "I honestly don't believe the love written about in all these tomes even exists."

Out of the corners of her eyes she saw Henrietta frown. "And your father is amenable to supporting you throughout your life?"

"He will grow accustomed to the idea," Ruby replied with a fervent wish she was right.

"Then you are more fortunate than most, Miss Hollingsford." She turned toward the door, and Ruby felt her stiffen. "Oh, good morning. I didn't know you were there, my lord."

Chapter Four

Ruby whirled to find the earl standing in the doorway. This morning he was once more dressed in his fishing clothes, a rough cravat knotted at his throat. Something stirred inside her at the sight. Had he sought her company, or was he looking for Henrietta Stokely-Trent? Or did that pleasant smile mask dismay to find his peaceful library disturbed?

"Good morning, Miss Stokely-Trent, Miss Hollingsford," he said, venturing into the room.

Henrietta Stokely-Trent went to meet him. "Do you not find that tedious, the whole Stokely-Trent business? Perhaps you could call me Henrietta."

Bold, Ruby thought, turning to pluck another book from the shelf at random and flipping to a center page, the leather rough beneath her fingers. Could she say such a thing to a fellow? *Hollingsford is such a long name. Call me Ruby.* She winced at the thought.

But Lord Danning didn't seem to be offended. "I would be honored, Henrietta," he replied, and out of the corners of her eyes Ruby saw him bow. "I am generally called Danning."

Ruby wrinkled her nose. *Danning.* His title. She'd

have preferred to call him Whit. It far better suited the angler.

"You have a fine library, Danning," Henrietta said. "An excellent mix of literature."

He chuckled, and the sound was like a warm wave, lapping Ruby. "I stock this room with some of my favorites," he confessed. "So I imagine it must seem rather eclectic. You should see the library at Calder House in London. My father was something of a collector. He had an early fragment of the *Odyssey* and a Shakespearean first folio."

Impressive, Ruby thought, glancing over at them despite her best effort.

Henrietta had clasped her hands in delight. "Oh, Danning," she said breathlessly as if he'd laid the riches of the Nile at her feet. "I would love to see them."

"Stop by anytime you're in London," he offered. "I'll tell my staff to expect you and your parents."

Generous. Was Whit truly as noble as he seemed? Henrietta must have thought so, for Ruby could see her blushing with obvious pleasure.

Ruby shifted, facing the bookshelf once more. She wished she could snatch up her apple and quit the room, let Whit get on with courting if that's what he wanted. Unfortunately, he and Henrietta Stokely-Trent stood between her and the door, and Ruby had been placed in the position of serving as chaperone.

"How kind of you, my lord," Henrietta murmured. "I wonder, would you recommend a book? I'm having trouble choosing among so many excellent tomes."

And there she went again! How well Henrietta played the game of flirtation. While Ruby enjoyed a good tease now and again, she balked at the veiled insinuations, the fulsome compliments, that seemed part and parcel to the way aristocrats talked to one another. Even her father had gotten into the habit of tossing out praise long before he knew whether it was merited.

"Is there something in particular you enjoy?" Whit asked.

Ruby glanced at the couple in time to see Henrietta flutter her lashes and lean closer. Was she actually asking for a kiss?

Well, if Ruby was stuck playing chaperone, perhaps she should embrace the role. She strode forward and thrust her book at Henrietta. "You might try this one."

Henrietta snapped upright, gray eyes narrowing to silver as if she knew exactly why Ruby was so eager to step between her and Whit. As far as Ruby could tell, the bluestocking ought to be glad it was only Ruby who'd caught her in such brazen behavior. Her mother would likely have boxed her ears!

Whit, however, glanced at the title on the spine, and his face lit. "*The Compleat Angler.* Excellent choice, Miss Hollingsford. One of my favorites. You cannot go wrong with Izaak Walton, Henrietta. He made this area famous."

Henrietta's gaze drew back to his, and she smiled. "Well, then of course I will read it, Danning." She accepted the book from Ruby with a reluctance that belied her words. "Especially as you praise it so highly. I take it the book wasn't to your liking, Miss Hollingsford."

She meant to disparage Ruby. Why did these Society women have to make everything a competition? "Oh, I'm sure it's an excellent book," Ruby replied with a smile as false as the bluestocking's. "It is only that I tend to prefer to learn a skill by doing. Driving a curricle, boxing, shooting."

Henrietta arched her dark brows as if she doubted Ruby could do any of those things.

"Do you know Mr. Walton agrees with you?" Whit put in smoothly. "He believes one can only truly become an angler by practicing." He brightened. "And speaking of practicing, would either of you care to join me at the river this morning for a short while before the others finish with breakfast?"

Ruby glanced out the window, where the gray light confirmed the tapping she could hear on the glass. "It's still raining."

"A mere passing shower," he assured her. "And the rain on the water further disturbs it so that the fish rise to feed."

He seemed to know what he was talking about, face shining in earnest anticipation. But Henrietta, unlike the fish, refused to rise to his bait.

"I fear I neglected to bring the appropriate attire," she said. "But I shall read about Walton's approach, and perhaps you would be so good as to compare it to your own when you return, Danning."

Whit inclined his head. "Delighted, Henrietta. Until then."

The bluestocking glanced at Ruby. "Coming, Miss Hollingsford?"

Though the request was a question, she seemed to expect instant obedience. After all, if she left, Ruby and Whit would be alone, for all the door was open. Ruby knew she should go, too, but she didn't particularly want to spend more time with the woman. "I need to pick a book," Ruby demurred.

Face tight, Henrietta excused herself.

Ruby felt Whit's gaze on her. His head was cocked as if he were trying to understand what she was about, his purple-blue eyes holding a sparkle as if he appreciated the way she'd handled herself. "And did you, too, wish a recommendation, Miss Hollingsford?"

Ruby shook her head. "I'm quite capable of determining what I like and don't like, my lord."

"And what do you like?" he asked.

You. Ruby felt her face flaming and dropped her gaze, glad that she hadn't spoken the word aloud. She knew the dangers of getting too close to an aristocrat. It never ended well for the cit.

But being little miss subservient would hardly help matters.

"I'm partial to Shakespeare," she said, forcing her gaze back up. "His comedies, like *A Midsummer Night's Dream* and *The Taming of the Shrew.*"

He raised a brow, but she couldn't tell whether it was from surprise that she'd be so well read or amusement that she might resemble that shrew a bit too much. "So you, too, prefer to spend the morning reading rather than fishing," he said.

"I fear I lack the dedication to stand in the rain, my lord," she replied. Then she grinned up at him. "But I'll be delighted to help you eat the fruits of your labors."

He laughed, and again she felt warmed. "Let's simply hope my labor bears fruit." He sobered as if remembering his duty. "Will you be all right until I return?"

What, should she swoon from lack of his uplifting presence? "I'm sure I can find ways to entertain myself, my lord. You must have more than fishing tracts in this library. Go, catch your fish. I'll try to keep the rest of them out of your hair for a half hour at least."

A half hour to fish! It was less than he needed but more than he'd hoped for when he'd descended the stairs that morning. And he couldn't believe how grateful he felt for the reprieve. He bowed to Ruby Hollingsford, quite in charity with her, and headed for his fishing closet.

Of course, it took him nearly a quarter hour to collect his accoutrements—his book of flies, his ash rod and brass reel and a leather coat slicked with paraffin to keep off the rain—and then reach the River Bell and set up for his first cast. Already rain ran in rivulets down his face and body.

Glorious. In the deep pool just beyond, he knew, the King of Trout lay waiting. All Whit had to do was cast.

He pulled out a length of silk line with one hand, then began to whip the rod back and forth, watching as the line lengthened. It floated across the stream. The fly kissed the top of the pool and hung there, tantalizing.

"Come on," Whit murmured. "Where are you?"

Something silver flashed in the depths, and his breath caught. He reeled in his line, checked that his fly—black body with white wings, one of the best he'd tied—was secure, then drew back his arm again. He'd been coming to this pool for twenty years, since his father had introduced him to the fine art of angling at ten. And still he hadn't managed to convince the wily King to take a bite.

He tried closer in, giving the rod an elegant flick. The fly landed as lightly as if it had been alive. He thought he saw another flash of silver, but the King did not rise.

"Come on," Whit urged him again. "I used to have all summer to play with you, my lad. Now I'm lucky to have a fortnight."

A fortnight he was going to have to share with his guests.

He pushed the thought away. He had now; that was all that mattered. He inhaled the scents of Derbyshire, brought out by the rain—damp earth, orchids, new growth. His hectic world dwindled to this place, this time. Something about fishing, the rhythm, the river, opened his heart, his soul.

He leadeth me beside the still waters; He restoreth my soul.

Prayer came naturally.

Lord, thank You for even this time to fish. Help me survive this house party. I know I must eventually wed to secure the line of succession. I only wish You'd send me a woman who would stir my heart the way my mother stirred my father's.

A memory rose through the rain. He'd been standing here by the river, fishing alongside his father, a few years after his mother's death. It had been early morning, the sun barely peeking over the hills to the east. Even the birds had been still.

Do you miss Mother? Whit had asked.

His father's arm had stilled in midcast. *Every moment of every day. That's what happens when your wife becomes a part of you, Whit.*

The devotion in his voice, the awe on his face, still spoke to Whit. He took a great pride in doing his duty, but when it came to marrying he refused to settle for anything less than that same love. Surely the Lord understood and would honor that.

"My lord! Danning!"

Whit pulled up his rod and glanced over his shoulder. The rain continued to pour, pounding the rocky shore and the grassy slope above it. Standing on the sodden hill was Ruby Hollingsford, an already bedraggled plaid parasol held over her head, her wine-colored velvet pelisse hanging heavily.

"My lord," she called. "It's been two hours. You are needed inside."

Two hours? Guilt added weight to his rod as he reeled in. A house full of guests and a truant host. Yet none of them had sought him but Ruby.

She shivered as he bent to retrieve his book of flies then moved to join her.

"Thank you, Miss Hollingsford," he said as they started up the slope. He reached for her elbow to assist her, but she was busy trying to angle the parasol to cover him, as well.

He waved her back. "Are my guests at their wits' end?"

"If they aren't, you soon will be," she predicted. "Lady Wesworth insisted that Lady Amelia practice on the spinet, the same song over and over for the last hour."

Whit inwardly cringed.

"Then your cousin Mr. Calder tried to interest everyone in another round of whist, but Mr. Stokely-Trent refused to continue playing and implied that Mr. Calder cheated."

He'd have to intervene there. Though Charles had perpetual trouble balancing his finances, he had too much honor to cheat.

"Not to be outdone," she concluded, "my father fell asleep while Mrs. Stokely-Trent was lecturing him on the proper way to discipline a daughter. I was the only one to be pleased by that turn of events."

Whit wanted to smile at the picture, but he could not help feeling a little responsible for the behavior of his guests. He was their host, after all. As far as they knew, he'd invited them here. If they were bored, it was his fault. Shouldn't he do something to see to their needs?

As if Ruby suspected his feelings on the matter, she laid her free hand on his arm. "You have two choices as I see it, my lord. Either give them some task to work on other than snaring you or provide them with some entertainment."

Whit nodded as they reached the house. "Excellent advice, but neither Lady Wesworth nor the Stokely-Trents strike me as delighting in a job well done."

"Unless it was for charity," she suggested as he opened the door for her to his fishing closet, the quickest way into the house. "The only place I've ever seen an aristocrat roll up his sleeves was in the name of a good cause. At the very least then he might take some of the credit!"

A rather dismal view of his kind, but he knew to his sorrow that some of the lords and ladies of London approached life in just that manner. He'd had to argue his peers out of some ridiculous plans for the orphan asylum that would have benefited them far more than the orphans they claimed to want to help.

"Has Derby no indigent farmers who need gloves knitted?" she asked, gazing up at him. "No aged widows who require a song to brighten their day?"

Her eyes were liberally lashed a shade darker than her hair, and he found himself drawing closer as surely as he did the call of the stream. He had to force himself to turn away to hang up his rod. "I fear Dovecote Dale is remarkably free of troubled souls."

Obviously caught by his gesture, she glanced about, then thrust out her lower lip as if impressed. "What an interesting room."

He supposed it was. He only knew of a few others

in existence. Originally designed as a sort of study, his father had replaced the papered walls with white paneling from which hung shelves, hooks and cupboards to store all their fishing gear.

"My father had it built," he explained. "Fern Lodge was his fishing retreat, after all. Why not dedicate a room to it?" He grinned at her. "And the staff is quite pleased to find my mud generally confined to one room."

She closed her parasol and hung it on the wall with a nod of approval. Then she looked over at him. "A shame you don't have more rooms in the house. At least then you could separate your guests. If there are no charities in the area, I fear entertainment it must be if you hope to survive this fortnight, my lord."

"Whit," he said, pulling off his dripping coat and hanging it up. "If I am to be on a first-name basis with the other ladies, I should be with you, as well."

"Whit," she said slowly as if trying it out, and something about the way she said it felt like a benediction. Then she frowned. "But you told Henrietta Stokely-Trent to call you Danning."

He had, but only because she'd been so bold as to force her first name on him. "Most of my acquaintances call me Danning. My father always called me Whit. He said I would be known by one title or another my entire life, so I should have a name that was mine alone."

To his surprise, she blushed and lowered her gaze. "Whit it shall be, then." Her fingers trembled as she undid the silver clasp at the throat of her pelisse.

Whit helped her pull the heavy velvet from her shoulders. When his chilled fingers brushed her neck, she shivered as she stepped away. "Thank you, Whit," she said, though the words came out breathless.

Whit felt unaccountably breathless himself. The fishing closet felt impossibly small, her body brushing his as she passed him for the door. He thought he caught the scent of cinnamon, and the dry, warm spice seemed the perfect complement to her personality.

A personality he appreciated more and more as the day wore on.

With Ruby's help, Whit rallied his guests for parlor games like charades and forfeits until tea, then had each lady take turns reading from *Guy Mannering,* a new novel by the author of *Waverly,* until it was time for dinner. After an excellent meal of duck in plum sauce with sundry fresh fruits and vegetables, he organized two groups for whist, being careful to keep Charles and Mr. Stokely-Trent on opposite sets.

For one round, Whit partnered Henrietta and found her a brilliant player, even though she had the habit of shaking her dark head when he played a little less brilliantly. For the other round, he partnered Lady Amelia, who, while competent, betrayed every emotion on her lovely face, from delight over an excellent hand to dismay when she could not follow suit.

He would have counted the evening a relative success if it had not been for Charles's behavior. His cousin partnered Ruby in the first round, opposite Whit and Henrietta, and his constant banter set Ruby to blushing and Whit's teeth on edge. That his cousin managed to gain her as his partner in the second round did not go unnoticed.

"It appears we know where one star is hitched," Lady Wesworth commented as she and her daughter made for the stairs and their bedchamber.

"Appearances can be deceiving," Ruby replied to no one in particular as she followed.

Whit caught his cousin's shoulder as he attempted to retire, as well. "Stay a moment."

Charles frowned but returned to a seat by the fire while the others made their various excuses and left. Whit closed the withdrawing room door behind the last and went to sit by his cousin.

Charles had his feet stretched to the fire, hands idly rubbing the wool of his black evening trousers. He resembled Whit enough to be his brother, and certainly they'd been raised as closely, attending the same schools, spending holidays together in Suffolk and at Fern Lodge. Their closeness made what Whit had to say so much harder. Yet he had promised himself to do his best for his guests after this morning's lapse, so he could not let his cousin's actions go unremarked.

"I want you to leave Ruby Hollingsford alone," Whit said.

Charles's blond brows shot up. "I beg your pardon?"

"It's hers you should be begging," Whit replied, giving the wrought iron fender a tap with his toe. "Don't you think some of your comments were inappropriate?"

"Not in the slightest, particularly when my intentions are entirely honorable." He adjusted his cravat. "A gentleman must move quickly if he wishes to pluck the rose before it blooms."

Ruby Hollingsford was no flower, though her hair was as red. "This isn't London, Charles," Whit informed him. "You needn't capture her heart in one night."

"Or at all, apparently." Charles leaned farther back in his seat to eye Whit. "Have you made up your mind, then? Do you intend to offer for her?"

"No."

Either the answer was too quick or too firm, for Charles's brows came crashing down again.

"That is," Whit amended, feeling his neck heat, "she didn't come here for an offer."

"Then why agree to attend this party?" Charles asked, obviously perplexed. "She must have some interest in marrying."

Whit could not help remembering how he'd first encountered her, leaping from a coach and marching down the river bank muttering about her father's perfidy. Such a temper! And such a strong sense of right and wrong.

"I believe she may have been persuaded to attend by her father," he told his cousin.

Charles rose and went to the glass-paned doors to peer out into the night as if the veranda held better answers. "Why would her father care about a house party in Derby?" he asked the view.

His cousin's shoulders were high and tight. Was he expecting Whit to confess some secret agreement? He'd already told Charles he didn't intend to offer for Ruby. "I suppose," he guessed, "he's hoping for a title in the family."

Charles turned with a grin, shoulders coming down. "Then he'll simply have to settle for charm instead."

Whit shook his head as his cousin returned to his side. "While he managed to get her here, I doubt he can force her to the altar. She's made it clear she doesn't wish to marry."

Charles waved a hand as he dropped into his seat. "Every woman wishes to marry. All that is required is the right bridegroom."

Whit wasn't so sure about that. When he'd first wandered into the library this morning, he had heard enough to be certain Ruby Hollingsford had determined that the single state best suited her. Besides, the same nonsense about marrying had been said of a fellow in possession of a fortune, or a title, that he must wish for a wife. Whit certainly didn't, at least not any wife.

"Nevertheless," he persisted, "I ask that you honor her intentions. If you wish to win a heart this fortnight, turn your attentions elsewhere."

Charles snorted, shifting in his seat as if the conversation was making him uncomfortable. "To Lady Amelia, perhaps? No, thank you. I have no wish to be eaten by her dragon of a mother."

"Lady Wesworth is protective," Whit replied. "But if her daughter pleases you and you her, she will come around."

"I wouldn't be so sure," Charles said, tucking his long legs under his chair as if to anchor himself. "And I prefer the bluestocking in any regard. At least she's willing to look you in the eye when she sneers at you."

Whit stiffened. "If any of my guests has had the temerity to sneer at you, she will be leaving in the morning."

One corner of Charles's mouth turned up. "Doing your duty, eh, Danning? Never you fear. None of them would dare sneer, to my face."

Whit leaned closer. "You're in an odd humor. Do you honestly think you're less than I am?"

Charles glanced up, then quickly down again. "Can you honestly say I'm not, *my lord*?"

Whit frowned. "There is that, of course, but only for certain circumstances would that make you less than me."

"Circumstances that are all too apparent," Charles insisted. "You have the title, and in addition you're taller, smarter and wealthier than I'll ever be."

"You forgot to add better looking," Whit teased, leaning back.

"And humble as well!" Charles grinned at him. "Even if I am the better fisherman."

"Ho! You know I cannot let that comment stand." Whit reached out to cuff him on the shoulder.

Charles chuckled. "No more than you could let my pursuit of Ruby Hollingsford stand. Admit it, my lad. You like her."

Of course he liked her. How could any man dislike energy and fire, all wrapped up in a pretty package? "As I said, Miss Hollingsford has no interest in courting, so my feelings have no bearing on this conversation."

"Maybe," Charles replied, slapping his knees and rising to leave. "But I think when you are performing your devotions this evening, you should ask the Lord why you're so set on protecting her, even from your own cousin."

Chapter Five

Ruby had cause to ask herself about Whit's intentions the very next day. Though the morning dawned gray and threatening, the air remained clear. When his guests had gathered in the dining room for breakfast, Whit announced his plans to take any who were interested to visit his neighbor down the Dale, Lord Hascot at Hollyoak Farm.

Ruby had never heard of the fellow, but her father filled her in as they sat together near the end of the table, partaking of the coddled eggs and salmon laid out for them.

"Horse mad, absolutely horse mad," he declared between bites.

"He raises riding horses," Whit supplied from the top of the table with a smile to Ruby. "Mostly hunters, with power and stamina. A gentleman knows he's made his mark when he obtains a Hascot horse."

"Indeed," Lady Wesworth intoned, poking at her salmon as if she would subdue it anew. "Lord Wesworth has even considered purchasing one."

"I'm certain Henrietta would do one justice," Mrs.

Stokely-Trent said with a nod to her husband, who har-rumphed and kept his gaze on his eggs.

"Indeed she would," Ruby's father agreed with a wave of his silver folk. "You might speak to Hascot when we visit today. It's not as if you'll meet him in town. He only comes off that farm of his once a year to bid at Tattersall's and perhaps commission a nice bit of gold."

So that's how her father knew the fellow. He must be a customer. "And he'll welcome a gaggle of visitors?" Ruby asked as the other women began arguing over who would sit where in the carriage.

"Only if they come to buy," her father predicted with a grin.

Ruby felt for Lord Hascot, but she felt more for Whit. He sat at the head of the table, interjecting in this con-versation, interceding in that argument. Since return-ing from the river yesterday, he'd done all he could to keep his guests happy. Unfortunately, the only thing that would satisfy most of his guests was the one thing he refused to offer—a proposal of marriage.

In the end, Lady Wesworth agreed to use her lan-dau, a portentous beast, with the hoods down so that her guests might better enjoy the scenery.

"My man had it from her maid that she takes it ev-erywhere," Ruby's father confided to her. "I don't envy the servants riding in it with the baggage while she and Lady Amelia travel in the larger coach. Those leather hoods can stink when they're closed for any time."

By the width of the two facing seats, Ruby guessed two abreast would be comfortable, but no one appeared content to be elsewhere. So Ruby found herself seated next to Henrietta and her mother, while the two fathers and Lady Wesworth sat opposite. By the set of their shoulders, she thought it a tight squeeze.

Luckily, Lady Amelia, Mr. Calder and Whit rode alongside, although, at Whit's suggestion, all the young ladies had changed into riding habits in case they might choose to ride one of Lord Hascot's famous horses. Ruby's was a slate-gray affair, tailored, with black braid across her shoulders and frogging down the front. With her plumed shako on her head, she fancied she looked rather dashing. Lady Amelia's plum-colored skirts were more practical than fashionable, and Henrietta's navy coat with its velvet lapels nearly matched the coat Charles Calder was wearing.

That gentleman didn't seem to notice. He urged his horse from one side of the carriage to the other, first flirting with Henrietta and then Ruby. Ruby shook her head at his antics. Though his compliments grew more fulsome each time he talked to her, she put no stock in them. Unlike Whit, his cousin seemed more interested in the art of flirtation than a commitment of lasting devotion.

Whit, of course, was the attraction of the day. He rode at the head of the cavalcade, calling back comments and occasionally stopping to point out a sight of greater interest. He wore a black felt broad-brimmed hat to shield his eyes from the sun, should it ever peek out from the misty clouds overhead, and his brown riding coat was conservatively cut across his broad shoulders. His nankeen breeches met brown-topped boots, his legs hugging the sides of his chestnut mare. Once again, she could not help thinking that the party was significantly lacking a portrait painter.

Whit had explained that Dovecote Dale was a hamlet tucked among the rounded hills, and Ruby felt as if she was sitting in a cup of verdant green as the carriage set off from the Lodge. The hills surrounded them, and the river chatted away like an old friend. Besides Fern Lodge, Lady Wesworth told them all, only three other decent-size houses speckled the valley. Bellweather Hall, home of the Duke of Bellington, was just over the rise from Fern Lodge, while Hollyoak Farm and Rotherford Grange lay deeper in the dale.

"Of course, the Grange is nearly empty now," Whit said, riding alongside as they took the bridge over the River Bell. "Sir Nicholas Rotherford's on his wedding trip to Vienna."

"Vienna," Charles Calder said with a wink to the carriage in general. "Now there's a place I've always wanted to visit. Perhaps it will do for my wedding trip. What do you say, Miss Hollingsford?"

"I have no idea," Ruby said, then couldn't help a grin to Whit, who was frowning at his cousin. "I suspect it would depend on the fishing."

Whit let out a laugh and urged his horse forward.

But though she'd never visited Vienna, she had to admit the Dale had its own beauty as the group made its way deeper. Tiny farmsteads hugged the rising hills; willows and ash hugged the bubbling stream. Twice deer bounded away at the sound of their approach, and when they stopped to let a farm wagon cross their path, Ruby heard doves cooing from the nearby bush.

Whit seemed to be in his element, pointing out the limestone spires rising on the other side of the river, the caves pocketing the cliffs. Lady Amelia rode beside him, glancing about with a smile of pleasure that likely had as much to do with the view as the fact that she'd escaped her tyrant of a mother for a time. The master of horse at the Barnsley School would have praised her seat, the effortless way she guided her mount. Ruby had to admit she was a fetching sight.

Beside Ruby, Henrietta seemed more interested in the scenery, throwing questions to Whit and his cousin about plant life and climate. Lady Wesworth nodded condescendingly, and Mr. Stokely-Trent was too busy arguing with Ruby's father over some matter of the Exchange to pay attention.

"And this is the village of Dovecote," Whit called as they rolled past a little stone inn with flower boxes under the windows. A few cottages crowded nearby, some with shops in front, but the village's crowning glory appeared to be its church. The stone chapel stood on a rise overlooking the area, the white walls holding up a gilded steeple that surely must be visible for miles. As they passed, the bell tolled the hour, and the sound echoed down the valley.

"A fine house of worship," Lady Wesworth pronounced it.

"I would not have expected such in this setting," Mrs. Stokely-Trent agreed.

"The Duke of Bellington has the living," Whit explained, "and each of the landowners has done his part to help."

Ruby could hear the pride in his voice. Though Lady Wesworth had said he owned a seat in Suffolk, Whit clearly felt that Dovecote Dale was home. But building a church?

While she attended Saint James's, Piccadilly, with her father each Sunday, and her father had been known to advance monies toward the church's upkeep, she could not say she was overly enamored of the place. The congregation, made up in large part of wealthy financiers and tradesmen, tended to flaunt their circumstances in the finest clothing, the costliest perfumes. At times she thought a few of them came more to worship themselves than their Maker. She wondered if it would be any different when she attended services with Whit and his guests this Sunday.

Shortly after the village, they crossed another bridge over the river, this one low and flat, as if the builder had felt even ornamentation too frivolous for his purposes. The road drew into a stretch of open pastureland gradually rising toward the hills. Elegant creatures nibbled at the emerald grass, their manes rippling in the cool, moist breeze. Ruby counted a dozen horses before the carriage reached the main house.

Compared to the charm of Fern Lodge, the main house at Hollyoak Farm was a rather boxy affair, three stories of reddish stone about as high as it was wide. Even the bow window jutted out squarely, as if giving no quarter. Stretching on either side behind it were gray stone stables with arched windows and wide polished doors, evidence of where the owner focused his attentions.

The carriage rolled past the house and came to rest in a graveled area behind it, between the two stable wings. Grooms came running to hold the horses for Whit, his cousin and Lady Amelia.

"Lord Danning, welcome," one groom said, holding the horse so Whit could dismount. Another groom scrambled to lower the step and help the others from the carriage.

"And where is your master?" Whit asked as his boots crunched against the gravel.

The groom pointed. "Just coming in now, my lord."

Ruby followed his finger. Out on the pasture behind the house, a set of obstacles had been erected: low wooden fences with ditches on one side and taller stone walls before small ponds. A powerful black horse, big chested, long limbed, was maneuvering among them. The man on its back looked completely in control, moving with the beast as it sailed over a wall and ditch and continued without missing a stride.

"Magnificent," Lady Amelia murmured as she stood beside the carriage, holding her horse's reins. When Ruby glanced her way, she blushed. "The horse. I've heard much of Lord Hascot's stock is descended from the Byerly Turk."

The name meant nothing to Ruby, but the fact appeared to impress Henrietta as well, for she craned her neck to get a better look as the horse and rider cantered closer.

"I doubt that one is," she said as Lord Hascot drew abreast. "Arabians are fine-boned fellows from what I've read. This creature has power."

Ruby might have said the same thing of the man astride him. His black hair waved about his sharp features; his dark brown eyes seemed to miss nothing as he reined in and slung a leg over the saddle to dismount.

"Danning," he said in a deep voice that sounded as if it was rarely used. "I wasn't expecting so many when you sent word you intended to visit."

"Neither was I," Whit assured him. "But it seems your fame precedes you, for all my guests wished to make your acquaintance." He went on to introduce the various visitors. Lord Hascot neither shook hands nor bowed, his dark eyes resting briefly on each person. But Ruby noticed his gaze remained the longest on Lady Amelia. As if she'd noticed as well, Lady Amelia dropped her gaze, her high-cheekboned face turning a pleasing pink.

"Good lines," Lord Hascot said with a nod in her direction.

"I'm not entirely sure he means her horse," Henrietta murmured to Ruby.

"The mount is not for sale," Lady Wesworth snapped, pushing her way forward. "Give the groom your reins, Amelia, and take Lord Danning's arm."

"It seems an earl in the hand is worth two barons on horseback," Ruby's father whispered to her as he passed. "Perhaps you should have ridden, my girl."

"I don't care much for horses," Ruby replied. She'd meant to keep her voice quiet, but it had evidently carried as far as Lord Hascot, for he turned and glared at her as if she had impugned his very honor.

"I would be delighted to wait at the carriage with you, Miss Hollingsford," Charles Calder offered. He had dismounted as well and now moved to join Ruby. His smile was its usual charm, but she certainly didn't want to sit in the carriage like some exotic plant in a conservatory while everyone else had all the fun.

As if he had the same thought, Whit came back to her side. "Allow me to escort you, Miss Hollingsford," he said. She could only wonder why he so carefully put himself between her and his cousin. "I'm sure seeing Lord Hascot's amazing creatures in the flesh will give you a whole new appreciation for the breed."

Ruby wasn't so sure about the horses, but if he kept smiling at her so warmly, she was afraid she just might develop a whole new appreciation for Whit Calder!

Whit could cheerfully have ordered his cousin back to Fern Lodge. What was Charles doing, asking Ruby questions about wedding journeys, offering to stay behind in the carriage with her as if he wanted nothing better than to get her alone? Had nothing Whit said last night penetrated his cousin's thick skull? Or was Charles truly bent on capturing Ruby's heart?

The question tugged at him as he led his guests into the nearest stable, Ruby Hollingsford tucked protectively beside him. He knew Charles needed money—his cousin's interests always outpaced his income. But surely he'd seen how the others had reacted to Ruby.

If she was to marry into upper Society, she needed a husband with sufficient consequence to overcome the prejudice against her father's trade. Even though Charles currently stood as Whit's heir presumptive, his cousin had to know the chances of him inheriting the title were slim. And lacking a title, his consequence would never be sufficient to shield Ruby from gossip. Instead of seeing a cherished wife, Society would claim he'd married Ruby for her money alone. She would never be accepted. If Charles cared anything for Ruby, he must consider that.

But Charles didn't seem troubled to have lost Ruby's attentions, if he had ever had them. He complimented Lady Amelia on her riding, her mother on her turn of phrase, Henrietta on her knowledge of horse breeding and Mrs. Stokely-Trent for having birthed such an amazing female. Perhaps Whit had no reason for concern. Perhaps his cousin had become so used to flirtation he no longer realized when it was inappropriate or inadvisable.

"I hope my cousin has not been annoying you with his conversation, Ruby," Whit murmured, making sure to keep the two of them at the back of the group as Hascot led them down the center aisle of the stable. Her only reply was a polite smile as she took in their surroundings. Around them, horses lounged in high-sided stalls, the wood lacquered in cream and topped by black lat-ticework. Along the walls, troughs offered clean water, fresh hay. Hascot had seen to every need for his beasts. A shame Whit had had less success with his guests.

Still, they seemed disposed to be congenial this morning as they questioned Hascot about his program and his animals. Though the baron generally answered in short sentences, he at least answered. Best of all, Whit noticed a spark of interest each time Hascot gazed at Lady Amelia, and the lady seemed to find it im-possible to directly meet his gaze without blushing. If Charles would just switch his allegiance to Henrietta, perhaps Whit really could finish this fortnight still a bachelor!

"Derby is uniquely suited to raising fine horses," Hascot was expounding as they progressed down the center aisle, the dry scent of fresh grain hanging heav-ily in the air. "Good pasturage, clear water, plenty of space."

Henrietta nodded as if she adamantly agreed. "It does seem quite ideal."

"And how do you bring your horses to market so far from London, my lord?" Ruby's father put in.

Lady Wesworth and Mrs. Stokely-Trent exchanged glances as if they had quite expected such a question from a shopkeeper.

Hascot did not seem to be troubled by the mention of crass commerce. A smile played about his mouth. "I have no need to go to market, sir. My market comes to me."

"I can see why," Ruby murmured beside Whit. "You were right, Whit. They're beautiful."

They were fine animals, grace combined with power and endurance, each one destined to be prized by its owner. But with Ruby gazing at them, green eyes wide, rosy lips pursed in wonder, he knew the horses were not the only beautiful sight in the stable.

Still, as Hascot directed their attention to this horse or that, Ruby said little. Indeed, in her gray riding habit with its military braid at the shoulders, she should have looked her usual perky self, yet she had one arm wrapped around her middle as if her stomach pained her.

"Is something troubling you, Ruby?" Whit asked as the group paused before a white mare that had Lady Amelia gushing with praise.

The plume in Ruby's riding hat bobbed as she nodded toward their host, who was stroking the mare's flank. "I fear I offended him."

Whit smiled as the horse breeder ordered Henrietta to back away from the creature. "It isn't easy to offend Hascot. He is more attuned to his animals than to people."

"But I disparaged his animals." She sighed, looking up at Whit through her cinnamon-colored lashes. "I did warn you that I tend to speak my own mind too quickly, or too loudly."

Whit put a hand on his heart. "Never say so!"

Ruby laughed, a sound as warm as her wit. Charles glanced back their way and shifted as if he planned to join them.

Oh, no. Whit was not about to encourage any further connection. He took Ruby's elbow and drew her away from the group. "Let me show you Hascot's pride and joy."

He led Ruby down the walk to the stall at the back of the stables. The massive horse Hascot had been riding when they had arrived had been rubbed down and given his oats already. Now the black stood, facing them, royal purple blanket across his broad back, sharp glint in his brown eyes.

"Miss Ruby Hollingsford," Whit said, "allow me to introduce Magnum Opus."

Ruby's look brightened. "His greatest work."

"Exactly." Whit smiled that she'd so easily understood the reference. A composer's magnum opus was generally his finest musical score, but Hascot obviously thought this horse the best of his breeding program.

Magnum must have thought the same, for he regarded Ruby regally a moment, then bobbed his head as if deigning to make her acquaintance.

"He has wise eyes," Ruby said. She lifted a hand, then hesitated.

"He has a wise heart as well," Hascot said, coming to join them. "Go ahead, Miss Hollingsford. He will suffer you to touch him."

As if cognizant of the honor, Ruby reached up and stroked the horse's nose. He shook his head, and she pulled back, but he took a step forward and nudged her shoulder.

"Why, I think he likes me!" The smile she beamed at Hascot made the fellow blink a moment in its glory. Then Hascot inclined his head, as well.

"Magnum is an excellent judge of character. You must have a good heart, too, Miss Hollingsford."

Whit felt himself standing taller. What, was he proud? He had no claim on Ruby that praise of her should so please him. Yet how could he not be pleased with the way she smiled, cooing at the massive beast as she stroked his cheek? Her every movement spoke of awe and delight.

How would he feel if she looked at him that way?

"What about this lady?" Charles called from across the way, and Whit could only be thankful for something else to consider besides his own odd thought. "I like a filly with a bit of fire."

Hascot turned, and Ruby pulled back from Magnum with a puff of a sigh to join the others across the aisle. Charles and Henrietta were standing next to a roped-off box where a roan horse stood, hind quarters pointed toward them. The coat was a shade darker than Ruby's hair. Whit could imagine her on its back, flying across the fields, her own hair streaming out behind her.

"You're quite right about the fire, Calder," Hascot said with a nod. "This is Firenza. I haven't found the right master for her."

Charles chuckled. "I do think she'd be a good match for you, Miss Hollingsford, if for no other reason than her color."

"Why don't you try her, Miss Hollingsford?" Henrietta encouraged, reaching for the brass hook that held the rope in place.

"Don't," Hascot barked, but it was too late. Firenza took a step back and bunched her haunches. Whit knew exactly what was about to happen so he shoved Ruby out of the way and met the brunt of the horse's hooves, right in his ribs.

Fire raged across his chest even as he felt himself stumbling backward into the aisle. His last sight before he hit the cobbles was of Ruby's face, staring at him in anguish.

Chapter Six

Ruby cried out as Whit flew past her, but the stable fairly exploded. Lord Hascot leaped the rope to calm his horse. Lady Amelia rushed to help him. Mr. Calder grabbed Henrietta and pulled her into his arms as if to keep her safe. Mr. Stokely-Trent and Ruby's father came running.

But Ruby reached Whit first.

He lay on the cobblestoned floor, blinking up at the ceiling as if he couldn't imagine how it had gotten there. His mouth opened and closed. She threw herself to the stones beside him, loosened his cravat with trembling fingers.

"Talk to me," she demanded. "Can you breathe?"

He sucked in a deep breath, winced, but nodded.

Relief lasted only a second. She put her hand behind his back to help him sit up. "Where does it hurt?" Ruby asked. "Your chest? Your ribs?"

"Here, my girl. Let me." Her father knelt on the other side, put one hand on Whit's back to steady him and began running his other hand over Whit's coat.

"It's all right," Whit said, and she thought he was

trying for a smile. "I'm more surprised than injured." He raised a hand to block her father's probes.

"You're sure?" Ruby begged, feeling as if the air of the stable was suddenly too thin for her, as well.

"Reasonably." He tried for another smile, then nodded at her father. "With your assistance, sir?"

Ruby's father positioned his shoulder under Whit's arm and helped him to his feet. By then, the others surrounded them, all visibly concerned.

"I'm so sorry, Danning," Henrietta was saying, hands worrying before her navy habit. "I had no idea the creature was so vicious!"

"You nearly scared the life out of us, Danning," Lady Wesworth scolded. "I thought Amelia would faint to see you fallen."

"Enough of that, my lad," his cousin declared, reaching out to clap Whit on the shoulder and forcing another wince from Whit. "I've no interest in inheriting the title this way."

Whit straightened, working his face into his usual poised smile. "It's nothing. Sorry to have concerned you."

Nothing? He acted as if *he* had inconvenienced *them!*

"You were kicked by a horse," Ruby said. "You should be seen by a physician. You could have broken a rib, cracked your chest bone."

Whit laid a hand on her shoulder kindly. "I'm fine, Ruby."

Even in her agitation she saw Lady Wesworth frown and Mr. and Mrs. Stokely-Trent exchange glances. They didn't like the fact that he'd used her first name. At the moment, she couldn't care less. He'd been hurt. He had no business shrugging it off, no matter now manly he thought he must appear. She was ready to argue the point when Lord Hascot pushed into the group.

"She's right, Danning," he said, a lock of dark hair falling into his equally dark eyes. "I keep a physician on staff. Come up to the house, and I'll have him look you over."

Ruby thought Whit would argue, but he'd been stretching his muscles and growing paler with each movement, as if he, too, wondered about the extent of his injuries. Now he nodded. "Very well. Charles, if you'll be so good as to escort our guests back to the carriage, I'll rejoin you shortly."

His cousin nodded as well, but the women immediately set up a howl.

"Amelia cannot be forced from your side at such a time, my lord," Lady Wesworth protested, pushing the blonde forward. Lady Amelia, paler than Whit, clasped her hands in front of her riding habit as if she were ready to pray the Lord into action on his behalf, or her own.

"You will require nursing, Danning," Henrietta insisted, stepping forward, as well. "I've read extensively on the subjects of anatomy and physiology."

"My physician won't abide amateurs in the room," Lord Hascot informed them before turning to Whit. "Can you walk?"

"I can." He stepped forward and nearly collided with his fawning friends, all of whom importuned him to allow them to accompany him.

Ruby's temper, which she'd guarded so carefully, snapped. She elbowed Lady Wesworth aside, stamped her boot down on Henrietta's instep and wedged her body between Charles Calder and Whit. Gasps echoed on all sides, but a sufficient hole opened to allow Whit to exit with Lord Hascot.

"Effective," Henrietta acknowledged before limping out of the stable.

"How dare you!" Lady Wesworth cried, recovering herself enough to point an imperious finger at Ruby. "She struck me!"

"And I might bite you, too, if you stick that finger at me again," Ruby warned, eyes narrowing.

Lady Wesworth yanked back her hand with another gasp.

"Here now, here now." Ruby's father waded into the group. "We're all concerned about Lord Danning. It's set everyone on edge. I'm sure a lady of your kind and generous nature must find this situation particularly difficult, your ladyship."

She inflated, chest pointing accusingly at Ruby. "Assuredly, sir. You would do well to remind your daughter of the proper way to behave under such trying circumstances."

Ruby felt her father's grip on her elbow. "Oh, I will, your ladyship. Right now."

Ruby didn't fight him as he pulled her out of the stable. She couldn't have abided another minute with the others anyway. She allowed him to tug her through a gap in the fence and onto the pasture. But as soon as they were safely out of hearing, she pulled out of his grip and stopped him.

"Don't you dare ring a peal over me," she scolded. "They were selfish and useless, the lot of them. He could be seriously injured, and all they could do was stand in his way!"

"And there's a fine physician seeing to him now," her father pointed out. "Edinburgh trained, no doubt. Nothing but the best for Lord Hascot's horses."

"Horses!" Ruby stared at him. "You mean the fellow is a veterinarian?"

"What other sort of physician do you think a horse farm needs on retainer?"

Ruby pushed past him. "That is ridiculous. I've a mind to speak to Lord Hascot this very minute!"

Her father pulled her up. "Ruby Hollingsford, you settle down. Animal doctor or human doctor, he'll know what he's about." He dropped his hold and shook his head. "What's wrong, girl? It's not like you to lose your head this way."

Ruby wrapped an arm about her middle. She wasn't sure why, but the gesture always calmed her. Now, however, every fiber of her being seemed to be protesting the idea of stopping and thinking, demanding that she act. She forced herself to take a deep breath, to feel the air brushing her cheek, to hear the whicker of one of Lord Hascot's horses as it passed beyond them.

Hateful, vicious things! Something that magnificent had no business lashing out like that! And she wasn't much in charity with Henrietta Stokely-Trent at the moment either. She thought she knew so much, even about a man's horses. Whit had to bear the price for her actions, and all because he had been trying keep Ruby safe.

"It's my fault," she burst out. "He was hurt because he was trying to protect me!"

"Now, then." Her father patted her shoulder with one hand and began rummaging in his waistcoat pocket with the other as if he suspected she would shortly need a handkerchief. "That's what gentlemen do: protect those they love."

Ruby sniffed, refusing to let a tear fall. "He doesn't

love me. And I don't love him, so don't start harping on that string."

Her father appeared to be assured she was not about to turn on the tears, for he dropped both hands. "Still, you must admit you're a bit touchy where he's concerned. Look at the way you lit into him the first day, just because the poor fellow had the misfortune to be born the heir of an earl."

Ruby couldn't help smiling, remembering. "It wasn't his birthright but the fact that he hadn't confided it to me that rankled."

"Ah," her father said, going to lean against the wooden fence that encircled the pasture. "Then you don't hold his title against him."

"I didn't say that." Ruby went to join him, bracing both hands on the wood. Across from them, the others were milling about the landau. Grooms were scurrying to close the hoods on the carriage in response to the thickening mist.

Her father blew out a breath. "You must put that incident with Lord Milton behind you. He was a scoundrel of the first order, title or no. I still wish you'd let me hire someone to thrash him."

Ruby leaned her chin on her hands. "You can't thrash an aristocrat, Father. That's a hanging offense for commoners like us. And I told you, I don't ever want to hear his name again."

"Fine, fine," her father muttered. "I'll say no more on the matter if you promise not to think of it further."

She wished she could promise that. She knew what was right. *Let not the sun go down upon your anger,* the Bible said. She was supposed to forgive Lord Milton. But how did you forgive someone who took your heart and spat on it?

"What are they doing?" she asked instead, straightening. One by one, Whit's other guests were climbing into the landau.

"Getting out of the rain," her father guessed. He glanced up at the sky and blinked as a drop hit the end of his nose and rolled down his chin. "Best we do likewise."

Ruby crossed her arms over her chest. "I'll wait until I know Whit is fine. Besides, I have no wish to join *them.*"

Her father shook his head. "Why must you be so pigheaded, girl? Why are you so defensive around these people?"

She could feel her temper simmering in the background, waiting for the least offense to boil over. "Perhaps I'm tired of pretending to be something I'm not."

Her father frowned. "What do you mean? You're a clever, kindhearted, pretty girl. Why should you need to pretend to be anything else?"

Ruby felt the rain on her cheeks. "I'm a clever, kindhearted, pretty daughter of a jeweler who grew up in Wapping," she told him. "I don't belong among the aristocracy, and they know it. Sometimes I think I must give off an odor. Or perhaps there's a sign pinned to my back: Watch out for this one!"

"Now, then, none of that," her father insisted. "You're better heeled than that Lady Amelia and a sight better intentioned than that Henrietta Stokely-Trent. They have nothing on you, my girl."

Ruby rolled her eyes. "Only titles and family connections."

"And aren't I trying to have you marry into both?"

Ruby started, then peered closer at her father. His craggy brows were drawn down, and water dripped from his long nose. But he had never looked more serious.

"Is that what you're trying to do?" she demanded. "Help me advance in Society?"

He shrugged, his brown coat hunching even as drops darkened the wool. "Why not? As you said, you have everything else. If I want the best for you, I must help you rise above your circumstances."

"Perhaps I like my circumstances," Ruby countered, pushing off from the fence and starting for the house. "Perhaps I'm content with my station."

Her father snorted as he followed. "You? Content? When you were a babe you crawled across the floor before anyone knew you could even sit up. You raced your pony the first day I put you in the saddle. Every task you mastered, at every game you excelled. There is nothing content about you, my girl."

Ruby didn't answer him, marching across the pasture toward the house. He was probably right, for at the moment she could not be content until she'd seen Whit. She let herself out the gate and hurried onto the stoop as the rain fell harder.

Inside the house, a helpful footman directed her to the library, where the veterinarian was apparently examining Whit. She barely noted the fine paintings, the thick carpet as she hurried down the corridor. She only knew she had to be certain Whit had taken no serious hurt. She'd never forgive herself otherwise.

She paused in the doorway. The room was dark—dark paneling, dark furnishings, heavy drapes drawn against any outside light as if the very air was trying to hide. Lord Hascot held a lamp for a tall, slender man with spectacles on his nose and curly hair nearly as red as Ruby's.

Whit was sitting on the back of a chair, coat and waistcoat gone so that only his linen shirt covered his chest, submitting to the fellow's inspection. Ruby couldn't tear her eyes away.

Lord Hascot looked up and scowled. Whit turned his head and smiled at her as if in encouragement, but the horse lord set down his lamp on a nearby table and stalked to the door.

"Wait in the withdrawing room," he directed her and shut the door.

Oh! She was certainly glad her father had fixed on Whit, for if she were forced to endure much more of Lord Hascot's company she'd likely end up shooting him in a fit of pique. Still, she consoled herself as she turned away, Whit did not appear to be suffering too much. She located the withdrawing room, an equally dark space that seemed somehow lonely, and plunked herself down on the brocaded sofa to wait.

Her father found her a short time later. "The others have gone back to the Lodge," he reported as he took a seat on a sturdy wooden chair nearby.

Ruby shook her head. "Couldn't they even wait to be certain Lord Danning is not seriously hurt?"

Her father shrugged. "Lady Wesworth says Lady Amelia's constitution is too delicate to be exposed to such inclement weather, and Mrs. Stokely-Trent had a case of the vapors and required her husband's and daughter's attention. They all went back in the landau with Lady Amelia's and Mr. Calder's horses tied behind."

Ruby threw up her hands. "So they expect Whit to ride back, injured and all! Never mind how we're to return. Why do you persist in courting these people, Father?"

Before he could answer, Lord Hascot strode into the room, Whit right behind him. Whit was dressed once more in his riding coat, but his waistcoat seemed broader and he moved gingerly, hesitantly. Ruby was on her feet and advancing before he spoke.

"I'm fine," he assured her with a smile. "The physician wrapped my ribs as a precaution, and I imagine I'll have a bruise or two, but nothing was broken."

Ruby breathed out a sigh. "Thank the Lord!"

"Indeed," he agreed. "I only regret that I gave you and my other guests such a scare."

"No harm done," her father declared, rising, as well. "The others have already decamped for the Lodge. I suggest we do likewise." He turned to Lord Hascot. "Would you be willing to loan us a carriage, my lord? I didn't come prepared to ride, which I tell you I regret, for there could be nothing finer than to be astride one of your marvelous mounts."

As usual, her father's flattery won the day, and the horse lord provided them with a fine carriage to return them to the Lodge.

Ruby watched Whit as he took his seat opposite her and her father on the leather-covered benches. She thought he was trying to be brave, but his mouth quirked as he sat, and he kept shifting as if searching for a comfortable position. His injury pained him more than he cared for her to know.

"You realize this is the perfect excuse to rid yourself of your guests," she told him as the carriage started off for the bridge, a groom riding Whit's horse. "Tell them the physician ordered you to rest."

"But he didn't," he replied with a smile that ought to have held more regret in Ruby's opinion. "Besides, I do little at the Lodge but rest, even with guests."

"Not these guests," Ruby insisted, edging forward on her seat to make her point. "They demand your time, your attention. They will be satisfied with nothing less."

He inclined his head. "I will, of course, do my duty."

Ruby shoved herself back into the seat in disgust. "Duty! Your duty, sir, is to yourself. You did not ask for this house party—you told me so. It would seem with your injury you will be hard-pressed to continue playing host. Send us all packing!"

Her father patted her hand where it lay on the bench. "Now, then, you heard his lordship. He is a gentleman, and he'll face his duty with honor."

Ruby pulled away. "You make it sound so noble. This isn't a war or some disaster. He has rights as well, you know."

"Thank you, Ruby," Whit interrupted. "Never have I had a more gallant defender."

Ruby's gaze snapped to his, but her frustration melted at the look in his purple-blue eyes. He wasn't being sarcastic. He truly admired the way she was trying to protect him. Heat flushed up her, and she dropped her gaze. She was being forward; she knew it. He was an intelligent, capable fellow, and if he said he could persevere, she should do what she could to support him.

But she would not confess she was glad he wasn't going to send them off. For something told her that if she never saw Whit Calder again, her life would be poorer for it.

Whit's chest ached. There was no way around it. He was thankful the injury wasn't serious, that the Lord had seen fit to protect him. He'd refused the dose of laudanum the physician had offered, knowing it would impede his abilities to return to the Lodge and interact with his guests. Yet he couldn't help thinking that the best medicine was sitting across from him, gazing at him with green eyes that were somehow as fiery as her hair.

How fiercely she championed him! He couldn't remember ever having a champion. In his life of privilege growing up, he'd never needed one. At Eton, he'd been one of the tallest and most athletic lads, and one of the smartest. He and Quimby had been a force to be reckoned with. And when his father had died, everyone had expected Whit to be the champion. Even the three men who had served as trustees and guardians until he reached his majority had believed that allowing him to make decisions would help him become the earl he needed to be to carry on after his father.

They would none of them have advised him to neglect his duty now for the sake of something as insignificant as his own comfort.

"I thank you both for your concern," he said, leaning against the seat back to lessen the tension on his ribs. "I cannot return your kindness by sending you and the others away."

Ruby puffed out a sigh and turned her gaze out the window, where they were passing through the village. Whit felt for her. She truly didn't want to be here. If he was the gentleman he claimed to be, he would give her leave to return to London. Yet the very fact that she was such an ardent supporter made him wish for her to stay.

"Wise fellow," her father said with a nod of approval, though his gaze rested on his daughter's head, and his smile faded as Ruby steadfastly said nothing.

Time to turn the conversation to other matters. "I see the rain followed us," Whit tried. "Perhaps it will be better tomorrow."

"No doubt," Ruby's father agreed, nodding with far more enthusiasm than the subject warranted.

Ruby sighed once more.

"And what of Hollyoak Farm?" Whit tried again. "Did you notice a horse that particularly interested you, Ruby?"

"After seeing what happened to you?" Ruby told the view. "No."

Oh, but her back was up. He glanced at her father, who shrugged as if to disavow all ability to sway her. Then he leaned closer, and Whit saw a decided twinkle in his gray eyes.

"Not much of a horse man myself, my lord," he confided. "I prefer the pleasures of the town. And I appreciate a fellow who helps make that town better. As such, I must thank you."

Whit frowned, but Ruby turned from the window to eye her father, as well.

"Oh, indeed, indeed," Hollingsford assured him. "Weren't you behind the recent renovations at the orphan asylum?"

Ruby looked to Whit, eyes widening. "*You* engineered the new wing?"

He refused to preen under her admiration. "I was one of several concerned about the state of the building," he replied. "It required little work on my part."

Ruby cocked her head as if trying to determine the truth of that statement, but her father shook his finger at Whit. "That's not what I heard. Gossip had it you were there twice a week, confirming that everything was going as planned, encouraging the children and the staff. Didn't the little ones throw you a party at the end?"

"They deserved a celebration," Whit said, smiling

in memory of the beaming faces, the little hands reaching to shake his. "For all they've been through, they are still children."

Ruby's mouth twitched, as if she were fighting a smile. Her father must have noticed, for he nudged her knee with his own. "Ruby's quite fond of children, too. Tell his lordship about your school, my girl."

She shifted away from him as if uncomfortable with his insistence, but she met Whit's gaze. "I am attempting to bring a free school to Wapping."

The height of her chin and the tension in her tone told him she expected him to argue with her. Some of the poorest of London's poor lived in Wapping, eking out a living along the Thames. He'd heard more than one lord complain that the area was a blight on the city and should be leveled. Few people were willing to take action to help the poor souls who lived there.

Whit applauded her, gloves thudding. "A bold venture, but one that will give those children opportunities for a better life." He dropped his hands. "I have supported the Thames police, headquartered in Wapping. If you have need for a Parliamentary bill for the school, I'd be happy to sponsor it."

Her smile curved, and he felt a constriction in his chest that had nothing to do with the wrapping on his ribs.

"You see?" her father all but crowed. "I told you you'd find support if you asked. Lord Danning even had something to say about the old sailor's home, from what I hear."

The fellow would have him a saint in a moment! He could not take such credit. He knew how often he struggled to manage the requests put upon his time.

"Interesting how well informed you are about my activities, sir," he said.

Ruby narrowed her eyes at her father, but Hollingsford chuckled. "Oh, I try to keep up with the doings of my clients," he said with an easy smile. "Never know when some bauble might be needed to commemorate an occasion, say a wedding." He winked at his daughter.

Ruby scowled at him. "Lord Danning isn't a client, from what I can tell. You both claim never to have met." She glanced at Whit for confirmation, and he inclined his head in agreement.

Her father smiled. "We never met before this visit, although I did undertake a commission, through your cousin, my lord."

The way he looked at Whit said he thought Whit would remember the occasion. But Whit had no idea what he was talking about.

"So that's how you know Mr. Calder," Ruby said, eyes gleaming in challenge. "Just what commission was this?"

"Now, then, you know I never betray client privilege," he said, leaning back and crossing his arms over his chest as if to put up a barricade to additional questions.

Ruby turned to Whit again. "As you were the client, you have every right to make him confess. What did you have your cousin do about a piece of jewelry?"

Whit shook his head. "I am unaware of any such commission. I fear you must be mistaken, Hollingsford."

Her father nodded, but he didn't drop his hands. "I beg your pardon, then. I only know that your efforts are laudable, my lord. I admire a fellow who tries to leave the world a little better than when he entered it."

"Only doing my duty," Whit assured him.

Ruby's frown didn't ease. But was it his activities or her father's that concerned her?

Chapter Seven

Ruby could barely sit still as the carriage trundled through the village and down toward the bridge that led to the Lodge. Though she couldn't help feeling impressed by all the generous actions her father ascribed to Whit and his humble response to the praise, she felt her temper stirring inside her.

Certainly, she had enough ingredients for a proper stew: her concern for Whit, her frustration about this visit, even the relentless rain that obscured the Derbyshire peaks as they crossed the bridge. If she didn't act soon, something was bound to spill out, and she knew the results would be messy. She simply had to find a way to let off some steam!

The best way to do that, she had always found, was to focus her attentions on something or someone else. That's what she'd done when Lord Milton had proved to be a scoundrel. That's what she did when she was lonely in London. There were always those less fortunate who needed help, a friend who could use cheering up.

And right now, the person in her opinion who needed the most help was Whitfield Calder, Earl of Danning.

He sat across from her, smiling at something her father said as the carriage pulled into the yard in front of the Lodge, but he didn't fool her. She saw the way he held himself, far too stiff in contrast to his usual easy grace. Despite his words, his injury pained him. And dealing with his guests wasn't going to help.

"Thank you again for your kindness," he told her and her father as the carriage drew to a stop and footmen came running to help them alight. "I appreciate you waiting for me and accompanying me home."

Did he know he called this place home? His duties, to his other estate and to Parliament, must require him to live many places. Yet this quaint stone cottage was where his heart lay. Ruby's temper bubbled up anew. It wasn't right that these people were spoiling his time here!

"Tell Mr. Quimby his master has been injured and requires his assistance," she murmured to the footman who helped her from the carriage. The fellow looked startled, but he hurried into the house ahead of them.

She made a point of linking her arm with Whit's, strolling along at half her normal pace to ensure he walked slowly, as well. Though she could hear Lady Wesworth's commanding voice, complaining as usual, even from the entry, she steered Whit toward the stairs.

Mr. Quimby was just descending. His head was high, his step measured, his clothes finer than those of most of the other gentlemen. Though his hair—a nimbus of yellow about his head—always looked a bit unkempt, it seemed to emphasize his haste in answering her call.

"Quimby," Whit said with a frown, removing his arm from hers. "Is something wrong?"

"There is an urgent matter requiring your attention upstairs, my lord," he said.

Good. That meant Whit would have a few moments away from the others, perhaps a chance to rest.

"There appears to be an urgent matter downstairs, as well," Whit replied, aiming his frown toward the withdrawing room, where Mr. Stokely-Trent's rumble had joined the hubbub.

"I'll see to it," Ruby promised. "Besides, you'll want to change."

He turned his frown her way, as if he could not understand what she was about. She returned her hand to his arm. "Please, Whit. Let me help. It will keep me from going mad."

His smile hitched up at one corner as if he thought her quite mad enough already. "Very well, Ruby. Thank you. I'll be down shortly."

She met Mr. Quimby's gaze around him. "Take all the time you need. It isn't every day a fellow is kicked by a horse."

She had the satisfaction of seeing the valet's eyes goggle. But he swiftly recovered and stepped aside to allow Whit to precede him up the stairs.

"See to it that he gets some rest, will you?" Ruby murmured to the valet.

Quimby offered a quick smile. "Not so easy with Lord Danning, I fear. But I'll do what I can. Thank you, Miss Hollingsford."

Ruby nodded and stepped back.

"That was nicely done, my girl," her father murmured as the valet followed Whit up the stairs. "What now?"

Someone struck the spinet's keys with excessive force. Ruby winced.

"For now," she told her father, "keep them from

eating their young while I get out of this riding habit, and then send the butler to me. I intend to tame those nobs, once and for all!"

Whit allowed Quimby to help him off with his coat, sucking in a breath at the pain the movement caused. Even wrapped in linen, his ribs felt as if they were on fire.

"I thought you knew better than to stand behind a horse," Quimby commented after Whit explained what had happened.

"I thought I knew a great many things I seem to have forgotten," Whit replied, sitting on the edge of the bed. Just the dip of the mattress set his body to protesting. "Such as how to manage a simple house party. Help me with these boots, will you?"

Quimby straddled his leg and tugged on the right boot. "I will send your excuses to your guests and request cool compresses from the kitchen."

"You will do neither," Whit argued, grimacing as the first boot came off and his body recoiled. "I know my duty."

In answer, Quimby yanked off the second boot and marched them to the dressing room.

Whit bit back a harsh word as he gingerly straightened. Without the tight-fitting coat, it felt easier to breathe. The chair by the fire beckoned, but he could not leave Ruby to the questionable mercy of his quarrelsome guests. Quimby may have invited them all here, but Whit was the host.

His valet returned with a quilted navy satin banyan picked out in gold thread and two cravats.

"Feeling puckish?" Whit teased as he stood and turned to allow Quimby to ease the loose coat up his arms and over his shoulders. "You haven't required more than one try at tying a cravat since we were lads."

"I have always said that if you cannot manage a decent fold on the first pass," Quimby agreed, coming around to the front, "cease trying. However, in this case, the second cravat is for your arm."

Whit frowned as his valet whipped off the wilted cravat, then set about neatly tying the new one around Whit's neck. "My arm isn't injured, Quimby."

"Are you certain?" Quimby asked, taking a step back and cocking his head. "A sling is accounted quite dashing and heroic, even if you don't need it. So, I've heard, is an eye patch, but I don't have one handy, worse luck."

Whit chuckled. "No sling and no eye patch. I have no wish to appear heroic before these people. Now, was something awaiting my attention or was that more of your posturing?"

Quimby allowed himself a sigh as he went to the travel desk set on a small table by the bed. "As to its urgency, only you can say. We retrieved the mail from the village while you were out, and you were forwarded several requests."

Whit sighed, as well. He had tried to hire experienced, capable men as the stewards and bailiffs over his holdings, but they each seemed compelled to defer to his judgment. He was thankful Quimby generally read all his mail and gave him only those which truly required his involvement.

"The steward at your seat in Suffolk is concerned about some recent rains," Quimby reported now, picking up a sheet of paper as if to refresh his memory. "He wants your permission to open the gates on the drainage ditches."

"Tell him to open them only if that will cause no

damage to our neighbors downstream," Whit said, stretching a bit to settle the bandage.

"Very good," Quimby replied with a nod, eyes on the parchment. "And there was a note from your cousin Lucretia asking if she might wear the Danning diamonds to an assembly in Kent in August."

Odd that Quimby thought such a request required Whit's attention, but perhaps Lucretia was one of those who insisted on only dealing with the earl and would not settle for Quimby's response. He waved a hand, taking a few steps and finding himself steadier than when he'd arrived. "Of course. Though why she wants to deck herself out for a country assembly is beyond me."

"The Danning diamonds are a magnificent set, my lord," Quimby reminded him, rather smugly, Whit thought. "No doubt she hopes to impress her friends with her connections."

"I'm only thankful Charles didn't inherit his sister's pretensions," Whit said, moving toward the door.

"As you say, my lord."

The sentence was clipped, beyond precise. Whit paused to eye his friend. "Has Charles done something to offend you, Quimby?"

His valet laid the note back on the travel desk and busied himself with smoothing the bedclothes Whit had disturbed. "Not me personally, my lord."

Whit strode back into the room. "When the number of *my lords* rivals the number of sentences spoken between us, I know something is wrong. Out with it."

Quimby offered him a tight-lipped smile. "I am merely concerned for Mr. Calder's finances. He seems acutely interested in marrying one of your ladies, all of whom have funds to spare."

Whit started laughing, until his ribs protested. "Is

that it?" he asked his valet. "You go to all the trouble of setting up a campaign to find me a wife, and you fear Charles will win a wife instead? If God intends me to marry one of these women, I trust Him to see it through."

Quimby beamed. "I'm very glad to hear you say that. For a while, I was certain you intended to get in the way of your own happiness."

Whit frowned. "What are you talking about?"

Quimby shrugged. "You have set inordinately high standards for marriage. You've told me about how your mother and father were so intricately linked that one could barely survive without the other. I've wondered if such a paragon as your mother can exist on this plane."

Whit stiffened. "I've never implied that my mother was a saint."

"You've hardly remembered whether she was sinner," Quimby pointed out good-naturedly. "And I'd be the last person to tell you you can't marry for love, my lad. But does it strike you that perhaps you have excessively high expectations for the emotion?"

"No," Whit said flatly. "I've had to manage on my own since I was fifteen, doing my duty at any cost. I know my responsibility to father an heir but the least I should expect is to marry a woman of my own choosing."

"Precisely," Quimby agreed. "Now all I ask is that you choose her."

Whit shook his head as he started for the door once more. "From the sound of it, you have the winner all picked out."

"Not at all!" Quimby protested, following him. "But you can't mind me praying that you'll have the wisdom to know the lady yourself."

Whit refused to respond as he quit the room. Quimby could pray all he liked. Whit would be the one to decide when he would give his heart. For now, he descended to the ground floor and steeled himself to deal with his guests.

He hadn't heard any shouts or crying coming from the nether regions, but that might only mean his guests were sitting in the withdrawing room glaring gloomily at each other. However, what he found inside the room stunned him, and he could only halt in the doorway, staring.

The space, which admittedly had a martial air to the furnishings, was for once the picture of placid domesticity. The elder Stokely-Trents, Lady Wesworth and Ruby's father were playing whist civilly and calmly. He even spotted a smile curving the marchioness's generally unforgiving lips as she laid down the ace of hearts. Lady Amelia was humming as her fingers ranged along the keyboard in a congenial air, and Henrietta and Charles had a pile of books between them on the sofa and were studiously comparing titles and contents.

Meanwhile, Ruby, now gowned in a russet day dress with puffy tops on the long sleeves and every edge trimmed in double bands of ecru lace, flitted from one group to the other, encouraging, inquiring about needs, offering support. He wasn't sure whether to join them or tiptoe back upstairs and leave them in peace.

But Henrietta spotted him and waved a hand. "Danning! You're among the living!"

His other guests immediately perked up, and he felt as if the temperature was rising in the room. Ruby moved to the center of the space. With the candlelight gleaming in her upswept hair, she commanded attention even before she spoke.

"How good to see you, my lord," she said, smile bright. "Lady Amelia has been practicing an air just to please you, and Miss Stokely-Trent has chosen a selection of books for you to enjoy while recuperating."

As if satisfied that their various offspring had been given their due, the parents returned to their game.

"How kind of you both," Whit said with a nod to either woman. As if that was all they had wanted as well, they, too, returned to their pastimes. He drew closer to Ruby.

A smile was playing about her lovely lips, and for once the light in her green eyes was more sparkle than fire.

"How did you manage this?" he murmured.

She winked at him. "Oh, a lady will do most anything for a little peace, my lord." She leaned closer. "I advise you to go listen to a song, then comment on the literary offerings. By then, an early dinner should be ready to be served."

Bemused, Whit did as she bid.

The peace remained unbroken through dinner. Several times he caught his butler or footman looking to Ruby for direction, and a lifting of her brow was all it took to set them back on course. She'd obviously enlisted their assistance in keeping the guests entertained. But Whit would like to have been standing in the kitchen to see how his mercurial chef took the news that the food was to be served a full two hours earlier than usual. Still, he could not fault the ragout of beef, braised asparagus and compote of summer fruit that was brought in for the first course.

He also wondered how his butler, Mr. Hennessy, felt about the change in the seating arrangements. Someone had written out the names of his guests on little

pieces of paper, elegant script on parchment, and set
them above the plates along the table. Whit was positioned at the head of the table and Lady Wesworth at
the foot as if to give them pride of place. Lady Amelia sat on Whit's right, Henrietta at his left, so neither
family could complain he was not giving them sufficient attention.

Whit was further buffeted from the older guests by
having Ruby and Charles sit opposite each other and
between the young ladies and their parents. With such
an arrangement, the conversation was as pleasant as
the food, and Whit didn't have to worry about Charles
continuing his flirting with Ruby.

Indeed, he noticed that his cousin spent most of his
time conversing with Henrietta, with only occasional
forays with her mother on the other side. Ruby said little, smiling as conversation flowed around her, helping
Lady Amelia to a particularly large piece of cake that
was served with the second course. He could not get
over the changes she had wrought.

In fact, it wasn't until Henrietta asked about tomorrow's activities that Whit felt himself the center of attention once more.

"I have several ideas," he told them all. "But whether
any come to pass depends on the weather."

His guests did not argue with that. As before, Lady
Wesworth led the ladies out first, and Whit and the
other gentlemen did not tarry long over their discus-
sions before joining them in the withdrawing room.
Lady Amelia all but pounced on him the moment he
entered, blue eyes bright.

"We are playing Consequences, my lord," she said,
handing him a piece of paper that had already been
folded over several times. "You are to write the name

of something a gentleman might wear, and I will pass this to Mr. Calder to have him write something a lady might wear."

Whit accepted the quill she offered and wrote "red waistcoat" on the slip. Lady Amelia then pursued Charles to the other side of the room to get his input.

"I'm not familiar with the game," Whit admitted as he took a seat on one of the armchairs by the fire. The two mothers were seated on the sofa, with Ruby's father flanking them on the other armchair. Charles and Mr. Stokely-Trent drew up the other two armchairs for Ruby and Lady Amelia before taking their seats on the chairs from which they had played cards earlier.

"It's been around since I was a girl," Mrs. Stokely-Trent replied. "Each person must answer a particular question, such as the name of a lady, the name of a gentleman, how they met, what they wore, what they said and what the consequences were." She smiled at Lady Wesworth. "We used to have such fun on rainy days coming up with the tallest tales."

Lady Wesworth actually smiled. "Yes, I remember playing it, as well. Ah, have you finished then, Amelia? Read it out."

Amelia hurried into the center of the circle but swiftly passed the paper to Ruby, who raised her brows in surprise.

"Do read it, Miss Hollingsford," Amelia begged. "You are by far the most brave when it comes to declaiming."

Remembering Ruby's attempt at a poem from earlier in the visit, Whit hid a smile. But Ruby rose agreeably and opened the paper.

"'Handsome Adam,'" she read, pausing to wiggle her eyebrows and gaining a giggle from Lady Amelia in the process, "'and sassy Firenza—' hmm, I wonder where that name came from?"

Mrs. Stokely-Trent concealed her smile behind her hand.

"'Met at church.'" Ruby paused to eye her listeners. "How very virtuous, to be sure."

Whit felt his face stretching in a grin as she continued with his contribution.

"'He wore a red waistcoat, and she wore a fetching brown dinner gown with ribbons down the front.'"

Henrietta stared down at her brown dinner gown trimmed with satin ribbons and craned her neck for a glance at Charles, who grinned, as well.

"'He said, "I believe I have made a fortune on the exchange."'"

"Smart chap," Mr. Stokely-Trent put in.

"'And she said,'" Ruby continued, clearly fighting a smile herself, "'"I should like the largest diamond available, if you please."'"

"Smart lass," Ruby's father added with a wink to his daughter.

"'And the consequence was,'" Ruby finished, "'they both went fishing in the rain!'"

Laughter ringed the room.

"Let's try another!" Lady Amelia cried as soon as the sound began to fade. Immediately, she glanced at her mother. "If that's all right with you, Mother."

Her mother waved a hand. "Certainly. Pass the paper about, in a different order this time, mind you, so we have a chance to think of a clever answer for another question."

Whit stood as Ruby returned to her seat next to his. "Well done," he murmured as Lady Amelia began circulating with a fresh piece of paper.

"It was actually Lady Wesworth's idea," Ruby explained. "I only encouraged her."

"You've done far more," Whit assured her. "I would never have imagined such a congenial evening was possible."

"Apparently your cousin agrees," Ruby said with a nod to where Charles and Henrietta had their heads close together. "If we were wise, we'd encourage that."

"Ah, so you're not opposed to courting," Whit teased. "So long as you're not the one involved."

She smiled, returning her gaze to his. "In truth, I once thought courting would be delightful. Gazing into each other's eyes, dancing at a crowded ball but feeling as if you were the only two there, standing out on a veranda talking while the stars turn above."

The picture resembled what he'd imagined it might be like should he fall as deeply in love as his mother and father. "What changed your mind?"

"It's cold on that veranda," she replied. "And you cannot simply stand about staring at each other. And crowded dance floors are simply crowded."

Whit shook his head. "I refuse to believe you have no romance left in your soul."

Lady Amelia appeared before them, holding out the paper. "Your turn, Miss Hollingsford. You are to write what the lady would say, and then, my lord, you are to prescribe the consequences."

Ruby took the paper and scrawled something, then folded it so Whit could not see and handed it to him. Given their conversation, he knew what he must write. He penned the words and handed the sheet to Lady Amelia.

"I'll read it this time," Henrietta volunteered, rising

and coming to Lady Amelia's side. Lady Amelia surrendered the page with a grateful smile.

"'Wealthy Hieronymus—'" she stopped to arch a brow, and Ruby's father snickered "'—and gorgeous Ruby met at Almack's.'"

Whit glanced at Ruby and knew the others were doing likewise. Her color was rising, but she kept a pleasant smile on her face as Henrietta continued.

"'He wore a sultan's turban, and she wore a jeweled snood.'"

"A snood?" Lady Amelia whispered to her mother. "Do I own one of those?"

Lady Wesworth waved her hand, but whether to encourage her daughter to hush or Henrietta to continue, Whit wasn't sure.

"'He said to her, "You are more beautiful than a sunset." She said to him, "I do not believe in true love, sir."'"

Whit knew that had been Ruby's contribution, but she did not glance his way.

"'And they lived happily ever after,'" Henrietta concluded.

"I say, I rather doubt that," Charles put in, and the others laughed.

"Mr. Calder," Ruby called. "I believe you promised to show the gentlemen your book of flies."

"I'd very much like to see that, as well," Henrietta said.

Charles hopped to his feet and drew Mr. Stokely-Trent, Ruby's father and Henrietta out with him to retrieve the book from the fishing closet. Ruby, Lady Amelia and the two mothers stayed behind with Whit. Lady Amelia wandered back to the spinet, and the two mothers began conversing about mutual acquaintances.

"They meant no harm by using your name," Whit said to Ruby.

She nodded, but one hand was wrapped around her middle. "It was only a game, Whit. I know that. This visit is nothing but a game to many of them. Unfortunately, they will do anything to win."

Chapter Eight

Happily ever after. Ruby shook her head as she climbed into bed that night after dismissing her maid. Did Whit truly think that was possible? Oh, she'd read books that promised such an end, but she no longer believed them. She'd had her happily ever after clasped in her hand, once, only to have it slip through her fingers like sand.

Or mud.

She lay on her back and gazed up at the underside of the bed's canopy. The curve of the lace covering was easy to follow even in the moonlight trickling in her window. But instead of the fine material, she saw that handsome face, that winsome smile of Phillip, Lord Milton.

They'd met at a ball on her first Season, and he'd soon become a frequent visitor to her home. He'd called her beautiful, his remarkable Ruby, the gem of London, and in his gaze she'd felt perfect. Her father was already planning the set of wedding rings he'd create for them.

Then one afternoon instead of taking her home from an outing in the park, he'd driven her to an elegant town house in Mayfair, ushered her through the opulent rooms and offered to make her its mistress.

And his.

Ruby had been certain she'd misunderstood, even as he took her in his arms and kissed her.

She'd pushed against his chest, hard, and then harder to make him disengage.

"Your mistress?" She'd nearly choked on the words. "I thought you were courting me! I thought you'd wanted to marry me!"

He'd adjusted his cravat as if maintaining appearances was truly the only thing that mattered to him. "Surely you understand that I could never marry a woman of your sort. But I promise I will take care of you for as long as I'm able. You won't get that offer from many men of my stature."

"I certainly hope not," Ruby said. Then she'd turned on her heel and stalked out.

It had been a long walk back to her father's, but she'd gone with head high, even as her eyes burned with tears she refused to shed. Phillip wasn't worth her tears. None of the aristocracy were worth her tears. None of them were worth the time of day.

And yet...

Whit seemed different. When he looked at her, she felt pretty, clever, useful. She knew she was all of those things, but it was refreshing to find someone besides her father who agreed with her. Perhaps that was why she liked Whit. He seemed to genuinely enjoy her company, to appreciate her efforts and her sense of humor.

She should be satisfied with that, she told herself as she turned to face the window. Until this house party, she'd convinced herself admiration was sufficient. There were always gentlemen willing to offer a compliment, escort her to the opera. The all-consuming fire of love wasn't true affection. Now something whispered there might be more. That she really could stand in the moonlight and kiss the one she loved.

Who seemed to bear an uncanny resemblance to Whit when she thought on it. She fell asleep with the vision on her mind and woke to glorious sunshine with a smile on her face.

While her maid set out her clothing, Ruby stood in front of the window in her dressing gown, catching the scent of orchids on the soft breeze that rustled the curtains.

A movement down by the stream caught her eye. Whit had evidently risen early to sneak in some fishing. He had waded into the water, the current lapping his boots. As she watched, he began moving his arm, backward and forward, backward and forward. Like the gossamer strand of a spider, his line lengthened, shining in the pearly light, to settle on the water.

Though the movement must sting after his injury yesterday, he was grace itself, a maestro conducting an orchestra, a seasoned coachman mastering a powerful team. Every movement, every step was poetry.

Then he leaned back, fingers hauling at the line, and his rod bowed. He'd caught something! Ruby stiffened, stood on her tiptoes to see what was on his hook. He waded deeper, pulling, then releasing, but always shortening the line until the sleek fish, scales flashing silver, leaped from the water.

Ruby threw open the window, leaned out. "Oh, well done, Whit!"

He turned from the river, glanced back, then up, and she knew when he'd sighted her by the way his smile broadened. He held up the fish, its tail flicking about,

and Ruby clapped her hands. He offered her a handsome bow, other hand spread beside him. Another man
might have fallen, stumbled on the slippery rocks. But
fishing, Whit was all confidence. She was still smiling
after she'd dressed and gone down to join him a short
time later for breakfast.

The others seemed to be in equally fine moods. Most
had beat her to the table. Only Lady Wesworth was
lounging upstairs, taking her breakfast in bed, while
Charles Calder had followed Whit's lead and gone fishing.

"Today we view the waterfall," Whit announced as
the rest of them tucked into the boiled eggs and bacon
laid out before them. His smile to Ruby told her he had
no doubt she would enjoy the sight. She smiled back.

"How far?" Mr. Stokely-Trent wanted to know, pausing before taking a sip of his morning tea from the fine
china cup.

"An easy walk of perhaps a mile," Whit assured him.
"And the view is well worth the effort."

Mrs. Stokely-Trent immediately demurred, and Ruby's father offered to stay behind with her and Lady
Wesworth, but Ruby was pleased to see the others showing interest. Anything to get them out of the house!
She was swiftly reaching the end of her ideas on how
to occupy them.

"I've read of the geologic formations in Derby," Henrietta said. "I'd very much like to see some of them for
myself."

"It sounds lovely," Lady Amelia agreed with a sweet
smile and a nod to Ruby. Ruby found she could like the
young lady well enough, so long as her mother wasn't
around.

The plan agreed, they all met in the entry a bit later

that morning. Ruby had spent little time in the country, but she thought she was dressed appropriately. She'd chosen a walking dress of heavier cotton, vertically striped in green and dun, with a white lace ruff at the throat and green kid leather gloves below the long sleeves. Her high-crowned bonnet covered in green and yellow plaid shaded her face from the sun, and her brown leather boots protected her feet from the dirt.

Henrietta was similarly attired in a sky blue walking dress with military braid along the edges. Lady Amelia's frilly muslin gown with its embroidered daisies at the hem and the butter yellow spencer on the top looked decidedly feminine and completely impractical, but both Mr. Calder and Mr. Stokely-Trent complimented her on it, setting her to blushing under her lacey parasol.

The gentlemen were all wearing practical wool coats of various colors, from Mr. Calder in fashionable navy to Whit in his spruce green. They, too, had donned boots and wore broad-brimmed felt hats to ward off the weather. And the sun certainly promised some heat, piercing the leafy canopy of the trees as they set out.

Fern Lodge rested on a shelf between the river and the hills. Nestled among a copse of trees, with the meadow filled with wild orchids close at hand, it was easy to feel as if the house was the entire world. But when Whit led them up the slope in front to its crest, the world opened wide. Hills rose green, one atop the other, mist clinging to the tops and so close Ruby thought she could reach out and touch it.

"What's that?" Lady Amelia asked, and everyone turned in the direction she was gazing.

Staring at the hills was a massive country house, sprawling in all directions. The stone walls glowed like gold in the sunlight, the windows winked like silver. Before the sweep of drive, a fountain bubbled, shooting crystal clear water into the air.

"That is Bellweather Hall," Whit offered. "Home of the Dukes of Bellington."

So, that was how a duke lived. The house must boast more than a hundred rooms, Ruby was sure.

"Is it open to tours?" Henrietta asked as if she, too, had been wondering what it must be like inside.

"Alas, no," Whit said, turning away. "The duke's mother and sister are uncomfortable having strangers view their things."

"Pity," Henrietta said, turning, as well. Ruby thought Lady Amelia sighed before joining them.

What a waste! At school, she'd been taken on tours of the estates of many fine families connected to the Barnsley School. Their homes were crowded with ancient statuary, classical paintings, medieval tapestries. They were happy to open their houses so that others might view the treasures.

But instead of sharing the riches that likely lay inside Bellweather Hall, Lady Bellington and her daughter clutched them close. Why were so many aristocrats so selfish?

Whit was obviously not among their number. As he had when they'd gone to see Lord Hascot, he took the lead, pointing out sights of interest, from the hawk soaring above to the flowers blooming along the path. Between the way he'd hooked his fish that morning to the way he moved easily along the ground, Ruby thought his ribs must not be troubling him. Or at least if they did, he was too proud to let on.

The path he followed was wide enough to allow three people abreast, and they soon fell into groupings. Ruby wasn't surprised to find Henrietta most often beside Whit's cousin, although Mr. Stokely-Trent seemed to be keeping an eye on the pair. That left Ruby and Lady Amelia to walk with Whit.

Everywhere, the recent rains showed their mark. Puddles dotted the path, and in places mud sucked at Ruby's boots. The daisies at Lady Amelia's hem were soon crusted, but she didn't appear to mind. She was gazing about her in wonder.

"Have you traveled much?" Ruby couldn't help asking her as they paused to rest beside a stream that ran down through a draw.

Lady Amelia watched a flock of wild ducks wheel above them before gliding down to settle on the stream. "No, indeed, Miss Hollingsford. My father isn't fond of his seat, so I grew up in London."

"I went to school in Somerset," Ruby confided. "But that wasn't nearly as wild as this."

Next to them, Whit inhaled so deeply Ruby was certain she felt a breeze. "Smell that?" he asked, closing his eyes. "Nothing but resin and water. No coal fires, no dust from carriages passing."

Ruby laughed as she lifted one of her boots free of the mud. "Dust wouldn't last long here."

Whit opened his eyes with a grin as Henrietta came up to them. She held some sort of large monocle before her, turned her back on the vista and gazed into the device.

"What is that?" Ruby asked.

"A Claude glass," Henrietta replied, lowering it a moment to allow Ruby and Lady Amelia to peruse it. "It allows one to better appreciate the picturesque."

It appeared to Ruby to be nothing more than a tinted mirror in a leather holder. Through it, the view seemed misty, plainer. "I think I prefer my sights uncolored," she said, leaning back. "This is glorious enough for me."

"Me, too," Lady Amelia said, glancing about with a shiver of obvious pleasure.

"Give me a moment," Whit said, smile widening, "and I promise you better."

He was true to his word. As they came out of the trees, Ruby saw that the land on their left rose to a cliff, set with rough formations of rock. Farther along, tumbling down its slope was a white freshet, ending in a fall of spray cloaked in rainbow mist. Ruby gasped and heard Lady Amelia do likewise.

Whit grinned at them. "It's even more spectacular up close. Come on."

Ruby shook her head as he loped forward. He was so delighted in his discovery, so eager to share it with them. How could she not admire a man like that?

Not to be outdone, Charles paused beside them and Henrietta. "See those rocks?" he said, pointing to dark blocks of stone jutting out from the cascade on the other side of the stream. "Basalt. Very likely from before the Flood."

"Interesting," Henrietta said with a nod of approval. "And how were they formed?"

He winked at her. "I'll never tell."

Shaking her head, Ruby turned away to follow Whit, leaving Lady Amelia behind with the others.

Whit had started up the slope leading to the top of the cliff and had paused to wait for them, booted feet splayed, hands on the hips of his chamois trousers. As Ruby drew abreast, she could hear the distant roar of the cascade.

"Where does it all come from?" she asked in awe.

"The snows at the top of Bell Tor finished melting

a month ago," he explained, "and the rain the last few days surely helped. All that water has to go somewhere."

"And this joins the River Bell?" she asked, following the freshet downstream with her gaze as it wound through marsh and meadow.

"It joins the Bell, and the Bell joins the Dove. Eventually, it all flows out to sea."

For a moment, standing there, she felt as if she were a tiny piece of an immense puzzle. What was one Ruby Hollingsford among stones from antiquity, hills that touched the sky, water that amassed an ocean? Did God even notice her among all that?

Wherefore, if God so clothe the grass of the field, which today is, and tomorrow is cast into the oven, shall He not much more clothe you, O ye of little faith?

Ruby frowned at the strange thought. But then, as if God had truly noticed her, she felt the oddest sinking feeling. Around her, the earth groaned, began shifting.

"Charles!" Whit shouted, grabbing her about the waist. "Stay back!"

Before she could protest, he heaved her up into his arms and ran.

Whit clung to Ruby as the ground sank under his boots. His ribs were on fire again. Each step was a stumble, each breath a prayer.

Lord, help me!

He made for the nearest outcropping of basalt and swung Ruby up onto it, then scrambled after her.

"What are you doing?" she cried, shoving herself to her feet beside him.

In answer, Whit caught her shoulders and turned her in the direction they had just come. He saw her mouth drop open as she gasped.

The entire hillside had slumped, grass disappearing under mud that was flowing thicker than treacle down to the stream. Already water pooled behind the makeshift dam, and Whit knew it was only time before the pressure burst it apart. The path they had followed was gone. On the far side of the devastation, Charles waved to him, the others crowded around him.

"Are you all right?" he called, voice echoing along the cliff.

"Fine!" Whit called back. "You?"

"Safe! Shall I come for you?"

Whit eyed the muddy mess between them. There'd be no crust. Every step would be difficult. And it was possible that their weight could trigger further collapse.

"No! Take the others back to the Lodge. We'll go along the Edge."

"Be careful!" Charles shouted, then he turned away to marshal the others.

"The edge?" Ruby eyed Whit, and he could hear the resistance in her voice, see it in her frown. "The edge of what?"

Whit nodded to the cliff top. "Calder Edge, that's the name for the grit stone form above us. The series of rocks is another way back to the Lodge, unless you want to cross that." He pointed to the ponding stream below.

She shook her head so hard her bonnet came askew. Or perhaps he'd done that when he'd carried her to the rock. Either way, he leaned closer and tugged it back onto her fiery curls, his fingers brushing the soft warmth of her cheek.

"You'll be safe with me, Ruby," he murmured. "I promise."

She eyed him a moment, face tight, mossy green eyes

as damp as the pool below. She bit her lip, then whispered, "I've never done this before, you know."

"This?" he asked, straightening.

She waved a hand. "This…this nature affair. I'm a city girl, born and raised. I don't know what to do out here."

He imagined merely confessing the fact disturbed his brassy Ruby. This was a woman used to solving problems, making decisions, acting sometimes without thinking because she was so sure of herself and her abilities. Now she was faced with something beyond her ken, and she didn't like it.

"Happily, I do know what to do out here," Whit said. "I've climbed all over these mountains for more than twenty years. I've followed this stream to its headwaters. I've chased deer up the draws. I know how to get us home, Ruby. You can trust me."

But she didn't. She shifted on her brown boots, glanced up the stream and back down again as if she might spy some way he had forgotten. He knew she'd reached the same conclusion he had when she gave him her hand to help her down on the other side of the rock.

Even then, her worries betrayed her. Before, she had walked purposefully, gazing about her with a smile on her face. Now her steps beside him were hesitant, each foot planted firmly, and her gaze kept flickering about as if she expected another calamity to come hurtling off the hill. Her very light seemed to have dimmed.

Whit paused to point the way ahead. "You see here, how the path is rocky? This is more stable terrain than what we've been following thus far." He stomped his foot to prove it, and she winced as if expecting the ground to crumble.

"It's solid, Ruby," he assured her. "As firm a foundation as you could ask for. We won't touch soft soil again until we start down the other side." When she didn't respond, he tried another approach. "Do you know the story in the Bible about the man who built his house on rock?"

She frowned as if trying to recall it.

"The rains came and the streams rose, but his house remained strong," Whit encouraged her. "Because it was built on rock. If we stay on rock, we'll be safe, too."

"I thought that story was about standing firm in your faith," Ruby said, but she followed him as he started upward once more.

"To be sure. But the Lord based many of His lessons on things His listeners could see in their world. I suspect He was trying to help them relate the truths to their everyday lives."

She picked her way around a boulder lodged in the hillside. "Do you think He still does that—involves Himself in our everyday lives?"

She sounded so wistful, as if she doubted such attentiveness could be true.

"Certainly," Whit said, offering her a hand around the next outcropping. "If He cared enough to help strangers then, why wouldn't He help His followers now?"

"Perhaps we don't need His help," she countered. "Perhaps He expects us to deal with the small matters ourselves."

Perhaps. Whit knew how little he liked his staff bringing him matters he thought they should be able to address. But the very fact that they brought him those problems said they doubted their ability or authority to solve them. Surely the Lord understood.

At the moment, however, he had more to think about

than the Lord's intentions. He had a promise to keep. Whit angled their path up the hillside for the crest. When they reached the top, he paused to catch his breath. The ridge ran for an easy mile, sharp rock on one side, falling ledges of greenery on the other. Up here, the wind whistled past, shaking the fine clumps of pale grass, the nodding wildflowers. He could smell moisture on the air.

The same wind rustling her bonnet, Ruby stared around her. She pointed ahead to where the softer grasses of the slope had slumped to the south, pulling away from the stronger rock. "Please tell me that wasn't the way back to the Lodge."

Whit felt a sinking feeling and knew it wasn't from the ground this time. "I regret to say it was."

Her shoulders fell as she dropped her hand. "So now what?"

Whit glanced around. The main ways back were closed, and they could hardly climb the craggy face of the Edge. Unless...

"There's another option," he said. "This way."

She said nothing as they crossed the Edge, the wind buffeting them. Whit only wished he could find a way to ease Ruby's concerns. While their situation was difficult, it was hardly dire. He had every confidence he could get them safely home.

A short while later, he found the spot he'd been seeking, where the rock sheared off cleanly for a five-foot drop. He leaped down and turned with lifted arms.

Ruby stared down at him. "Surely you don't expect me to jump."

Whit smiled. "Surely I do. Unless you think you can fly."

Her mouth quirked, and he knew her temper had

flared. Again she glanced up and down the Edge as if hoping some other answer would present itself. Then she took a deep breath.

And sat on the ledge.

Whit dropped his hands. "What are you doing?"

"Not jumping," she told him as if that should have been obvious. She wiggled this way and that until she was perched on the very lip of the rock. Then she craned her neck as far as she could with that silly white ruff at her throat and gazed down, as if trying to gauge the distance.

Whit raised his arms again. "Come on, Ruby. I'll catch you."

In answer, she rolled over onto her belly, feet dangling. "I can crawl down," she said, voice muffled by the rock.

Whit puffed out a sigh and waited.

In the end, she did climb down, slithering over the sharp basalt, digging her fingers into crevices Whit hadn't even known were there. She slid the last foot to land facing backward and stumbled to fetch up against him. Whit put his hands on her shoulders to steady her. Every inch of her was trembling.

"There," she said with a nod that knocked her bonnet askew again. She shoved it back into place and turned in his arms. "What now?"

She was more pale than the bit of torn lace hanging limply at her throat, her gown dusted with dirt, but she was ready to forge ahead if he asked it. Whit didn't have the heart to tell her that the path fell two more times before they'd reach the bottom.

"I could do with a rest," he said, dropping onto the stone and leaning his back against the wall. He patted the spot beside him. "Why don't you join me?"

She all but collapsed next to him. "All right, but not for long. We need to return. I wouldn't want Father to worry."

At the moment, he was more concerned about her. For now, the rock blocked the breeze as well as the sound of the cascade, sheltering and warming the spot. But the way would be more difficult before it got easier again. "Perhaps we need a little help after all," he joked.

Her lips tightened primly. "We've done all right this far."

She truly didn't trust the circumstances, but he could not believe she couldn't trust the Lord to help. Here, where the air was pure and sharp as cheddar, where the roar of the river often drowned out other voices, he felt closest to the Lord.

He allowed his gaze to stray out over the land dropping away before them.

Lord, show me how to get her home safely. I all but bragged about how I know this area, but You know every nook and cranny. You know the paths the animals take. You guide them to food, protect their young. Guide us, as well.

The breeze darted into their shelter, caressed his face, urged him on. He rose and held out his hand to Ruby. "Come along, then, my dear. Let's see what we can do."

Her determined look up to him said she intended to prove herself, no matter what lay ahead.

Chapter Nine

It seemed a day for revelations. First, that the ground could actually move faster than she could, a fact which still chilled Ruby. Second, that the world could dwindle to two people and a waterfall, a feeling which humbled her. And finally, that she could come to care about an aristocrat like Whit Calder, Earl of Danning.

And that shocked her the most.

Yet how could she not be impressed with him? But for his quick thinking and quicker action, she'd be squashed under a ton of mud or washed down the stream. She might not like the rocky path he chose to return them eventually to the Lodge, but he was right that it seemed to be staying in place. And he truly was trying to help.

When they'd first met, Whit's consideration had annoyed her. Now she had to admit she found it comforting. He kept an eye on her as they traversed the uneven path, pointing out safer places to set her feet, warning her of hazards she might have missed. He paused from time to time to draw her attention to the wonders around them, like the tawny-coated hare that bounded away from their approach, the nodding flowers that looked like tiny stars along the rock crevices. His consideration, she was certain, had as much to do with his wish to reassure her as his desire to share his love of the place.

And his love was evident, even in their circumstances. His gaze was bright, his steps assured. He knew his skills and this place, and she felt her confidence building just watching him.

Until he stopped to face her.

His broad-brimmed hat shaded his eyes as he braced one foot on a rock. "You're doing marvelously," he said, "but the way ahead is going to be considerably wetter."

She had noticed the path dropping, with Whit occasionally switching directions to stay on stable ground. Now Ruby eyed the swirling water at the base of the Edge. Swollen with the rains, the stream seemed to have overflowed its banks. The bushes on either side were partially submerged, their green branches waving farewell to the waters that tumbled past. She would guess the stream might reach to her thighs if she'd tried to wade it. She shivered at the thought. "I never learned to swim."

"You won't have to," he promised, offering her a smile. "The water I'm talking about will come from above rather than below. I mean to go behind the cascade."

Ruby gaped at him. "Is that possible?"

"Most of the time," he admitted, taking her elbow. "Though today is likely to be wetter than usual."

Something was pressing up inside her, making breathing difficult, taking a step impossible. "I don't know how to do that. I can't do that."

His smile was gentle. "It's all right, Ruby. There's nothing to fear."

Fear? Yes, that was what had been creeping over her from the moment she'd seen the emerald hillside descend into mud. The emotion threatened to drown her as surely as the turbulent waters.

It was an old enemy, one she'd sworn to vanquish. She remembered running through the streets of Wapping as a child, hiding behind boxes and crates while bigger boys pounded past, hunting anything weak they could bully. She'd vowed then never to be the weak one, always to walk with her head high and her step steady to show the world she was someone worthwhile.

Her years at school had threatened that vow more than once. Even sitting in a hired coach the first time, as it carried her to the Barnsley School, away from everything she'd known, had shaken her, as had the subtle sneers of so many of her classmates. She had fought through, refusing to give in to the black beast of fear. But then, she'd known she had herself to rely on. This time, she had to rely on someone else.

"Do you promise me," she said, staring up into the purple-blue of Whit's eyes, "you won't leave me? That you'll get me back to my father safely?"

His gaze was unblinking, solemn. "You have my word."

The word of a nob. Her father had lost thousands of pounds over the years taking nobs at their words. She'd had her heart broken because she'd expected too much from a nob.

But what choice did she have?

"Very well," she said. "Let's try it."

"That's my girl," he said with a grin.

"I am not your girl," Ruby replied, lifting her chin. "But I'll follow. Lead on."

They paralleled the stream, still sticking to higher

ground as much as possible where the rocks provided stability for the slope. The farther they went, the louder came the sound of the waterfall, until Ruby was certain the very air vibrated with the boom. As they came around a curve in the cliffside, she saw it. From a height taller than the crown of the Lodge, water spilled from the Edge to crash down into a foaming pool ringed by water-slicked rocks.

"Careful now!" Whit shouted over the roar. "Take my hand, and walk where I walk."

Ruby gripped his hand, all too aware of the sharp rocks below them. He took short steps, each foot carefully placed, as if anticipating her smaller stride. Her damp skirts, heavy from the mud and the spray that wet them now, pulled at her legs like frozen hands, but she kept moving. She was so intent on following that she bumped into Whit when he stopped, and he caught her in his arms to keep her from falling.

"Look," he called with a jerk of his head to the right.

Ruby gazed in wonder. They were behind the cascade. Tons of water fell in a silvery curtain beside them, the spray moistening her cheeks, her lips. She licked it away as she returned her gaze to his, waiting for him to take them through to the other side.

But Whit didn't move. He was staring at her, gaze fixed on her lips, and she felt her heart pounding again.

Slowly, as if fearing he'd frighten her further, he lowered his head and kissed her.

The cool of the mist was replaced by a warmth that went from her top to her toes. Instead of the waterfall, her emotions threatened to sweep her away—engulfing her in amazement, joy, delight. She clung to him, trembling, knowing she should tell him to stop and knowing she wouldn't.

As if he felt the same, he pulled away as slowly as he'd approached, then raised a hand to touch her cheek. His fingers were firm and cool, and they brought reality with them.

"Forgive me," he said. "I don't know what came over me."

Ruby wasn't sure what either of them had been thinking, but she had her suspicions. She waved an unsteady hand, and her gloves splashed in the silver water. "I know what came over you. This!" She flipped the spray toward him.

She thought he laughed as he ducked. Then he took her hand and tugged her forward along the path.

Gradually her heartbeat returned to normal, her steps steadied and she could think clearly again. He'd asked her to forgive his impetuous kiss, this man for whom every moment seemed another opportunity to do his duty. Of course she forgave him—how could she not? He deserved the chance to be spontaneous for once, without consequences. She knew full well that love had not motivated him. It was the relief of having made it so far, the beauty surrounding them. They'd both been caught up in their emotions. She shouldn't refine on it.

Lord, please help me not to refine on it!

She tried not to bother God with trivial matters like this, but she thought perhaps He knew that the kiss might not be so trivial for her. Surely He wouldn't mind a prayer about that!

She wasn't certain how long it took to return along the opposite bank of the stream. The ground was less rocky here, and Whit went even more carefully.

"Do you think it's going to turn to mud, too?" Ruby couldn't help asking at one point when he hurried her along a particularly damp stretch of path.

"Let's just say I prefer not to take chances," he replied with a glance up the slope that set Ruby's hackles to rising. Then he fired her a grin. "I am escorting a lady, after all."

Did he truly see her that way? He certainly treated her with the respect and solicitude the nobs generally accorded their female relations and friends. His hands were there to help her over every mud hole, his arms carried her over bigger rocks. He never faltered, never complained, though she knew he had to be tiring, as well. Surely his ribs must be aching! Yet he'd made her a promise, and he obviously intended to keep it.

"How much farther?" Ruby begged when they paused for a moment's rest. Her lips, once so moist in the spray of the cascade, now felt chapped in the sun, and her legs ached from the constant tramping.

He leaned over, braced his hands on his thighs and took a deep breath before answering.

"Not too far. Another half mile to the carriage road below Bellweather Hall, and then a short distance to the Lodge." He straightened to eye her. "Do you want me to carry you?"

Ruby blinked. "Absolutely not!"

He chuckled. "Forgive the assumption. I fear I'm unused to ladies who insist on taking care of themselves."

"Or who even know how," Ruby guessed.

He inclined his head. "True, but to do them justice, they were never trained otherwise."

She couldn't help the way her head came up. "And you think I was?"

"I would never presume to know your mind, my dear," he said, holding up his hands as if in surrender.

Ruby chuckled despite herself. "All right, I admit it. I may never have learned to hunt or fish, but I did learn to protect myself. I take boxing lessons at a ladies academy in London, and I keep a loaded pistol in my reticule."

His brows went up even as his hands came down. "My word. Why?"

Very likely, he couldn't imagine her upbringing. "When I was young," she explained, "we lived in Wapping. Father was a mudlark."

His brows quirked at the word. "Forgive me, but I'm not familiar with the profession."

Ruby smiled. "You wouldn't be. A mudlark is a fellow who combs the mud of the Thames at low tide for leavings—things of value that might wash up. He was gone for long hours every day to mind the tides, and I had to fend for myself."

He frowned. "Was there no schooling? No place where you could be protected?"

"If there was, I never knew of it. That's one of the reasons I want to charter a school there. But it wasn't all bad. Father sometimes took me along with him. You never know what you'll find among the mud." She looked down at the mud crusting her boots, remembering the black muck of the Thames shore.

"I wouldn't make the same claim here," he said with a smile.

She nodded, tucking back a strand of hair that had come free of her bonnet. "One day he found a ring he was certain was gold. He took it to one pawn shop and jeweler after another, but they wouldn't pay him what he thought they should. He wandered into a shop on the Strand, and the jeweler there knew worth when he saw it."

"And so your father started his fortune," Whit surmised.

"More than a fortune," Ruby replied. "Mr. Dirnbaum

the jeweler had just discharged two assistants in a row for theft. He wanted someone who would work hard and be grateful. He offered my father a position, and we moved from Wapping that very day. When Mr. Dirnbaum wished to retire, he left the business to my father, who has never failed to turn a profit since."

"An amazing tale," Whit said with a shake of his head in obvious admiration. "Your father should be proud of his accomplishments."

"I'm the one who's proud of him," Ruby said. "He made something of himself from humble beginnings. That's the sort of fellow who deserves praise."

Too late she realized Whit might take that as an insult. Aristocrats did not have to make anything of themselves. They inherited their titles, their wealth and consequence.

And now she had to rely on this aristocrat to get them safely down out of the mountains.

She took a deep breath. "We should go."

He eyed her. "Are you certain you don't want a little more time to rest?"

Did she look as peaked as she felt? Ruby straightened her spine. "No. I'm fine. Never fear, Whit. I won't stop until we're back at the Lodge. This is one lady you don't have to fret over."

Whit bent as he made the final climb up the hill to Bellweather Hall, one hand back to pull Ruby with him. She was right. He didn't have to fret over her. But neither could he seem to leave her to her own devices. While her strength held him in awe, he could see she was tiring. At times, it seemed she could barely put one muddy foot in front of the other.

Yet she kept walking.

He stopped on the top of the hill, let her come up even with him. Thankfulness welled up inside him, found breath in his prayer. *Thank You for seeing us safely through, Lord.*

She took one look at the vista ahead of them, and her face broke into a smile. "Oh, Whit!" she cried, pointing at the shine of the River Bell in the distance. "Look! We're nearly home!"

She fairly skipped along the hill, heading for the carriage road winding down from Bellweather Hall. Did she realize she'd called the Lodge home? He certainly thought of it that way. That Ruby might feel the same could only please him.

He caught up with her at the verge of the road, where she was attempting to wipe the mud off her boots on the grass.

"I thought I might remove a little now before it cakes even further on the road," she explained. "It's all downhill from here, isn't it?"

"An easy walk," he promised her. He nodded to the left. "We follow that curve into the trees, and then turn into the carriage drive for the Lodge."

She drew in a breath as if even the air smelled sweeter here. Then she took his hand and gave it a squeeze. "Thank you for seeing me safely home."

Her grip was firm, but her fingers felt so small in his—delicate, precious. He inclined his head, finding his throat unaccountably tight. "It was only my duty as a gentleman."

Ruby shook her head as if she refused to see him humble. "It was a necessity as a human being. I wasn't getting back any other way."

"Duty and necessity go hand in hand in my book."

He pulled away to usher her onto the road, the gravel rattling beneath his boots.

"Which makes you a rarity in mine," she assured him, walking beside him. "I know far too many aristocrats who are only too happy to shirk their duty, if it profits them."

Whit shook his head. "You have obviously met people I don't know."

Before she could answer, he heard the sound of a carriage coming up the hill toward them. The horses broke from the trees and thundered ahead. Ruby raised her head and darted forward.

Whit caught her arm and drew her to the side of the road. "Easy now. They'll be here in a moment."

Sure enough, the coachman reined in the horses right in front of them.

Ruby's father threw open the door. "There you are!" he declared, face alight with relief. "Half the servants are in the hills searching for you. The other half headed for the river in case you washed up."

Beside him, Ruby shuddered at the image.

"They shouldn't have risked their lives," Whit said, offering Ruby a hand to help her climb in. As heavy as her skirts must have been, she didn't object to his assistance this time. "I knew the way back."

"So it would seem," her father said with a smile as Ruby settled herself next to him. Whit took the facing seat. Another lady might have sat primly, hands folded. Ruby collapsed against the cushions and closed her eyes as if offering up a prayer of thanks.

Seeing that they were both settled, her father thumped on the roof, and the carriage set off again.

"I can tell you that you gave me a few bad moments," he said to Whit. "Ruby's my only child, you know, the only family I have left. Not sure how I'd get on without her."

Even in the dim light of the carriage, Whit could see the moisture in the man's eyes.

Ruby's eyes popped open. "Oh, Da!" she cried, reaching out to hug him fiercely. Whit could see her shoulders shaking. Everything in him demanded that he take her into his arms, hold her close, keep her safe until the tremors passed. Instead, he held himself still while her father patted her back and murmured assurances.

Why had he reacted that way? He'd been willing to accept that their brush with death and the glory of the cascade had combined to make him lose his head and kiss her. In the moment, though, he'd felt the stirring of something inside, something that went beyond the pleasure of kissing a beautiful woman, something that defied description. Now it seemed to rise up inside him, requesting a name, acknowledgment.

It couldn't be love. It was too soon. They were too different. She had no interest in marrying.

He had a feeling when a man needed that many excuses to avoid pursuing a goal, something was very wrong.

Across from him, Ruby straightened with a sniff. "I'm all right, Father," she said, accepting the handkerchief he offered. "Lord Danning kept me safe, as he promised."

"Glad I am to hear that," her father said, but the look he cast Whit spoke of doubts.

"And the others?" Whit asked as the Hollingsford coachman turned the carriage in front of Bellweather Hall. "I take it they reached the Lodge safely, as well."

"A full two hours ago," Ruby's father confirmed.

"Talking about how the earth opened and tried to swallow you all."

Ruby shuddered again as she dabbed at her cheeks. "I've never seen anything more frightful. I'm just thankful Whit knew what to do."

Thank You, Lord.

The praise was easy, especially as the coach drew down toward the Lodge. Whit had never felt so thankful. He hadn't been concerned for himself, but the thought of losing Ruby didn't bear contemplation. And by her admission, the trip had terrified her. Even the redoubtable Ruby needed help sometimes, it seemed.

So did his other guests, with their own concerns. The moment he and Ruby entered the Lodge, they were besieged by both his staff and his guests.

"My lord, we were so worried," Mr. Hennessy said, attempting to take Whit's water-damaged coat. "Mr. Calder marshaled a team to see if he could locate you."

"Amelia was so distraught she nearly had to be put to bed with a tisane," Lady Wesworth scolded Whit, having come out of the withdrawing room at the sound of the door.

"You should have taken Henrietta with you instead," Mr. Stokely-Trent insisted beside her. "She knows any number of facts that might have helped."

Behind him, his daughter nodded her agreement, face white and tight.

"And you would have returned a great deal sooner," his wife added with a glance at Ruby that implied it was all her fault.

"If you'll give us a moment to change," Whit said to them all, "I promise you a full explanation."

They did not appear mollified, but he held them off

long enough for Ruby to make her escape upstairs, then managed to break away, as well.

Quimby had him out of his wet things and into dry ones in the wink of an eye, tsking at the sight of Whit's boots.

"We'll have to send the clothes out to be laundered," he said as Whit stood before a fire that had yet to truly warm him. The Lodge boasted no laundry of its own. He was seldom there long enough to require one.

"And we should look on the bright side," Quimby continued. "At the very least, your guests can say it has been an interesting trip." He came to slip the blue banyan over Whit's shoulders again.

A knock on the door spared Whit from answering. Quimby went to open it and admitted Ruby's father. Unlike when Whit had seen him in the coach, Hollingsford's face was set in stern lines, his long nose pointing to his chin.

"My lord," he said. "I must have a word with you about Ruby."

Whit took a step forward, ribs reminding him of his exertions. "Was she hurt after all?"

Hollingsford held up a hand. "My girl's made of stronger stuff. I've no doubt she'll be fine, physically. I'm more concerned about her reputation."

"Won't you sit down, sir?" Quimby said, positioning one of the chairs closer to the fire he'd just stoked up. "Perhaps a cup of tea?"

"Neither, thank you," Hollingsford said, keeping his gaze on Whit. "You must know, Danning, that a lady's reputation is all she has. That's particularly true of my Ruby."

Whit stood taller. "I assure you, sir, that I have every respect for your daughter."

"And can you tell me that nothing untoward happened today?" Hollingsford challenged.

Their kiss came to mind. Any father might have taken exception to such a show of...devotion? Had it been devotion that had moved either Whit or Ruby? At the moment, he could not begin to name his feelings, and he rather thought Ruby felt the same way. But there was certainly nothing in his feelings to harm her reputation. Besides, no one but them knew about that kiss.

"Nothing happened that might affect Ruby's standing on the *ton*," Whit assured her father.

Hollingsford spread his hands. "Ruby told me the same thing. But the good London gossips will have it otherwise. A pretty young girl, alone for hours in the wilderness with a gentleman? You can imagine the tales Lady Wesworth and that Stokely-Trent woman will delight to tell."

Whit wanted to protest further. Neither his honor nor the circumstances would have allowed him to take advantage of Ruby. The trouble was, he could well imagine what others might say. From the beginning, Lady Wesworth and Mrs. Stokely-Trent seemed to take Ruby in dislike. Because Ruby was not one of them, she must somehow be less. They would take particular pleasure in thinking that their opinions had been confirmed in this instance.

"What would you have me do?" Whit asked. "I doubt a command from me will seal their lips."

"I share your doubts, my lord," Ruby's father replied, taking a step forward and narrowing his eyes as if with purpose. "I fear there's only one remedy. You must offer for Ruby. Immediately."

Chapter Ten

Ruby sighed as she snuggled deeper in the leather armchair by the fire. Her chilled feet, now clad in clean silk stockings, were finally starting to warm as she straightened them out before her. Her maid had taken away her mud-crusted walking dress and covered her in a fresh linen shift with a quilted dressing gown of spring green satin. The color reminded Ruby of the cliff she'd just climbed.

Her! Climbing cliffs. Crossing cascades. She grinned just remembering. She knew she'd have to make an appearance downstairs eventually, but at the moment it felt awfully good to sit and think.

Do You really listen to people like me, Lord?

The thought had been working its way up inside her ever since her talk with Whit. She took a deep breath and closed her eyes, hoping for a response. When none came, she opened her eyes and sighed again. Was He silent because He never spoke to people like her, or was God silent because she really hadn't expected an answer?

She shook her head. Some faith!

She tried again, the satin warm beneath her fingers as she clasped her hands in her lap.

Lord, I don't know whether You care what's happening in my life, if my concerns truly matter in the scheme of things. But if You do, if they do, will You show me what You want?

Someone tapped at her door.

Ruby stiffened even as her maid hurried to respond. It couldn't be! That was a remarkably quick answer to a prayer, particularly one as hesitant as hers.

She looked up as her father came into the room, and with him, Whit. Perhaps it was the blue banyan, but Whit's eyes looked darker, deeper, as if etched with sorrow.

Ruby jumped from her chair. "What's wrong?"

Her father nodded to Whit. "Lord Danning wishes to speak to you."

Ruby frowned at Whit. They'd had hours to talk. She couldn't imagine what was so important he had to come to her now, and with her father in tow. He was staring at her, and her fingers flew to her hair, which was unbound and flowing down her back. As if the movement awakened him, he bowed.

"Miss Hollingsford, I hope you took no ill from our adventure today."

Why was he being so formal? Even her father knew he was now in the habit of calling her Ruby. "I'm fine," Ruby assured him. "You brought me safely back to the Lodge, just as you promised."

He took a step closer. "I try to be a man of my word. I hope you believe that."

Where was this leading? "Certainly, my lord. You've proved yourself trustworthy."

His mouth quirked, as if he was trying not to smile.

Then he went down on one knee, gaze tilted up to hers. "Given your appreciation of me and my admiration for you, Ruby Hollingsford, will you do me the honor of becoming my wife?"

Ruby stared at him. His face was upturned, his gaze solemn, lips parted in expectation. He leaned forward as if her word alone would uphold him. It was the moment most girls dreamed of.

"No," Ruby said, feeling the panic rising. "Don't be ridiculous."

Whit blinked.

Ruby rushed forward and pulled at his shoulders. "Oh, do get up! You don't want to marry me, you know you don't."

As Whit climbed to his feet, she turned to her father. "This is your doing, isn't it? You put him up to this!"

"I assure you, Ruby," Whit said before her father could do more than open his mouth. "My admiration for you is real."

"As is mine for you," she told him. "But I don't wish to marry, and I thought you felt the same."

"Don't be daft," her father insisted. "There's no time like the present if two hearts agree."

"And *are* hearts involved?" Ruby challenged him before whirling back to Whit. "Is yours? Do you claim yourself in love, sir?"

One corner of his mouth hitched up. "With you in such a mood, I wouldn't dare do otherwise."

Ruby threw up her hands. "What an impassioned response. It must be love!"

Whit closed the distance between them and caught her hands, holding them in his own, his fingers warm and strong. "Good marriages have been built on admiration, Ruby. We are both intelligent people, dedicated to helping those we care about. I think we would do very well together."

She could not deny that. Practical, polished, he had the skill to calm her mad starts, and she knew she had the ability to help order the demands that seemed to be placed upon him. But Lord Milton had wanted a relationship built only on passion, and Whit seemed to want one with none. Was there no such thing as a happy medium?

"But what if I want more?" she murmured, gaze on his.

"Like what?" he asked.

That he had to ask made her fear he would never understand.

"Love?" she suggested.

He released her hands, and she knew the answer before he spoke. "That may come, in time."

"No," Ruby said, backing away from him. "I won't take that chance."

Her father sighed gustily. "What am I to do with you, girl? He's an earl!"

"That," Ruby replied, head high, "was never the issue."

"No," Whit agreed, "but there is another. Our adventure today could cost you your reputation."

Ruby glanced between her father's bobbing head and Whit's tight face. "Is that what this is all about? You are both determined to protect me. But my reputation, sirs, was never in peril."

Her father avoided her gaze. "Alone for hours? Some might find fault."

"Only an idiot would call struggling down a cliff seduction," Ruby countered. "We were outdoors the entire time, in full view of anyone who might have happened along."

"But no one happened along," her father insisted. "So you have no witness to prove yourselves innocent."

"No witness but our consciences," Ruby assured him. "Lord Danning saved my life today. I won't jeopardize his by saddling him with a loveless marriage."

"I would not see you harmed either," Whit said. "Are you certain this business doesn't trouble you?"

He was watching her, head cocked and hands hanging loose as if he wasn't sure what to do with them.

"Not in the slightest," Ruby said.

"Then why are you hiding up here," her father asked with a wave of his hand that took in her bedchamber, "instead of down with the others?"

She could not deny the attraction of avoiding their critical gazes, their sneering remarks. "I'm tired," she said and hoped he would leave it at that.

He didn't. "Ha!" he said, turning to Whit. "She knows she'll have trouble. You stick to your guns, my lord. Don't let her wiggle out of this."

Ruby stiffened, ready to protest, to fight. Whit moved to her side, took her hand once more and gave it a squeeze before turning to her father.

"No, sir," he said, "with all due respect. Ruby has refused my suit, and I admire her too much to go against her wishes."

Ruby raised a brow. Whit bowed over her hand. "Only know that I am your devoted servant, my dear. Don't be concerned about the other guests. There will be no more unkind remarks." With a nod to her father, he strode from the room.

Ruby sighed.

"You see!" her father crowed. "You do favor him!"

"What I favor is the fact that he listens to me." Ruby picked up her skirts and marched back to the chair. "Which is more than I can say for some." She plopped down on the seat.

"I listen," her father protested, following her. "I just don't agree with you. He's a fine man, Ruby, not like that Milton fellow."

Ruby glared up at him, and he held up his hands. "Right, right, not a word about him in your presence. But think about Lord Danning instead. He's not so top-lofty."

"He isn't the slightest bit toplofty," Ruby corrected him, gaze on the glow of the fire.

"Clever, too," her father pressed.

She could not deny that either. "Quite clever. You should have seen him navigate the cliffs today."

Her father leaned closer. "And you can't say he isn't kind on the eyes."

Heat flushed up her, and she gripped the carved wooden arms of the chair. "None of that matters, since I don't intend to marry at all, and certainly not without love." She eyed him a moment. "What am I going to do with you? You cannot keep pushing men at me. I won't have them."

"So what will you do?" her father countered. "Don't tell me you wish to care for me in my old age. You'd make a horrid nurse!"

Ruby couldn't help a laugh. "That's true enough. I haven't the patience. But are those my only choices— marriage or nursing? Perhaps I could go into trade, as you did."

He snorted as he turned away. "May the good Lord spare you from my path."

Ruby shook her head. "You're doing it too brown. I

know you struggled in the early years, but you've done very well for yourself."

He turned back. "And may I not want better for you?"

"Certainly, so long as your wants do not overshadow mine."

"Cheeky," he said. "Always have been."

"Always will be," she replied with a tight smile.

He sighed. "I suppose you'll be wanting me to take you back to London."

Two days ago, she would have jumped at the chance. Now, she couldn't help thinking of Whit. If she left, some of the tension in the house would likely leave with her, as there would be one less candidate for his wife. But without her here, he would be at the mercy of the others.

Her father had left her to the mercy of bullies when they lived in Wapping because he had had to make a living for them both. After their fortune was made and he'd sent her away to school, he hadn't known he'd left her to the mercy of her cruel classmates, as well. But she knew the feeling, and she couldn't abandon Whit.

"I'll stay through the end of the fortnight," Ruby said, then held up a hand as her father brightened. "But only to help Lord Danning."

"Oh, of course, of course," her father said with a nod. "Only natural you would want to help him, him saving your life and all."

"And you're going to help him, too," Ruby said. "On the first night, he laid out a plan for the visit. Do you remember?"

Her father ticked the activities off on his fingers. "Walk to the cascade, fish, visit his lordship's horse farm." His eyes widened. "My word, but he's nothing left!"

"And a full week remaining," Ruby agreed. "Services will take up some time tomorrow, but after that, they'll be at his throat."

Her father started pacing. "I don't know this area well. Might there be a summer fair we can venture to? Perhaps take them all on a picnic among those flowers?"

Ruby narrowed her eyes in thought. "We need something more original, something that will set them talking, capture their imaginations."

Her father started grinning. "I have an idea for you. I really did have a business purpose for bringing you up to Derbyshire. There's a new Blue John artist in the area just west of Castleton, perhaps an hour's drive. He's expecting me anytime this week."

Ruby smiled, as well. "Perfect! We'll organize a visit for all Lord Danning's guests. That ought to keep them busy, for a day at least!"

After her staunch refusal of his suit, Whit paused outside the door of Ruby's bedchamber, listening to the murmur of her voice. He was certain the events of the day had made his choice for him, yet here he stood a free man.

He could not understand her. In truth, most of the women he'd met would have latched on to his proposal and congratulated themselves on catching an earl. Certainly Lady Amelia or Henrietta would have been delighted to be victors in the wife campaign, or at least their parents would have gloated. Yet Ruby had stuck to her beliefs and refused. He was rather proud of her.

And disappointed.

He shook his head as he turned from the door, trying to push his emotions away. Yes, he found Ruby's company refreshing. Yes, their kiss had been stirring.

But in truth he doubted his fledgling feelings met the criteria for the kind of marriage he had hoped for. Besides, he was quite busy at the moment. Perhaps when the next round of renovations to the orphan asylum was completed, his estates in Suffolk enclosed and his tenant holdings improved, he might have time for a wife. Just the thought of what was waiting for him when he returned from Fern Lodge was enough to sober him. The weight of his responsibilities crouched over him, ready to pounce.

For now, he had another task that took precedence. He had guests to attend to, and he would need to make the appropriate appearance. He returned to his room long enough to affix the Danning diamond stickpin in his cravat, then located his guests in the withdrawing room.

He was pleased to see that Charles had returned. His cousin was standing by the doors to the veranda in conversation with Henrietta while the other ladies lounged closer to the fire.

Mr. Stokely-Trent, leaning against the mantel, spotted him first. "Lord Danning, welcome," he called, straightening.

The others looked his way and immediately expressed delight in his company. Whit remained where he was, so they could all see him.

"Thank you," he told them. "I'm sure you'll notice that Miss Hollingsford and her father were unable to return to our sides. There appears to be some concern that you will find her wanting."

Charles and Mr. Stokely-Trent frowned, but Lady Wesworth and Mrs. Stokely-Trent exchanged glances.

"I did wonder whether some might consider our time together today as scandalous," Whit continued, forcing his fingers not to fist at his sides. "Therefore, I asked Miss Hollingsford to marry me."

Lady Amelia gasped. Mrs. Stokely-Trent blanched.

Lady Wesworth pushed herself to her feet, skirts rustling against the carpet. "What a gallant gesture, my lord, but I assure you there was no need."

"Miss Hollingsford quite agrees with you," Whit informed her. "She refused me out of hand."

They all deflated.

"Is she leaving then?" Henrietta asked, and for once she sounded genuinely concerned.

"She has not confirmed her plans with me," Whit replied, although some part of him refused to think of Ruby leaving. "However, I hope I can count on everyone here to encourage her to stay for the rest of the visit. After all, none of us would want gossip to tarnish her reputation and require me to insist on a marriage."

Mrs. Stokely-Trent nodded. "Certainly not! Why, it's rubbish to think that dear girl would do anything scandalous."

"I always liked her," Charles put in, earning him a frown from Henrietta.

"You may count on my support, my lord," Lady Wesworth intoned. "With Amelia as her friend, no one will dare impugn Miss Hollingsford."

Lady Amelia nodded earnestly.

Whit inclined his head. "I was certain I could rely on your generous natures. I only hope the day's exertions don't prove too much for her."

"We should send for Lord Hascot's physician," Henrietta advised.

Having realized the limits of that physician's understanding of human anatomy, Whit could not agree. "I don't think that will be necessary," he replied.

"I could make her a licorice tisane," Lady Amelia offered.

"I'd be delighted to carry her to and from her bedchamber," Charles said.

Henrietta's face darkened.

Interesting. It seemed Charles's attentions had found their mark, and the bluestocking favored his cousin. They'd make a good match, if only Charles had the wisdom to see it.

"I believe she is able to walk," Whit said. "At the moment I would settle on persuading her to join us for dinner."

The women evinced their eagerness to try, and it was all Whit could do to keep them from marching upstairs right then and there to fetch her down. Indeed, the ladies were already quarreling about this and that, the gentlemen shifting uncomfortably on their feet as if unsure which side to weigh in on. The hours between now and dinner yawned unmercifully. What was he to do with them all?

What Ruby had done when he was unavailable.

"Lady Amelia," he said, loudly and firmly enough that the argument snuffed out and all eyes turned his way once more, "that licorice tisane sounds just the thing. Could I trouble you to instruct my chef on how to make it?"

She blushed, but rose. "It's no trouble."

"I wonder whether he will have the necessary ingredients here in the wilderness?" her mother mused.

"If you give us a list," Henrietta offered with a glance at Charles, "I'm sure Father would allow us to use his carriage to fetch the ingredients from the village. I would never trust a servant with so delicate a task."

"Certainly not," her mother agreed, rising with a look

to her husband. "We'll go with you." Mr. Stokely-Trent sighed, but came to join them.

Just like that, his guests were happily occupied. Whit bowed them out of the room and stood for a moment, basking in the quiet.

"Abandoned you, have they?" Ruby's father asked, coming up beside him.

Whit eyed him. "For the moment."

Hollingsford elbowed him in the ribs, heedless of Whit's wince. "Well, what are you waiting for, my lad? Let's go fishing!"

Fishing? Lady Wesworth and her daughter had invaded his kitchen. His cousin would soon be at the mercy of the Stokely-Trents, and Ruby was languishing upstairs. Surely there was something more important he had to do.

"Fishing," he said, feeling his grin forming. "Delighted."

And so Whit managed to reach the Bell again for only the fourth time in a week. Guilt tugged at his boots, but he tried to ignore it. Surely his guests could manage for a few moments.

The sun had already gone down below the crest of the hills behind the Lodge, casting the pool in shadow. The Bell welcomed him with a friendly gurgle. He and Hollingsford stood a few yards apart, casting in different directions to avoid a collision.

"You've done this before," Whit said after admiring the man's cast.

"Had a client invite me to the Dove once," Ruby's father said, watching his fly dance along the water. "Struck me as a peaceful way to spend an afternoon."

Whit smiled as he watched his own fly. "It is that."

Hollingsford must have heard the sigh behind the

words, for he eyed Whit for a moment before he began reeling in. "I take it you don't get too many such afternoons."

"Not nearly as many as I'd like," Whit confessed, giving the line a tweak.

"What you need," Hollingsford said, "is a wife."

Whit shook his head even as he drew in his line. Ruby was right. Her father was determined to make a match between them.

"My father," he told Hollingsford, "was also certain a wife was necessary for happiness. I find myself wondering."

"Oh, it's true," Hollingsford maintained, pulling back his arm to cast again. "God made us male and female. Stands to reason a fellow can never be complete without his other half."

That's how it had seemed to Whit about his mother and father. When his mother had died, his father had never been whole again. But were all marriages that way?

"Odd that you never remarried," he said to Hollingsford.

The fellow's fly drifted lazily along with the current. "Ah, when you've had the best, my lad, it's hard to stomach the rest. Even Ruby understands that. It seems she will settle for nothing less than love."

Neither would Whit. He cast as well, keeping his fly away from Hollingsford's.

"Of course, it doesn't help that she's gotten the notion in her head she'll never find love with an aristocrat. I blame that school." Ruby's father glanced Whit's way. "I thought it would be the making of her, a fine establishment catering to the aristocracy and gentry.

But poor Ruby was miserable so far from home out there in Somerset."

After what she'd told him of her upbringing, he could imagine Somerset must have felt odd indeed, and he said as much to her father.

"No doubt," Hollingsford agreed, pulling in his line once more. "But she did very well there—good marks in many areas, though she didn't favor music and such. Said she always felt as if she were on display. I was sorry to learn later that some of the other girls were unkind."

Like some of his guests. "If they could not appreciate her sterling qualities," Whit said, watching for a flash of silver in the pool that heralded the approach of a trout, "they were the losers."

Hollingsford beamed at him. "That's what I told her. It would have all blown over if it hadn't been for that prank in her first Season."

Whit frowned, reeling in. "Prank?"

"One of the girls from her school invited her to a ball. Fancy affair. Ruby had a new gown fitted, a garnet necklace just for the occasion. Like a princess she looked."

Whit's frown eased as he imagined Ruby's excitement. "So what went wrong?"

Her father sighed as if the memory hurt him, as well. "When she arrived, the girl asked her opinion on a tiara her father had given her, then ordered her to leave. Made Ruby think she'd only invited her as an appraiser, because of me being a jeweler. She made it clear that she'd never actually invite Ruby into her house as a guest."

Something hot pressed against Whit's heart. "That's abominable. I hope you spoke to her father."

Hollingsford's mouth was tight. "That's the thing.

Her father bought the tiara from me, not knowing anything about Ruby and his daughter. It was the girl's idea to turn it into that cruel joke—the father had nothing to do with it at all. He's been a good customer for years. Not much I could say."

While Whit appreciated his predicament, he couldn't help thinking that Ruby deserved a defender, someone who would take her side, no matter the cost.

And he was not entirely surprised to find that he wanted to be that defender.

Chapter Eleven

Ruby spent the rest of the afternoon in her room, her maid hovering at the ready. She'd hoped it to be a time for thinking, for planning, perhaps for pursuing this habit the Lord had of answering prayers willy-nilly. Unfortunately, some of the occupants of Fern Lodge had other ideas.

First it was Lady Wesworth demanding entrance, drawing her daughter along with her.

"We are making you a tisane," she announced as she stopped beside Ruby's chair and waved at her to keep her seat.

Such condescension was no doubt meant to be praised. "How very kind of you," Ruby said with a smile to the ever-suffering Lady Amelia, who stood just behind her mother.

"It's licorice," Lady Amelia confided, returning Ruby's smile shyly. "It smells delightful."

"I find it wise to ensure one's good health after such an ordeal," her mother said, noble chin as high as her generous chest in her creamy muslin gown. "And I think you were equally wise to refuse Lord Danning's misguided offer of marriage."

Lady Amelia paled and bit her lip as if to keep herself from commenting. Ruby had no such trouble.

"I didn't consider it misguided," she told the marchioness, shifting on the armchair to get a better look at her. "It was very chivalrous of him. I simply have no need to marry."

Lady Wesworth drew herself up. "It is every young lady's duty to marry and carry on the line. England advances through its sons."

"Through its daughters, too," Ruby corrected her. "Otherwise I fear there'll be no more sons born or married."

Laughter twinkled in Lady Amelia's blue gaze before she looked away.

"You are entirely too outspoken," Lady Wesworth declared, brown eyes narrowing. "However, I gave Lord Danning my word that we would support you, and I intend to keep it. Come, Amelia."

"One moment, Mother," she promised, lagging behind.

Her mother was so used to instant obedience she didn't notice. Lady Amelia watched her out the door, then took a step closer to Ruby, lowering her platinum head and her voice, as well.

"Please excuse my mother, Miss Hollingsford. She has strong opinions about the place of marriage in a woman's life."

"Obviously," Ruby drawled, pulling her dressing gown closer.

Lady Amelia eyed the fire as if unable to meet Ruby's gaze. "I suspect it's because she married above her station. No one in her family had a title, you see. She doesn't like to be reminded of the fact."

"I would think that would make her more in charity with others in the same position," Ruby argued.

"Ah, but if she approves of them, Society might remember her more humble beginnings. No, her only hope is to pretend disdain." She reached out and squeezed Ruby's hand, meeting her gaze at last. "Only know that I admire you, Miss Hollingsford. We'll be back shortly with the tisane." With a smile, she pulled away and glided out.

Ruby shook her head. So Lady Wesworth had married up and now could not condone anyone else doing so. Small wonder she pushed so hard for Lady Amelia to marry a title. Every alignment drew attention away from her past. But how miserable for Lady Amelia, forever pushed and pulled for her mother's sake!

Still, because of her mother's demands, Lady Amelia had likely never had to fight simply to be treated fairly. And scoundrels wouldn't dare approach her for fear of her father. She'd never had her heart broken with silken promises that proved utterly false.

Oh, but Ruby refused to dwell on that. She shifted on the chair, but Philip's face persisted in coming to mind, first smiling so sweetly as he handed her a bouquet of violets, then scowling at her when she'd refused his proposition. She was almost thankful when her maid went to answer another knock at the door. This time, it was Mr. Quimby who entered.

The valet offered her a bow. "Miss Hollingsford, I just wished to say how sorry I am that our usually delightful Derbyshire countryside chose to be fractious today. Is there anything you need, anything I might do for you?"

He was all contrition, hands clasped before his silver shot waistcoat, head bowed. She could hear her maid behind her, fussing with the bedclothes, twitching the curtains farther off the window. It wasn't often the woman entertained such a presentable gentleman.

"I'm fine, Mr. Quimby," Ruby told him with a smile. "Thank you for asking."

He inclined his head. "And even before this happened, I understand that you were not enjoying your time with us."

She was no doubt supposed to assure him on that score, too. "Not a great deal," she admitted instead. "I'm still not entirely certain why I was even invited."

He straightened in obvious surprise. "Why, I invited you, Miss Hollingsford. This house party would have been dreary indeed without you."

Ruby frowned. "You invited me? On whose orders?"

"On my own, I promise you. You will not recall having met, but I saw you once when I was at your father's shop. You struck me as just the sort of young lady he needed to meet."

Ruby leaned back against the seat. "Why? I'm not an aristocrat."

He shrugged. "Neither am I."

"Yes," she pointed out, "but you're a valet."

He raised a golden brow, look imperious. "And do you find fault with that profession, Miss Hollingsford?"

"No, in truth, Mr. Quimby," she assured him hurriedly. "I'm certain it's a very noble profession."

He wrinkled his nose. "I wouldn't go so far as that. You haven't seen the mess Lord Danning makes of his boots." He rolled his eyes.

Ruby laughed in spite of herself. "You bear your burden with distinction, sir."

"Of course. It is my enviable duty to see to all Lord

Danning's needs, whether it is a perfectly tied cravat or a perfectly arranged marriage."

Ruby raised her brows. "And does he agree to such a wide scope of duties?"

"Not in the slightest. Hence the need to set up this house party without his knowledge. I only hope he'll play his role well and pick a suitable bride."

"I think you go too far," Ruby declared, slapping her hands down on the arms of the chair. "No one should have to marry unless they so wish it."

"I fear that isn't entirely true when it comes to the aristocracy," Quimby said with a sigh. "The Danning estates are many and varied, requiring a steady hand at the tiller, if you will. The only other male in direct line is Mr. Calder."

He stopped just short of maligning Whit's cousin, but Ruby saw his point. Charles was such a butterfly, flitting from one lady to another, always with a joke on his lips. Would he have the strength to lead an earldom, to help lead the nation?

"I suppose Mr. Calder would find his way, if necessary," Ruby said.

Quimby wandered to the window, straightening the curtains with an apologetic smile to Ruby's maid. "Such lovely weather we're having, don't you agree? And, if I'm not mistaken, here comes your father back from fishing."

Her father had gone fishing? Ruby rose to join Quimby at the window. Sure enough, there came her father, all smiles, a brace of trout hanging from one hand. Whit clapped him on the shoulder as they laughed.

Oh, but she wondered what those two had been discussing besides fish!

"If you'll excuse me," Quimby said, stepping back

from the window, "I will be wanted shortly. Please let me know if there's anything else I can do to assist you, Miss Hollingsford." He bowed, Ruby nodded and he was out the door a moment later.

Ruby glanced out the window again, but Whit and her father had already entered the Lodge. Her father was so intent that she marry Whit. Was he pressing Whit to propose again? Didn't he understand how the thought of marriage, especially marriage to an aristocrat, concerned her? She might have forbidden him to mention Phillip's name, but that didn't mean he had to forget how the fellow had betrayed her! Then again, her father certainly had evidence of his own to indicate that the upper class had as many wiles as wealth, based on the actions of his clientele.

And why had Quimby been at her father's shop? On a commission for Whit? Her father claimed it was Charles who'd come calling, and Whit disclaimed all knowledge of the transaction. It made no sense.

Whichever way she considered the matter, she only had more questions! But one thing was certain. Despite Lady Wesworth's pompous statement, Ruby would do just fine without marrying. She returned to the chair by the fire and sank onto the seat to stare at the glow in the hearth. She could spend time doing good works, like Lady Thomas DeGuis…who was, of course, *married*. Or enlist additional support for her school in Wapping, perhaps from her friend Eugenia Welch, whose *engagement* had been announced shortly before Ruby and her father had headed north. Or maybe pursue a profession. Sir Trevor Fitzwilliam's wife was rumored to have been an apothecary, before she *married*.

Oh, this was maddening!

It was possible, she supposed, that she might marry,

someday. But only to a man who loved her with all his heart, despite any shortcomings. And there was nothing her father or Whit Calder, Earl of Danning, could do to change her mind.

Whit found Ruby much on his thoughts as he changed for dinner that evening. He had tapped on her door after returning from fishing, but Lady Amelia and Lady Wesworth were in the middle of administering the hard-won tisane, so he had merely sent in his regards and a hope that he would see them all at dinner. Indeed, he didn't much relish the thought of facing the others without Ruby's smile down the table to encourage him. And he wanted to assure himself that she had taken no harm from the day's adventures.

His heart couldn't help lifting when he sighted her standing by the veranda as they all gathered before dinner. She was dressed in a blue-on-blue-striped gown, with a pointed lace at the collar and long white sleeves tied with blue ribbons. He couldn't help thinking that the triple bands of lace along the hem would have been frightfully impractical on their walk that day, for all that they swung fetchingly as she came forward to greet him.

"And I see you were so very tired from our troubles today that you promptly went fishing," she accused him, pretty face alight with a smile.

Whit shrugged. "If the trout are biting…"

"A gentleman must bite back," Charles quipped, coming into the room behind him. "Ah, Miss Hollingsford, our heroine! Ready to take on another cliff, I've no doubt." He bowed over Ruby's hand. "All I can say is that I pity the cliff."

Whit took Ruby's hand from his cousin's. "See Lady Wesworth in to dinner, will you, my lad?"

Something crossed his cousin's face, but Charles inclined his head, and Whit had the satisfaction of walking with the woman of his choosing for once.

He was a little sorry to find when they entered the dining room that his butler had kept the same seating arrangements from the previous night, with Lady Amelia on one side of Whit and Henrietta on the other. While it maintained the peace, he found he would much rather have sat next to Ruby. The short distance between them, however, didn't keep his gaze from frequently seeking hers.

She seemed to have no trouble conversing with those around her, whether with Lady Amelia on her left or her father and Mr. Stokely-Trent on the right. In fact, she spoke with her usual spirit. Perhaps that was why he wasn't surprised when she announced she had a diversion planned for them.

"My father and I would like to invite you all to view the work of a promising new artist," she said, glancing around at the other guests before returning her gaze to Whit's as if seeking approval. He nodded for her to continue. "He works in stone, Blue John to be precise."

Henrietta frowned, and Lady Amelia cocked her head. But Mrs. Stokely-Trent clapped her hands, causing her husband to raise a brow.

"Oh, Blue John!" she cried rapturously. "The Dukes of Devonshire had two entire columns at Chatsworth made of it. Remember, Winston? We saw them when we visited."

He nodded. "Purple-blue stuff with veins of yellow. Very pretty."

"Very popular as well," Ruby's father put in. "Going

back thousands of years, I'm told. The Roman emperors favored it for vases and such."

Whit caught Ruby smiling at how Lady Wesworth perked up at that.

"How is it formed?" Henrietta asked. "Where is it mined?"

"I can't answer the question about its formation," Charles said, "but I believe the only source is here in Derbyshire."

"Quite right," Hollingsford agreed.

They all began to talk at once then, asking questions, exclaiming over the idea. Ruby grinned at Whit.

Minx! She was clearly pleased that she'd caused a hubbub, but he couldn't fault her for it. For once his guests seemed happy to be discussing the same subject. She and her father had found a way to keep them occupied, and he was grateful for it.

Unfortunately, with the next day being Sunday, they could not embark on the trip until the day after. But Whit knew a few options for the meantime.

"Who's for services tomorrow?" he asked over a second course of pineapple from the duke's conservatory and apricot ice.

Lady Wesworth immediately agreed, gaze appropriately pious, and Whit knew that meant Lady Amelia would be coming, as well. Charles looked ready to demur until Henrietta agreed, and her parents added their acceptance.

"I'd very much like to go," Ruby murmured, so carefully he could only wonder what was going through her mind. He had seen no sign of unkind behavior toward her. She had fought for her right to be among them. What made her hesitate now?

He received the start of an answer when they attended Saint Andrew's in the village the next day. Whit knew the church was a little grand for a country chapel, with fine stone walls and a gilded steeple, but he couldn't help being proud of it. The gentry of the area had all contributed to make it finely appointed. The carved oak seats inside had been donated by an earlier duke. The Rotherfords had endowed the alabaster cross along with the stained-glass windows on either side of the pews.

Whit had contributed the linens that draped the altar and the gold plate used for communion as well as an organ, which had recently been installed. Now the sound of the pipes rolled through the chapel, setting the Reverend Mr. Battersea to grinning as he took his place at the lectern, wispy white hair in direct contrast with his practical silver-rimmed spectacles.

With the Duke of Bellington not yet returned and the Rotherfords on their honeymoon, Whit and his guests made up most of the aristocracy in attendance. He spotted Lord Hascot on the opposite wall, gaze steadfast on the vicar as Mr. Battersea led the congregation through the service.

Normally, Whit paid particular attention to the lesson, looking for insights he could apply to his life. Today, the reading was in First Samuel and started with a mother's prayer of thanksgiving for what God had done for her. For some reason, the words felt emotional, speaking of a joy he couldn't recall feeling. His gaze was drawn down the pew, where Ruby stood beside her father.

While the other women worshipped with backs stiff and gazes raised, her head was bowed. One gloved hand rubbed against the other before her wine-colored pelisse, as if she were trying to wash away some concern.

She seemed to be truly touched by the words. Had she, like Hannah in the reading, found a fervent prayer answered? Or had she some problem that required divine intervention even now?

Her heartfelt look remained on his mind as the service ended.

The others were making for the carriages, which waited just outside the churchyard in the summer sun, and Whit found himself beside Ruby. Her head was still bowed; only her chin showed below the lace edge of her bonnet.

"Fascinating flagstones," he offered with a tap of his toe against the path through the churchyard. "And nicely flat, too."

She glanced up at him with a smile, but he couldn't help noticing the gleam in her eyes, like a stream that had flowed over mossy rocks.

"What's troubling you, Ruby?" he asked.

In answer, she caught his hand and pulled him off the path and among the tombstones. Whit had been in any number of churchyards where the chest-high slabs leaned at precarious angles, but the grave markers at Saint Andrew's stood as firm as the convictions of its congregation.

Ruby's convictions, however, seemed to be wavering. "I'm sure what I'm going to say is too forward or too personal or will break some rule of Society I never learned, but if I don't confide it soon I think I will explode!"

Whit felt his brows rising. "I'm honored you'd consider confiding such a thought to me."

She shook her head, then had to reach up and readjust her bonnet. "You may change your mind once you hear me out. Tell me, do you think God cares about us individually or more as a group?"

Whatever he had been expecting it was hardly that. "I hadn't thought to question the matter," he confessed.

"That's entirely the problem!" She set about pacing back and forth between the stones. "I didn't attend services when I was younger. Even the church hesitates to set foot in Wapping. I always thought God was an infinite being who guided the affairs of nations." She waved at the sky, then stopped and glared at Whit. "But today, that reading. It seemed to me He answered a very personal prayer, what some would say was a self-seeking prayer. Why?"

Whit adjusted his cravat, shifting on his feet, and still found it difficult to meet that outraged gaze. She acted as if someone had kept an important truth from her, as if even the church had lied. "I wouldn't presume to guess the Lord's purpose."

She threw up her hands. "But if He does care about each of us, shouldn't we so presume? Shouldn't we ask what He expects of us?"

The question hung in the air, and he felt humbled. All his life, he'd done his duty—stepping into his father's shoes at fifteen, managing the estates, attending Parliament, helping the less fortunate. He'd taken it for granted that that was the sum of expectations placed upon him, and they were heavy enough some days. He had asked the Lord for wisdom, for help. Yet when had he asked what the Lord expected?

"Yes, Ruby," he said, meeting her gaze solemnly. "We should. Thank you for reminding me of that."

Pink brightened her cheeks as she dropped her hands. "I didn't mean that to sound like a scold. I was just trying to reason it out. This place, all this grandeur—" now her wave encompassed the hills, the river and the church "—makes you think about your place in the scheme of things."

He chuckled. "I fear sometimes it has the opposite effect on me. When I'm at Fern Lodge, I often forget my place in the larger world."

Ruby linked arms with him and drew him back to the path. "And then you found yourself surrounded by guests, including an impertinent chit who demands answers to impossible questions."

With her smiling up at him again, no question seemed too large. Yet the very idea of discussing his feelings on religious matters raised a wall inside him. He was actually glad to see Henrietta's father approaching through the thinning crowds.

"What about fishing this afternoon?" Mr. Stokely-Trent asked, stopping before Whit and Ruby and rubbing his large hands together before his fine green coat. "I've been itching for a chance at the Bell. I've heard it's second only to the Dove for trout."

Pride forced the answer from Whit's mouth. "I find the Bell preferable."

Ruby smiled as if she knew why.

"Preferable?" Stokely-Trent said, face lighting. "Excellent! Perhaps we three gentlemen should take the opportunity, now that the ladies seem to be getting along better."

Three gentlemen? Last time he'd checked, there were four men staying at Fern Lodge, counting himself. As if she recognized the slight to her father, Ruby drew herself up.

Whit moved to intervene. "I'd be delighted to share the stream with any of my guests who are interested," he said, eyeing Stokely-Trent. "Gentlemen as well as ladies."

The fellow laughed. "Ladies, eh? Excellent jest, Danning."

"Didn't your daughter express an interest in learning to fish, sir?" Ruby put in, far too innocently.

His look darkened. "Henrietta was merely being polite to express interest in a gentleman's pastime. My daughter does not fish."

"Pity," Whit said with a wink to Ruby. "And what of you, Ruby? Would you care to join us?"

Stokely-Trent's mouth opened and closed. Whit had seen a similar look on the face of the fish he caught. Then the fellow glanced at Whit and snapped his mouth shut.

At least Henrietta's father was making an attempt to be polite. As if Ruby thought so, too, she smiled at them both. "Sadly, no. The Barnsley School for Young Ladies did not extend its curriculum to the fine art of fishing."

Whit smiled back, but Stokely-Trent frowned. "Barnsley School, you say?"

"Miss Hollingsford is a graduate, I believe," Whit supplied, feeling a sense of pride in her accomplishments.

"Two years ago," Ruby confirmed.

"Excellent school," Stokely-Trent said with a nod of approval. "I was hoping they'd take Henrietta, but she had other ideas." He glanced to where his daughter was chatting with Charles, her face alight as the breeze pulled a strand of her dark hair free from her velvet hat. "Still does."

"Your daughter is a well-informed woman," Whit offered. "She is a credit to you."

He puffed himself up to his usual bluster, chest swelling in his green-patterned waistcoat. "Yes, she is. I'm glad you noticed, my lord. I'd feared your cousin had stolen a march on you." He laughed as if the very idea was a great joke.

Whit could feel Ruby watching him. Did she think he was intent on pursuing the bluestocking? Clearly Stokely-Trent hoped to hear such a confession, for he was watching Whit, too.

Whit inclined his head. "I cannot blame your daughter for seeing Charles's many excellent qualities," he told Stokely-Trent. "He is loyal, good-natured and well mannered."

Ruby snorted. "You make your cousin sound like a well-trained spaniel, sir! He is also handsome, witty and charming."

Surely Charles could not have captured her heart! Whit peered closer, but she had already turned to Henrietta's father. "And he is certainly intelligent enough to have seen the diamond in your daughter, sir," she added.

Stokely-Trent scowled at her. She'd put him in a difficult position, and Whit thought she knew it. The man could not disparage Charles without making it seem as if he maligned his daughter, as well.

"I shall look forward to fishing, my lord," he said instead with a nod that barely included Ruby. Then he turned and strode to his carriage, ushered his wife and daughter into their coach and shut the door in Charles's face.

Whit shook his head. "And just when I thought everyone was getting along nicely."

"It's plain he wants a title for her," Ruby explained. Then she grinned at him. "A shame you're not allowed to loan your cousin yours."

She clearly meant it for a joke, but Whit could not

help his sigh as his cousin ambled toward them. "A very great shame, Ruby. I assure you, there are times when, if I could short of dying, I'd give him my entire inheritance!"

Chapter Twelve

Ruby had call to remember those words the next day on their trip to Castleton. That Sunday afternoon, the men had indeed abandoned the others for a couple of hours, leaving Ruby, Lady Amelia, Henrietta and the respective mothers to sit on the veranda sipping lemonade, reading, listening to the birds call from the trees and peering down at the gentlemen as they fished.

Of the four fellows, Whit moved with the greatest confidence, picking his spot with care and casting his line with his usual grace. Ruby counted at least four fish he brought to shore. The men returned sun-reddened and laughing, their lines hung with trout, which Whit's chef cooked for dinner.

"Had I realized you might actually catch so many fish," Ruby teased Whit over the succulent dinner, "I'd have been more tempted to try fishing myself."

"What did you think our purpose, Miss Hollingsford?" Charles Calder asked with a perplexed smile from across the table.

Ruby grinned. "Exercise, Mr. Calder. Until today, most of what I've seen you all do is throw string at the water!"

They all laughed at that. Indeed, it was a merry evening with Charles and Henrietta leading a reading from one of Shakespeare's comedies, and everyone taking a part. Ruby found herself sharing a smile with Whit when Mr. Stokely-Trent boomed out a line only to be outdone by Lady Wesworth's enthusiastic performance.

Indeed, sharing her thoughts with Whit had never been easier. It seemed everyone knew that a proposal had been made and refused, which put her out of the running as a candidate for his wife. Henrietta appeared to be developing an affection for Charles, for she seldom left his side. And Lady Wesworth no longer felt the need to thrust her daughter forward, as it was clear she was the only lady left to win Whit's heart.

Had the roles been reversed, Ruby wondered what she would have done. If she had never given her heart to Phillip only to see him crush it, would she be willing to sit beside Whit, fluttering her lashes? To show off her skills for him so that he would see her as the woman to manage his home, bear his children?

She nearly snorted aloud. That would mean she'd actually have to have excelled at some of the arts Society expected from a wife besides managing a staff. But she'd never particularly cared for the playing of music, the singing of a country air, or painting imitations of flowers onto firescreens. While pleasant to observe on occasion, the pastimes seemed rather pointless. Give her action any day!

Whit did not seem to agree, for he smiled as he helped with the reading, then applauded Lady Amelia's sweet rendition of a popular hymn that ended the night. As the ladies excused themselves and started for the door, he rose to intercept Ruby.

"Are you all right?" he murmured, frown settling on his face.

He'd removed his hat while fishing, and she could see fine lines at the corners of his eyes where the sun had kissed him.

"It was a relaxing afternoon," Ruby assured him.

He hesitated a moment, then lowered his voice further. "I found our talk after service much on my mind. I feel as if you expected more from my answer."

Ruby shook her head with a laugh. "I can hardly expect you to answer a question to which there may be no answer."

Again he hesitated, and she wondered what he found so difficult to say. Was he, too, struggling to understand this new concept of God? Or did he think her foolish for even considering such matters?

Then he straightened, once more the charming host. "I hope nothing further troubled you about our adventure yesterday," he said.

Ah, the obligatory asking after health. She stomped her feet against the carpet. "Hale and hearty, my lord. You need have no fears."

His smile hitched up. "I'm glad to hear it. I can't help thinking another lady might still be abed from her exertions."

Lady Amelia came immediately to mind. "And what of you?" Ruby asked. "Are your ribs healed from your accident at Hollyoak Farm?"

He stretched as if to make sure, and she was suddenly aware of the breadth of his shoulders, the length of his arms. "I can reasonably say that I've returned to my usual health."

Which was rather good health at that, Ruby thought,

then blushed at the impertinent thought. "Then I'm sure you'll acquit yourself well on our trip tomorrow."

He took her hand and bowed over it, his grip sure. "I look forward to it, Ruby."

With her fingers tingling in his, she found herself looking forward to it, as well.

Indeed, it was an eager group who assembled before the carriages the next morning after breakfast. The sun shone down from a cloudless sky, as if the Lord was giving His blessing to the event. The gentlemen in their navy coats and fawn trousers, their boots spotless and cravats immaculate, looked as if they were ready to call upon the Prince Regent himself.

Ruby had chosen one of her few white muslin gowns but covered it with her favorite pelisse—a sky-blue twill lined with dun satin, with puffed sleeves inset with lace and a lace collar that ran in a deep V front and back. The satin ribbons wrapping her high-crowned bonnet were the same shade of blue, and the lace at her hem just covered her practical half boots.

The distance they were to go made taking one carriage impossible. Ruby had hoped that Whit might join her in her father's carriage, but Lady Wesworth had other ideas, as usual.

"You will ride with us, Danning," she said, offering him her hand to escort her to the closed travel coach.

Whit's mouth quirked, but he put out his arm. "An honor, Lady Wesworth. Lady Amelia, if I may?" He held out his other arm as well, and the blonde beauty simpered as he led her to the waiting carriage.

Ruby bit back a sigh. She had refused his suit. She must not allow herself to mind when another lady saw his worth.

"I fear you will have to make do with the cadet

branch, Miss Hollingsford," his cousin said, offering her his arm.

Ruby smiled at him. "Cadet? Surely a captain at least, sir."

"Perhaps major general," he said with an answering smile.

Ruby glanced to where Lady Amelia had invited Henrietta to join them, to the obvious chagrin of Lady Wesworth. "Surely you would prefer to ride with Miss Stokely-Trent," she told Charles.

He followed Ruby's gaze, and she thought his arm slumped just the slightest. "The marchioness's travel coach will only seat four." As if he knew how that might sound, he immediately patted her hand. "And aren't I a lucky fellow to have been forced to ride with the reigning beauty as a result?"

It was a nice response, but for once it seemed utterly hollow. Had the flirt truly developed deeper feelings for Henrietta? As the Stokely-Trent parents climbed into their own carriage, Ruby let Charles Calder help her into hers. She was a little surprised when he took the seat next to her, leaving her father to sit opposite.

"I've told Davis to start out slowly," her father explained, "and to make sure to keep the other coaches in view."

And so the cavalcade set off. The road led over the stone bridge below the Lodge and out of the Dale to travel south along narrow country lanes. Trees crowded on either side, heavy from the recent rains. Once in a while branches brushed the carriage tops, sprinkling water down the glass. Through the sheen, Ruby could see tall spikes of flowers blooming in the grasslands, purple and white. Wooden bridges spanned the little rivers, and stone walls crusted with moss marked property lines.

"You wouldn't know it," Mr. Calder supplied as they came out onto a flatter expense of pastureland, where sheep grazed among the green, "but there's a stone quarry just beyond." He leaned closer to point to a dip in the ground, and a flowery smell wafted past Ruby—his cologne perhaps? She kept her gaze on the window.

"Do you know this area well, Mr. Calder?" she asked.

"Only around Fern Lodge," he said, making no effort to move away from her. "Like Danning, I've been coming here to fish since I was a boy." He nudged her shoulder with his own. "And like Danning, surely you can call me by my first name."

She truly wasn't willing to pursue that intimacy, so she was glad when her father spoke up across from them.

"Interesting your family should own the Lodge," he said. "I'd have thought the land belonged to the Duke of Bellington, given that it's such prime acreage along the river and so close to Bellweather Hall."

"It does belong to the duke," he said, leaning back at last and allowing Ruby to breathe easier. "The current duke's grandfather and ours were great friends growing up, and he granted our family a hundred-year lease on the Lodge as a wedding present."

"Odd wedding present," Ruby said with a frown. "It seems to be an entirely male bastion, a place for you all to escape."

"Indeed it is, my dear Ruby." His fatuous smile said he had taken it for granted she had agreed to allow him to use her first name, as well. "And if you had ever met my grandmother, you would know exactly why my grandfather required an escape."

Ruby shook her head at his audacity, but her father laughed.

Charles continued his attempts to be witty as the carriage rolled south past cozy stone cottages. Ruby tried to enjoy his company, but she couldn't help comparing him to Whit. He might be handsome and charming, but he seemed to lack substance, depth. By the time they stopped to rest the horses just outside Chapel-en-le-Frith, she had lost patience with him.

She was thankful that Lady Amelia requested her and Henrietta's company to stroll along the road looking at wildflowers. Lady Amelia seemed to have bloomed during the carriage ride in Whit's presence, for she held her lace-edged confection of a parasol over her head and gave it a twirl. She made a very pretty picture in her muslin gown, and Ruby could see that the gentlemen had noticed by the glances they cast the lady's way.

"You seem to have captured Danning's attention," Henrietta said to Lady Amelia as they paused before a patch of purple and blue flowers that somehow reminded Ruby of Whit's eyes.

Lady Amelia blushed. "He is very kind. But I'm not sure we will suit."

Ruby's brows shot up. "Why ever not?"

"You really are the most outspoken woman," Henrietta said as Lady Amelia's color deepened, and Ruby couldn't tell whether the bluestocking was annoyed or envious.

"Perhaps I am," Ruby replied. "But I see a very fine man in Lord Danning, and I cannot understand why you would think the two of you would not suit, and on remarkably short acquaintance."

Lady Amelia regarded her with a frown. In the shade of her parasol, her eyes looked more slate than blue.

"How odd, Miss Hollingsford. You already determined the two of you would not suit, and on nearly as short an acquaintance, I believe."

Now it was Ruby's turn to blush. "You're right, of course. But we both know there are reasons why a match between Lord Danning and the daughter of a jeweler would be inadvisable. There exists no such impediment between the two of you."

Lady Amelia cocked her head. "Are you counseling me to pursue him, Miss Hollingsford?"

She should say that. They were aligned in social status; in fact, marrying Lady Amelia might even give Whit a boost in society, as her father's title was higher than his. She'd already decided Lady Amelia was a sweet person, and no one could complain about her looks. By all accounts, she and Whit would be an excellent match.

But something kept her from answering.

"And what is that lovely flower, Henrietta?" Charles asked, coming up beside them. "It puts me in mind of little cups on a stick."

"Foxglove," Henrietta supplied readily, turning to beam at him. "The Latin name is *digitalis,* and the plant has been extracted to help cure heart palpitations."

"How perfect," he said, leaning closer to her as if *she* were the most perfect thing he could see at the moment. "For I find my heart positively pulsing every time I am near you."

Ruby rolled her eyes, but Lady Amelia put a hand to her mouth as if to keep from laughing.

However annoying Charles Calder might be, it was Whit's behavior that most amused Ruby as she returned to the larger group waiting by the carriages. He moved among his guests, asking after their health and enjoyment, offering encouragement and suggestions. And somehow, when the carriages set off again, Ruby found him sitting beside her.

She couldn't stop the frission of pleasure at the sight of him. "And what have you done with your cousin?" she asked as the carriage turned for the east toward Castleton.

"Allowed him to ride where he will be most appreciated," Whit replied, leaning back against the squabs as if well satisfied with himself.

"You will have to pay for this later," Ruby predicted with a shake of her head.

"Very likely," he agreed, tipping his top hat down so he could rest his head, as well. "But at the moment, I find I cannot care. Besides, I have a duty to all my guests, not just those in the other coaches."

Duty. Was that what she was to him, another task to be performed, another role to be fulfilled? Immediately she chided herself. She hadn't wanted to be a candidate in this wife campaign. She should be glad he wasn't here to pursue her.

But she had to own she enjoyed the second half of the drive more than the first. Whit pointed out places of interest, such as enclosed farms near Sackhall, the stone fences marking off the territory of each tenant, and the rising behemoth of Mam Tor that dwarfed the rest of the countryside. He chatted with her and her father about the usefulness of the Exchange, the need for reforms in the House of Lords and the role of women in the Courts of Law. She was surprised when she felt the coach slowing.

Ruby looked out the window. It was as if the countryside had shrugged, green hillocks bumping up on either side and rising in the distance. The coach had pulled into the muddy yard of a farmstead that was tucked against the side of one such hill. The gray stone cottage had windows that sparkled in the summer sun as if in greeting.

The owners must have heard the carriages coming, for an older man and woman immediately came out to greet them, followed more slowly by a younger man with a thatch of brown hair and a tense, pale face. Their clothes were more serviceable than fashionable, brown wool and rough linen. Ruby liked the family straight-away.

Whit alighted first and turned to help her from the carriage. As the rest of the party exited the carriages and gathered in a circle, the couple introduced themselves to Ruby's father as Mr. and Mrs. Greaves and their son Albert.

"A very talented young man, I hear," Ruby's father said as he shook Albert Greaves's hand. "I had the good fortune to purchase one of your pieces from a fellow who had been up this way. So, of course, I had to come meet you myself and bring a few friends along."

Introductions were swiftly made, and Mr. and Mrs. Greaves bobbed and blushed with pride that so many fine people had come to see their son. Albert, how-ever, turned paler and shuffled back a few steps, and Ruby wouldn't have been surprised had he fainted dead away. Beside her, Whit frowned as if he had noticed the same thing.

As the Greaveses bowed and curtsied to Lady Wes-worth, Ruby nudged her father. "You take the parents, I'll take Mr. Greaves," she murmured.

"Done," he murmured back. "Try to put him at his ease so I can make sure he hasn't reached an agreement with anyone else." He stepped forward and raised his voice. "Such a pleasure to meet you all. I wonder, might we see some of Mr. Greaves's exceptional work?"

His parents bubbled happily as they led the others toward their humble home. Whit offered Ruby his arm, but she shook her head. "See to the others, will you? I have work to do."

His frown deepened, but he inclined his head and moved toward the cottage with only one look back to her.

Albert Greaves positively dragged his booted feet as he followed.

Ruby caught up to him with a smile. "Bit much, aren't they?"

He raised his brows as if surprised by her candor, then hastily dropped his gaze to the ground. "Honored to have them here, your ladyship."

"Ah, too many names for you to keep us all straight, as well," Ruby said with a tsk. "Let's start fresh." She stopped, forcing him to stop, as well. "I'm Ruby Hollingsford, just plain Ruby, no lady. In fact, I'll probably answer to anything, with the possible exception of 'eh, you daft girl!'"

He smiled at that. "A-A-Albert Greaves," he said, then blushed and dropped his gaze again.

"Albert Greaves, artist," she amended. "I saw the candelabra you made. It's beautiful. I can't imagine how you could work the stone that way."

"It's not so hard," he said with a shrug, still avoiding her gaze. "The stone is soft. You turn it, like wood on a lathe." He glanced up at her. "Would you like to see where it comes from?"

"Very much!" Ruby beamed at him. "I know the others would like to see it, too. They came all this way, after all. Seems like it would be a shame for them to miss it."

He nodded. "It would, at that. All right, miss. If you fetch them, I'll show you where I get the stone."

Whit stood in the doorway of the cottage while the others exclaimed over the bowls, vases and gems Mr. Greaves had carved from the purple-blue stone. No one else seemed to have noticed Ruby's absence. He watched as she approached the artist, saw the fellow's slim shoulders come down, a shy smile play about his lips. How easily she melted resistance, his own included.

He had spent the first half of their trip sitting beside Lady Amelia, trying to draw her out. She was an excellent listener, but she couldn't seem to understand that conversation was better when two participated. The trip had seemed interminable, until he'd escaped to Ruby's carriage, and then he didn't know how they'd crossed the distance so quickly!

Well, that wasn't altogether true. He suspected the trip had seemed shorter because he'd been with Ruby. Like the gemstone for which she was named, she positively sparkled. Watching her now, something poked at him again.

Have I mistaken my way, Lord? Are these feelings for Ruby something You want?

He received no answer, but he stepped out of the doorway as the young artist approached with Ruby on his arm.

"Mr. Greaves would like to show everyone the cavern where he extracts his stone," Ruby told Whit with a smile to the man on her other side. "Would you invite them, Lord Danning?"

Mr. Greaves was too lost in her smile to appreciate the fact that she just made an earl his errand boy.

"Delighted," Whit said, holding his appreciative chuckle until he was out of hearing from Mr. Greaves.

The others were equally delighted. They kept up a steady stream of comments and questions as the entire Greaves family, Albert in the lead, brought them up the hill behind the cottage.

Ruby dropped back beside Whit on the rocky path. "And here we are on another adventure, my lord."

Her excitement was palpable. "Because of you," he said. "You never cease to amaze me. When we first arrived, I wasn't sure whether Mr. Greaves was going to run or expire on the spot."

"Poor man," Ruby murmured, gaze going ahead as if to make sure her darling was safe. "I think he just needs a little encouragement."

Something she excelled at giving, Whit realized. From the seating arrangements at dinner to the activities she'd planned, she'd helped manage the demands of an overfilled house with poise and grace. Indeed, this entire house party could have been a disaster without her.

But now was not the place to acknowledge that. The rest of the party had gathered before a wooden door set into the side of the hill. He couldn't help his sense of anticipation as Mr. Greaves senior took a brass key and opened the portal so they could all file past him into the very hill itself.

Gray rock enclosed them immediately, lit from above by an iron chandelier set with thick candles. The drippings littered the rough floor at their feet and scented the still air with tallow. But wax wasn't the only thing to drip. Nearby Whit heard the sound of water on rock, slow and steady.

"Watch your step, now," Mr. Greaves senior was saying, lighting lamps and handing them about. Ruby accepted one from him, as did Stokely-Trent and Charles.

From there, the path angled down on stairs carved into the rock, and the walls rose around them veined in dun and black. Their shadows followed the rough curves. In places, it appeared that clay had melted and run down in rivulets, but when Whit put a hand to it, he found the material hard. The voices of the others quieted, as if awe filled the narrow way in the still, cool air. Ruby gazed about her, wide-eyed, as if she'd wandered into a cathedral.

And then they did.

The space before them opened up into a vast cavern, the top and bottom of which were lost to view. Yellowed spires hung down from above and poked up from below, glittering in the light from the lamps. The path hugged one wall, leading them along past underground mountains and streams. It was as if the Lord had granted another earth below the one where He had walked.

In the stunned silence, Ruby spoke first. "How do you even know where to start?" Her voice echoed into the darkness.

Albert seemed to be in his element at last, his feet as sure on the rock as those of a goat. "It all depends on what you want to make," he explained. "If you're after a cup, this small piece might do." He took a little hammer from a stash of tools along the wall and tapped at the stone here, there and there. The force seemed insufficient, but a chunk broke off and fell into the lad's outstretched hand. Albert turned the dark stone to show them the underside. The purple, blue and yellow of Blue John gleamed in the light.

"Amazing," Lady Amelia breathed.

"What if you want something larger?" Charles called from in front of Whit.

"Perhaps those columns Mother and Father saw at Chatsworth," Henrietta agreed, moving closer to him.

Charles stepped back to make room for her on the crowded path. "Say this size," he explained, gesturing with his hands to show the shape he imagined. His hand hit Whit on the shoulder, and Whit moved aside to get out of the way.

"Watch out!" Ruby cried, darting forward, lamp wavering.

Whit felt his right heel sinking into the path. He flailed for purchase, but the soft limestone crumbled, pulling him down. Then he was tumbling backward into the unforgiving depth of the cavern.

Chapter Thirteen

Ruby snatched Whit's hand as he fell, heart in her throat as she locked her fingers around his. Her feet slid, and for a moment, she thought she would follow him over the side. She dropped the lamp, which hit the ground with a tinkle of metal, clasped her other hand to his and braced her feet against the rock.

Whit hung, his back out over the chasm beside them, mouth open as if to cry for help. An answering cry rose up inside Ruby.

He said You were rock, Lord. Be that for us now!

Before she could cry aloud for help, Charles whirled to stare at her. Why did he hesitate? Couldn't he see they were about to go over? Ruby felt every second straining her arms, yet Charles paused to set his lamp carefully on the ground, as if it were more important than his cousin's very life.

Then he was crowding next to her, reaching past her. She could feel his muscles bunching where his shoulder pressed against hers. With a heave, he brought Whit up beside them.

Ruby released her grip, stumbling back to fetch up against the stone wall behind her, breath ragged. As she embraced the strength of the rock, Charles caught Whit close for a moment before letting him go and putting out a hand to steady him.

"Well done," Whit said, clapping his cousin on the shoulder.

At the sound of Whit's comment, Henrietta looked back with a frown, as if wondering what was keeping them. The others didn't even notice the short-lived disturbance, peppering Albert Greaves and his father with questions about the cavern, their cheerful voices grating on Ruby's overshot nerves. They had no clue that a tragedy had just been averted. Beside her, Whit adjusted his cravat as if it had been the most affected by the incident.

Ruby wasn't fooled. Even in the golden light from the lamp Charles bent to retrieve, she could see that Whit's face was ashen. He knew the danger he'd avoided. He was simply trying not to frighten her.

But she was frightened. He could have been killed! Just the thought of his body dashing against those yellow spires made her stomach clench, her breath stop. Her hands were shaking so hard she didn't dare bend to pick up her own lamp.

Her one consolation was that Charles Calder looked even more shaken than Whit did.

"You must watch yourself more closely, cousin," he said, rubbing his free hand along his leg as if to try to still the trembling. "You've had a few too many accidents of late." He offered Ruby a smile. "And you won't always have a lady knight to look out for you."

She inclined her head at his quip, but it was his first comment that held her against the stone. There *had* been a number of accidents on this visit. Too many accidents.

Was someone trying to kill Whit?

Ridiculous! Much as she had come to dislike and distrust nobs, much as some of Whit's visitors had treated her unkindly at first, she could not see his guests as homicidal. Surely these accidents were simply a factor of putting too many people in too small a place—the stables at Hollyoak Farm, the path by the Edge, the way through the Blue John cave. Few of the accidents could have been planned. Very likely, Whit would be fine as soon as they all left him in peace.

Yet she would know no peace until she was certain.

"Ready to move along?" Charles asked, glancing between the two of them.

Whit shook his head. "Give us a moment. We'll catch up shortly."

Charles eyed him as if uncertain of Whit's state of mind, then he inclined his head and turned to follow the others, the glow of his lamp dimming.

Whit watched his cousin move away, then turned to Ruby. With her lamp out, she could not be sure of the look on his face.

"What were you thinking?" he asked. His voice shook, but she couldn't name the emotion it held.

Ruby raised her head, pushing away from the rock at last. "I saw you start to fall. Would you have me simply stand and watch you die?"

"I would have you show some care for your own life!" As if he knew his voice was rising, he puffed out a breath and ran his hand back through his hair. "Surely you must realize how dangerous that was. I outweigh you by a stone and a half at least. If Charles hadn't grabbed my other hand, I could have pulled you over with me."

She hadn't thought of that when she'd reached for

him. All she'd known was that he was in danger, and she'd acted.

"But you didn't," she protested. "So no harm done." She tried for a smile as she took a step forward.

He pulled her against him, held her close, his arms as warm as a wool blanket in the cool of the cavern. For a moment, she allowed herself the luxury of leaning against his strength, feeling his chest rise and fall against hers, inhaling the clean scent of him.

He was the first to break away. She searched his face in the deepening twilight, but she could find no sign of an emotion. "We should go," he said, bending to take up her battered lamp. He stepped aside to allow her to precede him up the path. It was as if he meant to ensure she'd have no opportunity to help if he fell again.

But he didn't fall. She could feel him following her as she hurried up the narrow path to join the others and finish the tour of the cavern. He even carried a chunk of Blue John back to the cottage for Albert Greaves. Several of the others held stones as well, and Lady Wesworth and Mr. Stokely-Trent commissioned items. Ruby's father rubbed his hands together as they waited before the carriages.

"You see?" he all but crowed. "I knew Albert Greaves would be popular. I spoke to him on the way back from the cave. He's agreed to sell everything through my shop from here on out. A very promising beginning."

Ruby was glad for her father, but she couldn't help wondering as they traveled back to the Lodge whether her father's promising beginning would mark the dismal end to her friendship with Whit. He was polite and congenial to everyone, but she caught him gazing at her from time to time with a slight frown, as if he wasn't entirely sure what to make of her.

As he had when they'd traveled out, Whit rode the first stretch of the way back to the Lodge in the Wesworth coach, leaving her to the mercy of his cousin. At least Charles had no trouble filling the time. He positively glowed as he described the sights he'd seen. Unfortunately, his monologue only gave Ruby more time to stew.

She thought perhaps Whit would switch coaches again when they stopped to rest the horses, but he returned to Lady Amelia's coach after only the most polite conversation with Ruby.

She'd clearly offended him. How?

She could not believe he was so proud as to refuse the help of a woman, or that he disdained assistance from the daughter of a shopkeeper. And if he thought she should mind her own affairs when he was in danger, he had better think again!

"Is everything all right, Ruby?" Charles asked as they headed north toward the entrance to Dovecote Dale. "You seem uncommonly quiet."

Her father barked a laugh, and Ruby couldn't help smiling. "Is that your polite way of telling me I generally talk too much, Mr. Calder?" she teased.

He held up his hands. "No, indeed. I find your conversation delightful."

"Ah, you better watch out, Ruby," her father joked. "It seems you've made a conquest."

"Not at all, Father," Ruby said with a look to Charles. "I believe Mr. Calder's heart is already engaged elsewhere."

He had the good grace to look away. "If it is so obvious to you, I can only wonder why she doesn't seem to notice."

"She notices," Ruby said, remembering how the bluestocking brightened every time Charles was near. "But she may not wish to let you know, for fear of the reactions of her parents, who clearly expect an announcement of another sort."

"Sweet on the Stokely-Trent girl, are you?" her father asked, leaning back. "She's a rare handful."

Charles agreed with such a wistful sigh that Ruby was sure he'd taken the ambiguous term for praise. He was clearly smitten. The only question was whether Henrietta would have the courage to defy her parents and declare her feelings for Whit's cousin.

Ruby did not have a chance to spend time with Whit again until the group reassembled that night for dinner. Most of his guests laughed and reminisced about their trip as they ate the braised lamb the chef sent in as the crowning glory of the first course. Whit rarely looked her way, spending so much time in conversation with Lady Amelia that Lady Wesworth positively beamed from her place at the foot of the table.

Ruby knew she should leave be. If he annoyed, her silence would give him time to calm. Certainly a young lady of the *ton* might be expected to ignore such behavior, to rise above it, to focus on some other gentleman instead. But Ruby wasn't a young lady of the *ton*.

So after dinner, while Lady Amelia played at the spinet, the older people played cards and Henrietta played at flirting with Charles, Ruby approached Whit.

He was standing by the door to the veranda and looking out at the night as if wishing he might be down at the stream fishing even then.

"Have I offended you?" Ruby asked without preamble.

He turned from the view to eye her. Tonight he was

the perfect gentleman host, his evening black as spotless as his pristine cravat. Mr. Quimby must be proud.

"Not in the slightest," Whit assured her, although his smile did not quite reach his purple-blue eyes.

"Something's wrong," Ruby insisted. "You've been remarkably quiet since the accident in the Blue John cave."

He inclined his head, but she had the feeling the movement had more to do with a desire to keep her from seeing his emotions than from any attempt at politeness. "Forgive me. I hadn't realized my thoughts were so apparent and so easily misconstrued. You could have been killed today, Ruby. I find that disturbing in the extreme."

Ruby frowned. "You're still worried about me?"

"How could I not be? When I think of you falling, of seeing your joy snuffed out…" He turned his gaze out the window as if he didn't want her to notice the concern on his face.

But she had seen it. She'd heard it in his voice, as well. He was more shaken by the possibility of harm to her than to himself.

"Well, you wouldn't have seen my joy snuffed out," Ruby pointed out. "You'd have been dead first."

He humphed. "Small comfort."

Ruby touched his sleeve, drawing his gaze back to her. "I am fine, Whit. You are fine. We have much to be thankful for."

He took her hand, raised it to his lips. "I am well aware of that."

The caress of his lips against her hand made her breath catch. Ruby pulled back.

"Perhaps that's why I'm quiet," Whit said, straightening. "Coming so close to death made me realize how fortunate I am, in my family, my friends and my circumstances. With such blessing comes responsibility. And one of those responsibilities is to marry and ensure the line."

Ruby wrapped an arm about her middle. "I thought you said you weren't looking for a wife."

"After today, I am forced to change my mind. Charles isn't ready to be earl. If I die, there's no one else to inherit."

Ruby made a face. "Practically speaking, if you were to marry tomorrow, there wouldn't be anyone mature enough to inherit for a good nineteen years."

"Sixteen," he countered. "I became earl at fifteen."

She still found that ridiculously young to be expected to shoulder such responsibilities. Small wonder he'd all but forgotten to do other than his duty, that he chose to run away from time to time.

"Sixteen, then," Ruby acknowledged. "That seems a great many years to be concerned about today."

One corner of his mouth lifted. "But if I don't begin the process, it will be longer still."

Ruby swallowed. He was right. She knew he was right. It shouldn't hurt so much to think of him marrying another. She was the one who had removed herself from consideration. If she had other thoughts, now was the time to state them.

"Your cousin Charles is enamored of Henrietta Stokely-Trent," she heard herself say. "It appears you are wise to focus on Lady Amelia instead."

He said nothing, merely gazing down at her. In the candlelight, his eyes were as deep as the Blue John cave, and as dangerous.

"Perhaps," he said. "But I find myself more drawn to another young lady."

Ruby's mouth was dry. "Then by all means, pursue her."

He did not move, but her heart started beating faster. "I'm not assured she would be amenable to another proposal. She's already refused me once."

"Perhaps she isn't certain either." The words came out in a whisper, and she could not look at him. All her reservations rushed up, shouting for her attention. He was a nob; no one in his social circle would accept her place at his side. She'd be belittled, ridiculed, made the target of every jibe and insult Society could invent if she married him. And what solace would she find in her husband? He would come to see the gulf between them, and his affection for her would fade.

Then there was the matter of the money she'd receive on marriage. He would squander it on gambling. No, drink. No, fishing accoutrements. And he would expect her to be the perfect Society wife, smiling even when her heart was breaking, no more than an ornament on his arm. He didn't love her.

He lowered his head, even as his fingers lifted her chin. "Allow me to court you, Ruby. Please."

Please. A decided concession from any aristocrat, and said so sweetly, so yearningly. How could she refuse?

Here You go, God. The thought popped into her mind. *Here is the perfect opportunity for You to show me what is right, to prove You care about my life. Would I be right to accept him or would I be diminishing my convictions? Is this something You've planned as my father keeps saying, or am I on my own as usual?*

"Have you no answer for me?" Whit asked.

Have You no answer for me? Ruby begged.

Something urged her to respond. Perhaps it was

Whit's look, or his words, or a quiet voice inside her. She swallowed. "Yes, my lord. I would very much like you to court me. I can only hope we won't live to regret it."

Whit felt as if someone had offered him the deepest trout hole in the river and an entire lifetime to fish it. He wanted to lift Ruby in his arms, twirl her around the room, shout at the ceiling for the sheer joy of it.

But such were not the actions of a belted earl or a gentleman. So, instead, he bowed over her hand, held it only slightly longer than was reasonable and offered to escort her back to her father.

She raised a fiery brow as if he ought to know full well she was capable of walking on her own. "I'll go talk to my father," she conceded. "After that last chortle over his win, he's likely to undo all the good you've done in keeping them happy."

She hurried off to the card table, and Whit thought that, despite her brave words, her trim figure seemed to waver just the slightest, as if his request had shaken her.

It shook him, too. In truth, that day in the cavern, when he'd realized Ruby's attempt to rescue him had put her in danger, the world had seemed to tilt on its axis. He had never considered himself afraid to face adversity, but the thought of losing Ruby had terrified him. Somehow, she had become important to him.

So, on the trip back, while nodding to conversation instigated by Lady Wesworth, he'd offered a prayer for wisdom, for understanding. The answer had come from an odd direction, and he'd blinked in surprise.

"What did you say?" he'd asked Lady Wesworth, interrupting her strident monologue that had made her daughter sit with knotted hands and set Henrietta's soft face to hardening.

"What?" she'd said, frowning.

"You quoted something. I'm sure of it," Whit had insisted.

Her brow had cleared. "I said a gentleman must look at breeding and accomplishment when seeking a wife. We are told a woman of valor, a lady of accomplishment, is a crown to her husband."

A woman of valor. Could there be any better description for his valiant Ruby?

His heart had swelled at the thought. But in his world, such feelings had only one proper outcome, an outcome Ruby had refused, until tonight.

He felt a smile growing and realized that Lady Wesworth was regarding him in a decidedly odd manner, as if she could not tell whether he was mad or dyspeptic. He turned to the windows but immediately realized why she might be concerned. He couldn't remember such a grin on his face!

He was going to court Ruby Hollingsford.

She wouldn't make it easy. Something frightened her—her, his redoubtable Ruby! Whatever it was, he was determined to surmount it. And if there was something lacking in his own heart, if he struggled to express some concepts to her satisfaction, then he'd have to work on that, as well. He hadn't led an earldom for fifteen years without learning how to persevere.

Of course, he still had five days of this house party to survive first.

They all spent the evening playing whist again, and he was able to partner Ruby at last. She was a quick player, tossing her card out the second Charles on her right played his. Yet as quickly as she played, she always played exactly the right card. As a result, they won two rubbers by the time the parents began making noises about retiring.

"Allow me a word before you go," Charles murmured to him as they bowed the ladies and older gentlemen out. Whit nodded absently, more interested in the smile Ruby offered on her way out the door than in his cousin's request. The room seemed to cool as she disappeared, and he suggested that Charles join him in the library instead.

His cousin spent a moment checking behind the drapes and around the larger furnishings before joining Whit on one of the leather-bound armchairs in the center of the room.

"Is there a French spy at large?" Whit teased.

"Very likely," Charles said with a rueful smile. "Though not in Dovecote Dale, I would imagine." He glanced at the paneled door as if to make sure it was closed, then lowered his voice all the same. "I would prefer to keep your guests ignorant of this conversation."

Whit raised a brow but waited for his cousin to continue.

Charles cleared his throat, adjusted his spotless cravat, stroked his hands down the arms of the chair, then snapped his gaze to Whit's.

"I must ask you, Danning, about your intentions toward Henrietta Stokely-Trent."

Whit leaned back, smile quirking. "I have none. And you?"

Charles grinned. "I have far too many."

"Do you claim yourself in love, then?"

Charles nodded. "Hopelessly so. She's so clever, Whit. You never know what fact will pop from her mouth. And she is forever curious, about any number of things. Do you know she asked me to teach her to shoot? What other woman would even show interest?"

Ruby came to mind immediately. She'd said she boxed and could fire a pistol. He had no doubt they could find any number of interesting pastimes to pursue together.

"Have you spoken to her father?" Whit asked.

Charles fiddled with the brass tacks that held the leather to the wood of the chair. "I have not. For one thing, I wanted to make sure your feelings weren't engaged, as well."

"Not in the slightest," Whit assured him.

Still Charles avoided his gaze. "And for another, I was hoping you'd speak for me."

"Why?" Whit challenged, sitting straighter. "You can't fear him."

Charles made a face. "*Fear* might be too strong a word. But his reaction concerns me. He's so set on a title, Danning, or at the very least a fortune. Lacking both, I am not encouraged about my chances."

He edged forward on his seat, raising his gaze at last. "I thought if you were to talk to him, explain my expectations, my admiration for his daughter, he might be persuaded to see me differently."

Surely Henrietta's father would have greater respect for Charles if his cousin spoke to the man outright. Yet, given Winston Stokely-Trent's respect for a title, Charles was probably right that he'd be more likely to listen to Whit.

"I'll speak to him," Whit promised. "But see that you do so, as well. To marry Henrietta, you may have to fight for her."

Charles clapped both hands on the armrests. "I will,

Danning. Count on it. Whatever it takes to win the fair maiden, I intend to do, no matter the cost."

Whit admired his determination, for he very much felt the same way about Ruby. He could only hope he could find a way to overcome her reservations.

Chapter Fourteen

Whit managed to catch Henrietta's father at breakfast the next morning and requested a moment of his time in the withdrawing room before the others rose. He was hoping for a quick conversation so he could wait for Ruby. He could imagine any number of ways to spend the day with her: showing her the intricacy of casting, taking a picnic among the orchids. But Stokely-Trent had other ideas.

"I've been meaning to speak to you, my lord," he said, coming into the room behind Whit and stopping just short of the fireplace, legs splayed in his chamois breeches. "I do believe you're attempting to pawn your cousin off on my girl." His paisley waistcoat-clad stomach jutted out as if it protested, as well.

"And I take exception that you would consider my cousin the inferior man," Whit countered. He crossed his arms over the chest of his brown wool coat as he stood by the hearth and was pleased his ribs only murmured a minor objection.

Stokely-Trent waved a plump hand. "Of course he's inferior. He lacks a title, he lacks a fortune and he lacks property. My girl could do better on her family name alone."

Interesting that he put the title before the stability of fortune and property. The Stokely-Trents moved in high circles, yet it seemed they, too, felt the need for a title to be fully accepted.

"Charles may lack a title," Whit countered, "but he has true affection for your daughter."

Henrietta's father shook his head. "Perhaps too much affection, for any number of things. I understand he has accumulated a sizeable debt gambling."

Would the gossipmongers never cease making up tales? "Interesting," Whit replied, lowering his arms and shifting on his booted feet. "I wonder how he managed to finance his gambling if he has so little to his name."

Stokely-Trent blinked, then recovered to raise one finger, pointing it at the ceiling. "Very likely on his expectations, my lord. Everyone knows he is your heir, and you are not yet wed."

"At thirty," Whit replied dryly, "I can reasonably be expected to sire an heir."

Henrietta's father puffed out a sigh as he lowered his hand. "The very fact that you're speaking to me about your cousin tells me it won't be with my girl. Have you settled on that Hollingsford chit, then?"

Whit drew himself up. "I asked you here to discuss Charles's matrimonial hopes, not my own."

Normally, when he gazed down his nose and drew down his brows, using what Quimby called his lordly look, his staff and those with lesser titles jumped to do his bidding. Stokely-Trent took a step forward, narrowed his eyes as if about to make a business deal.

"Think, Danning," he ordered. "You need a woman who will do you credit, who can help advance your influence. I can see the attraction of that red hair, but you must look at pedigree to find a proper wife."

Was everyone in his class a snob? Whit met him gaze for gaze. "Ruby Hollingsford is clever, capable and caring. She has the skills to help manage my affairs, the confidence to stand beside me in any social setting. I would feel fortunate should she respond favorably to my suit."

He snorted. "She's the one who's fortunate, to think of catching an earl. She may have been educated at the Barnsley School, but she isn't our kind."

Whit's jaw tightened. "If by our kind you mean a title-hunting bully, I quite agree."

He puffed up like a dead fish left too long in the water. "Now, see here, Danning."

Whit closed the distance between them. "No, *you* see here. If I choose to marry Ruby Hollingsford, it will be because we love each other deeply, share the same values and are willing to work side by side. That, sir, makes a marriage, not the prestige or power that might accrue from it, not the benefits that might be provided to the parents. Now, are you willing to discuss my cousin and your daughter, or should I tell Charles he would be wiser not to associate with your family?"

Stokely-Trent held his gaze a few moments, eyes narrowed, but Whit saw the doubt that slowly replaced the determination. He looked away with another shake of his head. "Very well, my lord. I'll say no more about your infatuation with Miss Hollingsford. But do not expect me to toss my girl away, merely because some son of a second son shows interest."

Whit told himself to accept the first victory and focus on gaining another for Charles. "I believe it goes beyond interest. Charles would like to pay his addresses.

He has my blessing. He and his family will always be welcome at my table. And I plan to give him one of the unentailed estates on his marriage. He will be able to provide for his wife and children."

Stokely-Trent nodded slowly. "That is something, I suppose, though I still say my girl is worth more."

"Every father wants the best for his children," Whit acknowledged, taking a step back. "But her happiness is not a minor consideration, and I do believe she cares for Charles, just as he cares for her."

He nodded again, then blew out a breath. "Very well, my lord. I'll listen to the fellow, if he is so bold as to approach me."

"That's all I ask," Whit replied, inclining his head. "Now, if you'll excuse me, I have other guests I should see to."

The smirk on Stokely-Trent's face said exactly which guest he thought Whit had in mind. In that case, he would not be wrong. Whit felt as if he'd stepped in mud and couldn't wait to be with Ruby's refreshing honesty instead.

Ruby came down to breakfast filled in equal parts with anticipation and anxiety. She'd spent half the night tossing and turning, wondering what she'd done by agreeing to let Whit court her. He was an aristocrat, for pity's sake! There would always be those who would whisper she'd married him for his title or he'd married her for her dowry, that she was beneath him. Did she want to spend the rest of her life subjecting herself to such nonsense?

She'd even thrown the matter to God.

"Is this really what You want?" she'd asked the ceiling of her box bed. "Did I understand You right? Why won't You say something?"

"Oh, go to sleep, you silly girl!" Lady Wesworth had bellowed from next door.

She had finally soothed herself to sleep by assuring herself it was not a fait accompli. Whit could court her all he wanted. In the end, she did not have to accept his proposal.

But it was not Whit's voice she heard as she approached the dining room that morning. Lady Wesworth's demands echoed down the paneled corridor.

"You are not making enough of an effort, Amelia," she was complaining. "You must take every opportunity to spend time with Danning."

Lady Amelia murmured something in response, as quiet and agreeable as always. It did not assure her mother.

"Playing the piano and listening to a fellow are not enough. That bluestocking at least is original. I never thought to say it, but you must be as bold as Miss Hollingsford."

Ruby bit her lip to keep from laughing. Lady Wesworth may never have thought to say something admirable about Ruby, but Ruby had certainly never thought to hear it!

She stamped her feet the last few yards of the corridor before entering to make sure they knew she was coming, then smiled at them both from the doorway. "Good morning, Lady Amelia, Lady Wesworth."

"Good morning, Miss Hollingsford," Lady Amelia murmured, gaze on the table linen and graceful hands hovering over the silver teapot next to her. "There's some lovely chamomile this morning. Shall I pour you a cup?"

"That's very kind of you," Ruby said, coming into the room.

Lady Wesworth glowered at her daughter, and Ruby could only wonder what the poor girl had done wrong this time. Was there some Society rule about being too friendly?

She ventured to the sideboard and filled her plate with shirred eggs and spinach, buttery rolls and fresh raspberries with cream, then went to sit at the table near the young lady. Lady Amelia handed her a china cup patterned with bold iron-red leaves edged in gold.

"And where are all the gentlemen this morning?" Ruby asked after a few bites in silence. "Out fishing so soon?"

Lady Amelia shuddered, but whether for the early hour or the thought of the pastime, Ruby wasn't sure.

"I do not believe they have risen," Lady Wesworth said as if this were some great moral failing.

"Then we don't know what they have planned," Ruby surmised, taking a sip of the chamomile.

"Lady Amelia," Lady Wesworth announced, "is going fishing with Lord Danning."

Lady Amelia choked. Indeed, she sputtered so hard, Ruby rose from her seat to help her. Lady Amelia held up a hand to forestall her and managed to catch her breath.

"Yes," she said, swallowing convulsively. "I am going fishing. Do say you'll join us, Miss Hollingsford."

"I hardly think that's necessary," her mother protested.

It wasn't necessary. Lady Amelia would not require a chaperone. The anglers would be outdoors, in ready view of much of the house, as well as anyone passing along the road. But Ruby recognized desperation gazing back at her from the lady's sapphire eyes.

"I'd be delighted to join you," Ruby said, returning to her seat and picking up the damask napkin she'd dropped in her haste. "Perhaps between the two of us, we can endeavor to catch something."

"I have no doubt," Lady Wesworth said, anger simmering in every syllable.

Ruby simply smiled at her and took another sip of her tea.

She was thankful that Whit joined them shortly after. He didn't appear to have spent a sleepless night. His golden hair was pomaded in place, his eyes twinkled and his cravat was casually tied above his coat as if he were ready for adventure. But then, she supposed Mr. Quimby would not have allowed him to go out looking less than perfect.

He didn't even finish his greeting before Lady Wesworth informed him of her plans for Lady Amelia.

To do him justice, he only hesitated a moment before smiling at the lady. "How delightful," he said to Lady Wesworth. "And will you and Ruby be joining us?"

She sat up straighter. "I have correspondence I must catch up on." Her look to Ruby dared her to say otherwise.

"I'll join you," Ruby piped up with a grin.

He seemed to settle on his feet. "Excellent," he said, smile growing so dazzling she nearly forgot the topic of the conversation. "Give me a moment for some sustenance, and we'll see what can be done."

Because Lady Amelia had been so kind when Ruby had entered, Ruby thought the lady would offer Whit a cup of tea, as well. But Lady Amelia sank lower in her seat, long fingers crumbling her roll, as if she rather hoped everyone would just forget about her existence.

Whit set his plate down beside Ruby's and pulled up a chair. "And how are you this morning, my dear?"

Nervous, concerned, absolutely mad. She smiled back. "Fine. You simply couldn't wait to fish again, could you?"

He smiled as he forked up a mouthful of the eggs. "I am a creature of habit."

"Perhaps we shouldn't disturb you then," Ruby offered, watching how his hands shaped around the silver fork, his body leaned forward over the table, so strong even in repose. "I'm sure Lady Amelia and I can find some other way to entertain ourselves if you'd prefer to go alone."

Lady Amelia's head came up. "Oh, certainly, my lord."

But of course he was too much a gentleman to agree. "Nonsense," he said with a smile to Lady Amelia before focusing back on Ruby. "Nothing would make me happier than to share my favorite pastime with you."

Lady Amelia sighed.

Ruby had to admit she shared the woman's trepidation. She'd seen Whit on Sunday. He'd stood so patiently, so intently, as if every part of him was attuned to the water rushing past.

She didn't think she had the same patience, and she truly didn't want to disappoint him. Besides, she and Lady Amelia could hardly follow his example and wade into the water in skirts!

He seemed to have considered their inexperience at least, for when they all gathered in his fishing closet a short time later, he immediately began explaining.

"I was hoping one of the other practiced anglers

could join us," he said as he selected various pieces of equipment from the shelves and hooks of the room. "Unfortunately, Charles has already gone out shooting, Mr. Hollingsford is still abed, and Mr. Stokely-Trent felt the need to converse with his daughter."

Ruby wondered what that was all about, but she managed to keep herself from asking.

"So," he continued, turning to them with a smile, "you will have to make do with me. I take it neither of you have fished before."

Ruby shook her head and saw Lady Amelia do the same. While Ruby was wearing a gray walking dress and brown boots, the lady wore another of her frilly muslin gowns, this time with a spencer as blue as her eyes over the top. Ruby refused to comment on the impracticality of standing on a rocky shore in the matching blue slippers peeking out from under the lacy hem.

"Then allow me to instruct you." He took down a narrow, leather-bound book and opened the cover. Lady Amelia shrank back against the wall with a gasp.

"Easy, my dear," he said. "These are not what they seem."

Ruby looked closer. What had at first looked like dead flies stuck on brass pins were instead bits of string and feather cleverly tied together to resemble nature's pests.

"Did you make these?" Ruby asked, reaching out a hand to touch the one constructed from a mallard's feather.

"Many of them," he replied, and she could tell by his smile he was trying not to sound too proud of the fact. "Some belonged to my father and a few to my grandfather. Never fear, Lady Amelia. You gave me a great compliment by assuming they were real."

She ventured closer as well and peered down into the book of flies. "They are very convincing."

"They must be. Their sole purpose is to deceive the fish so that he will take a bite, and when he does, we have him."

"Notice that he said 'him,'" Ruby teased. "A lady fish would surely be wiser."

Lady Amelia dimpled.

Whit smiled as he pulled three rods from the rack and handed them around. About eight feet long, with a grip covered in cork, the thing was light and flexible in Ruby's fingers. She gave it a flick of her wrist, imagining how it would feel to toss the line out over the stream.

"I knew you'd be a natural," Whit murmured in her ear before he turned to help Lady Amelia untangle her line from the feather on her bonnet.

A sliver of anticipation ran through Ruby. She could hardly wait to see what happened next.

Whit led them the short distance to the stream and set a wicker basket and the book of flies well above the water on the pebbled shore. The day was bright again, heat already rising, though shade dappled the pool before the bridge. Whit eyed the water, then bent to the basket.

"I don't think flies will be our best choice today, ladies," he said, rummaging in the basket to pull out a glass vial. "This time of year we sometimes have to use brandling."

"Brandling?" Ruby asked, as she and Lady Amelia peered closer. Inside the vial, long, reddish tubes squirmed over each other.

"A worm," Whit replied, poking a finger in the tube and pulling one out.

Ruby was rather proud of Lady Amelia for merely turning white and gripping her pole like a staff.

"They are generally found beneath dunghills," he continued, bracing his pole between his booted feet and grabbing up the brass hook with his other hand, completely oblivious to the panicked look on the lady's face. "The best way to ensure they stay on the hook is to start at the middle and poke the hook in and out as if you were sewing, so that the prick of the hook comes out the head. Like so."

He held up the hook with the impaled worm.

With a strangled cry, Lady Amelia threw down her rod and fled.

Whit raised his brows as the hook fell.

Ruby put a hand to his shoulder. "Fish. It might be the only chance you get. I'll go after her."

His look softened, and one hand came down to touch her cheek in her bonnet. She tried not to think about those fingers touching a dunghill worm. "I was hoping to spend time with you," he murmured.

She wanted to sink into the pool of his eyes. Instead, she forced herself to take a step back. "We will," Ruby promised. "Give me a moment, and I'll be delighted to have you show me how to subdue a trout."

He dropped his hand with a nod, and Ruby turned and started up the bank.

She wasn't sure how far Lady Amelia would go. Would she run to her mother or all the way to London? But she found the lady just over the rise from the river, head bent and shoulders shaking in her blue spencer.

Ruby slowed her steps, then came to a stop beside her and put a tentative hand on her arm. "Messy thing, fishing. Who would have imagined it would be so barbaric?"

Lady Amelia shuddered. "Or that I would be so faint-hearted," she murmured with a sniff. "How you must despise me, Miss Hollingsford."

"Of course I don't despise you," Ruby declared, coming around to face the woman. Tears left delicate tracks down her pearly cheeks, made her rosy lips look redder. Even pitiful, she was a beauty!

"How could you not?" Lady Amelia begged, blue eyes swimming. "I despise me!"

Ruby recoiled. "Why? What horrible thing have you done?"

Her lower lip trembled. "It is not so much what I have done but what I have *not* done. I have always tried to do what was expected of me. But some expectations are simply too much. I lack the will for what's required."

"Perhaps the expectations do not suit you," Ruby guessed. "Perhaps they are not worthy of being met."

Lady Amelia sighed, gaze drifting to the shrubs nearby, though Ruby thought she didn't see the balls of snowy white flowers bobbing on the stems. "These particular expectations suit me not at all. But I have tried all my life to be a dutiful daughter. I cannot be that person if I refuse my parents' wishes for me."

"Funny thing about parents," Ruby said, brushing her hands against her skirts. "In my experience, they get the oddest notions on what will make us happy. A shame they can't trust us to see to our own happiness."

Lady Amelia nodded. "That's it exactly, Miss Hollingsford. Left to my own devices, I would marry…" She blushed and ducked her head.

Ruby moved closer and nudged her with her elbow. "Go on. Who would you marry?"

Lady Amelia glanced up at her as if she were about to say something quite daring. "Someone I loved."

Ruby smiled, stepping back. "Nothing wrong with that."

"Tell that to my father," Lady Amelia said with another sigh.

"Happily," Ruby agreed. "Simply give me his direction."

Lady Amelia laughed, a soft, musical sound. "Then we'd both be in trouble." She sobered as she turned from the shrubs to face Ruby fully. "How I envy you, Miss Hollingsford. You seem so free—to speak your mind, to choose your husband."

Ruby had never considered the matter from that point of view. Oh, she knew monarchs had arranged marriages, for the good of the nation. But all those girls she'd gone to school with, the ones from titled families who snubbed her on her first Season, were they also locked into their lives, marrying to please their families? Did they labor under a weight of expectations? She still could not condone their behavior, but perhaps there had been a reason for their dislike of her. Perhaps they envied her her freedom.

Surely at least some of the men of the *ton* felt the weight of those expectations, too. Perhaps that was why Phillip had refused to marry her, the scoundrel. She'd thought he could not appreciate her for herself, but perhaps it had been the need to meet these dratted expectations that drove him. It did not excuse the insult of his offer to become his mistress, but it did explain why he'd felt he could never consider her as his wife.

And what of Whit? Didn't he have to meet expectations, as well? How could he possibly marry someone like her?

"Choosing who to marry is a serious decision," Ruby said, fully realizing the truth of the statement for the first time. "For anyone. But as for love, I think it a highly necessary factor in the decision. I know others will disagree, but there you are."

Lady Amelia gave her a tight smile. "I cannot argue with you, Miss Hollingsford."

"Then don't," Ruby said with a grin. "Save your arguments for your parents."

Lady Amelia nodded. "You're right." She straightened her spine, bonnet brushing the top of the overhanging shrubs and causing a flurry of petals to fall like snow. "Yes, quite right. If I hold love to be sacred, I must stand my ground. Thank you, Miss Hollingsford."

"Happy to help," Ruby assured her. She looked so determined—head high, gaze clear—that Ruby couldn't help asking her her plans. "So will you pursue Lord Danning?"

Lady Amelia smiled. "No. I somehow think his heart is already engaged in any event. I wish you the best of luck."

Ruby felt herself coloring, unsure for once how to answer. Then, close to hand, came a large bark of a noise. Doves leaped from the trees.

Lady Amelia pressed her fingers to her chest, glancing about. "What was that?"

"A shot!" Ruby cried, heart pounding in her ears. "I'm sure of it! Come on!"

Chapter Fifteen

Whit pulled in his rod and shook his head at the shattered piece. Snapped! What rotten luck!

Trusting Ruby to settle Lady Amelia, he'd taken her advice and waded into the stream. But he'd only managed a few casts before the rod had broken. Now he took the remains and waded back to shore to pull in the line by hand.

"Whit!"

He turned to see Ruby and Lady Amelia rushing down the rise. The look on Ruby's face—eyes wide and color high—spurred him to meet her, dragging the rod and line with him.

"What's happened?" he demanded. "Are you hurt?"

"No, but I feared for you." Her green eyes searched his face. "Did you hear that shot?"

A shot? He found it hard to believe a noise would frighten his Ruby, but the concern on her face was matched by the look on Lady Amelia's. He put on a smile.

"In truth, I didn't hear anything until you called out my name. When I fish I often lose track of all else. But very likely you only heard Charles firing. He was going shooting this morning."

Lady Amelia relaxed with a sigh of acceptance. Ruby, however, frowned.

"Shooting so close to the house?" she asked, setting her hands on the hips of her gray grown. "Surely that isn't wise with so many people likely to be about."

He doubted Charles was that close to the house. Sound carried in the hills.

"Charles will be careful," he assured her. "He knows the dangers of ill-using a firearm."

"I'm sure he does," Ruby muttered darkly.

Before he could ask her what she meant, Lady Amelia spoke up. "Thank you for putting our minds at ease, Lord Danning." She offered him a pretty smile. "We're sorry to have disturbed your fishing."

Ruby's frown only grew, but Whit turned to Lady Amelia. "I wasn't doing a great deal of fishing. I seem to have snapped my rod." He held up the raw end as evidence.

Ruby leaned forward to eye the broken piece, but Lady Amelia's eyes widened. "That must have been a tremendous fish!"

Whit knew plenty of anglers who liked to embellish the tales of their exploits. He'd never been one. Of course, he seldom had to make up a story—he generally caught the fish!

"Sad to say, I didn't even have a fish on the line," he confessed, lowering the rod. "It's a jointed rod. They snap fairly frequently, I fear."

"Let me see it," Ruby ordered.

Surprised, Whit handed her the rod. She aimed her frown at the breakage, turned the rod in all directions.

"I didn't realize you were an expert on the construction of fly fishing rods, my dear," he teased.

Ruby scowled as she handed it back. "I'm not an expert on anything to do with fishing. But I do know a thing or two about guns."

Now it was Whit's turn to frown.

"I don't understand, Miss Hollingsford," Lady Amelia put in. "What does the break in Lord Danning's rod have to do with firearms?"

Ruby focused on Lady Amelia as if suddenly remembering her presence, then put on an overly bright smile. "Lady Amelia, might I enlist your assistance?"

Lady Amelia blinked as if surprised by the change in her, as well. "Certainly, Miss Hollingsford. What do you need?"

"I left my reticule upstairs on the table by my bed. Be a dear and fetch it for me, would you?"

Lady Amelia frowned. Very likely she'd never been sent on an errand in all her privileged life.

"What about you?" she asked Ruby. "What will you be doing?"

Ruby smiled sweetly, fooling no one, Whit was sure. "I'd like a word with Lord Danning. Never fear for my reputation. After all, Mr. Calder is nearby, and I'm certain you'll return shortly."

Lady Amelia eyed her a moment more as if trying to determine Ruby's game, then she straightened. "Very well." With a nod to Whit, she lifted her skirts and climbed the bank.

As soon as she was out of hearing, Ruby rounded on Whit.

"Your rod didn't break. It was shot."

Whit shook his head with a chuckle, then bent to

rinse his hands in the cool water. "Ruby, you get the oddest notions."

She took a step closer, raising her voice as if to make sure he heard her clearly over the rushing of the river. "It isn't a notion. Look at your rod. If it had snapped, the break would be clean. This one looks as if it had been made with force."

Whit straightened and glanced at the broken end of the rod more closely. The wood *was* splintered. Still, a lead ball?

"It can't be," Whit said, lowering the rod again. "Hitting something so narrow as a fishing rod, particularly when it was in motion, is impossible."

Ruby shook her head. "Difficult, but not impossible. And I don't think the shooter was aiming for your rod, Whit. I think he was trying to hit you."

Whit's hand tightened on the rod. "Nonsense."

Ruby gazed at him. Her catlike green eyes were narrowed, her mouth set firmly. "You have to admit there have been a lot of 'accidents' recently—the incident with the horse at Lord Hascot's, for one."

Whit chuckled. "As my valet pointed out, I should know better than to stand behind a strange horse."

"And what of the landslide?" Ruby countered, face paling as if she disliked remembering. "Someone hereabouts must have known the slope was dangerous. Why were you never informed?"

Whit bent closer and tweaked a curl inside her bonnet. "I rather think the rain had more to do with the landslide than anyone wishing me ill."

"And the fall in the Blue John cave?" she pressed, catching his hand as he withdrew and giving it a squeeze. "You very nearly lost your life."

"Because I had the misfortune to step where I

shouldn't," Whit replied, cradling her hand in his. "I appreciate your zeal for my safety, Ruby, but it is misplaced."

She looked ready to protest, rosy lips compressed and eyes snapping fire, but a movement on the bank caught his attention. As he raised his head, she pulled away from him to whirl in that direction as if expecting trouble.

Lady Amelia was picking her way down the slope, Ruby's reticule clutched in one hand. Ruby hurried to meet her and took the bag from her. "Thank you so much. Now, would you return to the house and determine the safety of all Lord Danning's other guests? I wouldn't want them to be concerned after hearing that shot."

Whit doubted any of them had even noticed. Lady Amelia must have wondered as well, for she stopped with another frown. "Is something wrong, Miss Hollingsford? You seem to wish me out of your way."

The girl was more clever than he'd thought. She would not be sent away with an easy excuse again. Ruby evidently gave up the attempt, for she motioned Lady Amelia to follow her down to Whit's side by the water, then turned to face her.

"I must swear you to silence on this matter," she said. "You can reveal none of what I'm about to relate, not even to your mother."

What now? Whit thought.

Lady Amelia's blue eyes widened, and she nodded solemnly. "I would never betray the confidence of a friend."

Ruby's mouth quirked, as if she couldn't believe Lady Amelia would count her as a friend, but she nodded, as well. "Good enough. I believe someone is trying to kill Lord Danning."

Whit groaned as Lady Amelia pressed a hand to her bosom. "Oh, my word!"

"It's nonsense," Whit assured her. "Ruby, I must ask you not to persist in this. I'm fine."

In answer, she reached in her reticule and pulled out a pistol.

Lady Amelia fell back against Whit with a gasp.

Ruby rolled her eyes. "I'm not going to use it on either of you," she said, bending quickly to check the powder and cocking the gun carefully.

"You carry a pistol even here?" Whit demanded, highly tempted to remove it from her grasp before she shot herself, or him.

"In London I carry it everywhere." She glanced around, then pointed the pistol at a branch hanging over the stream on the opposite side. "What say you, Lord Danning? If I can hit that branch, will you believe me that your rod was shot in two?"

Whit puffed out a sigh. Part of him just wanted her to cease her wild speculations, but another part was curious. Could she really hit so small an object?

"I shouldn't encourage you," he started.

"And I should encourage you," she argued, "to pay more attention to those around you." She spread her feet, raised one arm, elbow bent, and balanced the pistol over it. Then she squeezed the trigger.

Lady Amelia cried out as the pistol roared, then buried her head in Whit's chest. He was more interested in the branch. As the powder drifted downstream with the breeze, he saw that the limb was pointing straight down at the river. She'd done it!

Pride surged up inside him, only to be followed by dismay. Was it possible? Could she be right?

Ruby relaxed her arms and turned to eye Whit. "You see? If I can do it, surely anyone with some knowledge of a gun could do the same. And that person, may I remind you, was likely aiming for a much bigger target."

Whit felt cold, but he knew it wasn't because Lady Amelia had pushed away from him with a shudder.

"It is monstrous," she told Ruby. "What should we do? Is there a constable in the village? A magistrate nearby?"

"With no villain in hand? I doubt either would listen." Ruby tucked her spent pistol back into her reticule.

This had gone far enough. Just because such a shot was possible did not mean he believed any guest at the Lodge had done so.

Whit stepped between them. "Ruby, Lady Amelia, there's no need to call in a constable. Surely none of my other guests could make a shot like that." Trying to ease the moment, he smiled at Ruby. "I doubt many marksmen could do it. Where did you learn to shoot?"

"I asked my father to hire an instructor," Ruby said, raising her head as her reticule hung down beside her. "After someone tried to kidnap me."

Anger raced through him. She'd been forced to learn the skill to protect herself. What was the world coming to that a woman was placed in such a position?

"How horrible!" Lady Amelia cried. "And how brave of you to take such measures." She shuddered again. "I don't think I could bear to so much as lift a piece."

"Which is one of the reasons you are not a suspect," Ruby assured her, then she narrowed her eyes at Whit. "But I reserve the right to consider everyone else."

"You need not go to such trouble," Whit said. "I can look out for myself."

Still she regarded him, her skepticism clear. She had agreed to his courtship, so she must have some feelings for him. Perhaps the thought of him in danger concerned her as much as the thought of her in danger concerned him.

He met her gaze. "If I promise you I'll investigate the matter, will you trust me to see things right?"

Her gaze darkened, held. "Very well, my lord. It is your life, after all." She turned to smile at Lady Amelia. "Shall we rejoin the group, dear? I'm sure we can find other ways to amuse ourselves."

That was exactly what Whit feared.

Ruby was more than a little put out with Whit for refusing to acknowledge the danger he was in. Had he no concept of the perfidy of his own class—their devious natures, their manipulative ways?

It was patently obvious to her that someone wished Whit dead, and she was fairly certain Charles Calder was the villain. Look at the way he had hesitated to save Whit in the Blue John cave. And hadn't he been near the horse when it had kicked? He coveted the title, most likely, and knew it would never be his if Whit followed through on his plans to marry.

She accompanied Lady Amelia back to the house, Whit walking just behind them with the fishing gear. Ruby made sure to stay close and talk loudly so his dastardly cousin would know he had a witness to any more cowardly deeds, but her mind kept humming.

Whit was terribly close to his cousin. And from what she'd seen, the affection between them was mutual.

Perhaps he was right, and Charles was innocent. She supposed it was possible one of the others had motive.

Lady Wesworth might feel slighted Whit hadn't appreciated her daughter. While Ruby couldn't see her pulling the trigger, the marchioness could certainly have asked her coachman or groom to lie in wait. Mr. and Mrs. Stokely-Trent could have similar motive and ability to send out servants. Why, even Ruby's father could have engineered the deeds, intending to injure rather than kill Whit to encourage Ruby's protective nature!

Her thoughts must have been written on her face, for Whit stopped her at the door from his fishing closet to the corridor, allowing Lady Amelia to hurry into the house.

"It's still bothering you," he murmured, hand on her elbow.

"Of course it's still bothering me," Ruby declared, glaring at him. "You could have been injured, killed. If you will not take things seriously, then I must."

"Ruby."

The tender tone in his voice held her captive. He reached up, touched her cheek, look softening.

"While I appreciate your zeal on my behalf," he murmured, "I would not see you harmed. If there is danger, you must let me handle it."

She opened her mouth to protest, and he pressed a finger to her lips, the touch warm, intimate. "Trust me," he said.

He was telling her, politely of course, to mind her own affairs. Normally, she would have agreed. He was clever and strong enough to catch the villain if needed. But if he refused to believe in the possibility of danger, how could he protect himself?

She stepped back, away from his distracting touch,

and dipped a curtsey. "Of course you are capable, my lord. Forgive me if I seemed to imply otherwise. Now, pray excuse me while I go put away my pistol."

He inclined his head, and she managed to quit the room. She should let the matter be, reload her pistol and find another way to spend the rest of the day without worrying about Whit. She trudged up the stairs, steps as heavy as the reticule swinging beside her. Inaction was so very dissatisfying. However did women like Lady Amelia abide it? Was this what Whit would expect of her as a wife, to sit idly by while he solved the world's problems? She'd go mad.

"Something wrong, Miss Hollingsford?"

Ruby paused at the top of the stairs. Mr. Quimby had just exited Whit's chamber, soiled coat draped over one arm. Very likely he was heading for the kitchen to clean it, but Ruby narrowed her eyes.

"And where were you this morning?" she demanded.

He raised his brows. "I had an argument with a recalcitrant cravat, and then I attempted to beat Lord Danning's black boots into submission. Is there an article of clothing you desire pummeled, Miss Hollingsworth? I must say I'm in the mood for it."

He did not look the least bit militant, smiling at her, his eyes crinkled at the corners. She could not find it in herself to suspect him.

"No clothing, alas," she replied. "But I wonder whether some person hereabouts requires pummeling. Do you know anyone who might wish his lordship ill?"

She thought he would protest as Whit had, assure her she was mistaken. Instead, Mr. Quimby moved to her side, put a hand on her elbow and lowered his voice.

"What have you seen?" he asked, gaze searching hers. "Who do you suspect?"

Ruby's voice came out quietly, as well. "Then you think something's wrong, too?"

He nodded. "I have only one bit of proof to offer and a great deal of conjecture. Tell me, have you ever heard of the Danning diamonds?"

The way he watched her said he expected that she had. Ruby nodded her head.

He released her. "Have you seen the stickpin his lordship favors? It's part of a set—a necklace, tiara, earbobs, stickpin and bracelet. They're worth a small fortune."

Ruby shook her head again. "I don't understand. What has this to do with an attempt on Lord Danning's life?"

Quimby paled. "Someone tried to kill him? When? How?"

"This morning." Ruby explained about the shot at the river. When she finished, his jaw was tight and his gaze had lost its usual twinkle.

"And he wouldn't listen, would he? I feared as much. That's one of the reasons I included you and your father in this house party. You see, I suspect the diamonds have been exchanged for paste."

Ruby clutched the newel post with both hands, her reticule banging against the wood. "You included me so I or my father might attest to the value of the Danning diamonds?"

Quimby made a face. "Not entirely. I did see you at your father's shop when I took him the stickpin to verify its makeup, and I thought you would be good for Lord Danning. But I wanted your help in this matter. I observed Mr. Calder taking the diamonds from the safe where they are normally stored and later replacing them—with paste copies, I feared. Lord Danning would never accept my word over his cousin's. I could only hope you or your father might be willing to speak up."

Once before she'd been invited to an event for the sole purpose of valuing jewelry. Then she'd felt humiliated, betrayed. Now all she could think of was how the truth would affect Whit.

Mr. Quimby could not know it, but he'd piled another weight on the scales against Charles Calder. If Charles had indeed stolen one of his cousin's most precious possessions, he might well wish to keep Whit from discovering his crime.

The valet clearly thought Ruby could convince Whit of the truth. But would Whit listen to her, especially when she'd promised to trust him and leave the matter in his hands?

Chapter Sixteen

Whit put away his fishing gear, pausing as he came to the broken rod. Jointed rods had a lamentable habit of breaking, even with the brass screws that were sometimes used to keep the sections together. Surely Ruby must be wrong to see a more violent reason for the break.

Given her treatment by her peers, he thought he understood why she'd rush to judgment. But to see a murderer in the quiet of Dovecote Dale? Unthinkable. He could remember no reason for anyone to wish him ill.

Still, the need to reassure her was strong, so when he finished, he went in search of her. Unfortunately, he ran across Lady Wesworth, chest at full sail, in the corridor as he passed the withdrawing room.

"My lord," she said, face set and gaze challenging, "something must be done about Miss Hollingsford."

He quite agreed, but he could only wonder what had set off the marchioness this time. "I'm sure there must be some misunderstanding."

"Oh, undoubtedly." She nodded, setting her silvery curls to trembling. "Entirely on her part. Do you know she ordered my Amelia about as if she were a servant?"

Her chest was puffed so high Whit was surprised she didn't bark her chin when she spoke.

"If you are referring to Ruby's request at the river," he said, trying for a congenial tone, "I was there when she spoke to your daughter. She requested Lady Amelia's assistance, which your daughter granted with her usual grace and kindness."

She seemed to settle below him, and he wondered whether she had been standing on her toes, as well. "Amelia is ever kind. Perhaps too kind. She does not always notice when others are taking advantage of her." She narrowed her eyes at him as if she suspected he was among the number seeking to impose upon her daughter. "That lot falls to me, as her mother, and I assure you I know a conniving creature when I see one."

Whit was highly tempted to ask if that was because she saw one so often in her mirror, but he refrained. He knew the pressures of the Jacoby family—their many estates, their various financial interests, their influence in Parliament, and all with no son to inherit. In her mother's eyes, the entire future must rest on Lady Amelia.

"And I assure you that Ruby is no conniving creature," he said instead.

Lady Wesworth fisted her hands alongside her muslin gown. "She has pulled the wool over your eyes! Why, she dissuaded Amelia from accepting your suit, encouraged that Stokely-Trent girl to look at your cousin. And now, based on what little I could understand from my distraught daughter, Miss Hollingsford seems to be implying that something dastardly is afoot."

That was how rumors spread. He had to put a stop to it. "As I said," Whit replied determinedly, "all a misunderstanding."

She refused to believe him. "I misunderstand nothing, my lord. This tale of danger is merely a pretense to end this house party early and prevent you from fixing your interests elsewhere. Why can't you see that?"

"Because it is a fiction." When she raised her brows at his pronouncement, Whit took her hand in his own. "Miss Hollingsford is mistaken about the danger, but that does not change the fact that she is concerned for my well-being. Indeed, of all my guests, she has distinguished herself by attempting to make things easier for me. Why, madam, can you not see *that?*"

"Well, I never!" She yanked back her hand and raised herself up again. "I trust when you have had the opportunity to reflect, you will beg my pardon, sirrah." She turned and swept back down the corridor.

"When pigs fly," Whit muttered. The impertinent phrase reminded him of Ruby, and he couldn't help grinning as he started up the stairs.

His grin vanished when he saw her waiting outside the open door of his bedchamber.

Her face was pinched, and one arm was wrapped about her middle. The way the reticule hung heavily against her skirts told him she had yet to divest herself of her pistol. Before he could ask what was wrong, she raised her free hand and thrust his stickpin at him.

"Paste," she declared.

Whit accepted it with a frown. "I don't understand."

"It's paste. Fakery. False. Just, I fear, like your cousin's loyalty." She trembled as if she could not abide her own accusation.

Neither could he. "What's this all about?"

Quimby appeared in the doorway, clearing his throat. "Allow me to explain, my lord. I had a particular purpose in inviting Miss Hollingsford to this house party."

"Because you thought I would like her," Whit remembered. "And you were quite right."

If anything, his statement seemed to distress Ruby further. She clutched the cords of her bag so tightly he thought they might snap like his rod.

"Oh, Whit," she said, voice tight. "You like everyone."

She made it sound like some sort of failing. Whit spread his hands. "I thought it a virtue to live at peace with others, so far as that is possible."

Her face scrunched further. "And could you perhaps have taken that to extremes?" She waved at Quimby. "Your valet set up this house party to force you to choose a bride. Such an infraction would seem to require drastic action."

Even Quimby raised his brows at the idea.

"What did you have in mind?" Whit said, still trying for a lighter tone. "The stocks? Perhaps a flogging?"

Quimby cocked his head as if he'd like to see Whit try, but at least the jest brought some color to Ruby's cheeks. "I cannot help but wonder why you didn't consider sacking him."

Whit shot Quimby a grin. "Oh, I considered it. But Mr. Quimby and I go back many years. I would miss his otherwise sound council."

"Not to mention my ability to tie a cravat," his valet said with a critical eye to Whit's throat.

"See how well he knows me?" Whit returned his gaze to Ruby. "Which is why he understood exactly what sort of woman I need in a wife."

She steadfastly refused to take his bait, raising her chin with a touch of defiance. "But that trust you have in him—and in all your other acquaintances—is why he knew you wouldn't believe him if he brought you a concern, particularly about your cousin Charles."

Whit felt his smile fading and glanced at his valet again. Quimby shifted on his feet as if uncomfortable, fingers brushing at the coat that draped his arm.

"Do you have something you wish to say to me, Quimby?" Whit asked.

"Only what Miss Hollingsford has already related, my lord," he replied, avoiding Whit's gaze. "The diamond in your stickpin is paste."

"Of course it is," Whit replied and had the satisfaction of seeing them both blink owlishly at him. "Do you think I'd be so foolish as to bring a diamond fishing with me? I had a paste copy made some time ago. The real diamond pin is in the safe in Suffolk."

"But, my lord…" Quimby started.

Ruby interrupted him. "Why bring a paste copy with you? Who did you think to impress, the trout?"

Whit chuckled. "There's a thought. Perhaps I should consider trying it for bait. That might encourage the King of Trout to take a bite."

When she merely frowned at him, clearly perplexed, he shrugged. "The Earl of Danning has worn the diamond stickpin for five generations, Ruby. It is part of my heritage."

"You mean wearing it is expected," she said, arm stealing about her waist again. "I have recently become aware of how many expectations are put upon you, my lord. It seems your life is laid out from the moment you are born—how you will act, what you will wear, even the woman you will marry."

Was that her fear? That she somehow didn't conform to the expectations he had for a bride?

She didn't. She shattered them.

Understanding came in an instant. All this time, he'd been waiting for the right woman to stir his senses, warm his heart. He had assumed his love would blossom in an instant, the moment he saw the woman who was right for him. Instead, the feelings had crept up on him, building from admiration, shared trials. This tenderness, this concern, this was what his father missed when his wife had been taken from him. Surely this was the beginnings of love.

"Perhaps I am a creature of habit," he admitted, moving closer to Ruby. "But I have only ever had one expectation for my bride, Ruby, and that is that we can truly say we love each other. You asked me about my feelings the other day, and I regret that I responded with a quip. The truth is that I am falling in love with you, Ruby Hollingsworth."

She gazed at him, mouth pursed in an *O* of wonder. It was the most natural thing in the world to give action to his feelings. He took her in his arms, angled his head and kissed her.

All the fire that was Ruby kissed him back. This was what he'd yearned for; this was what he'd dreamed might exist. This closeness, this hope for the future. *Thank You, Lord!*

From some distant place, he heard a cough. Quimby. Whit raised his head, but he refused to let Ruby out of the circle of his arms. She stood there, smiling at him as if he'd given her the sun and the moon, and he wished he knew a way to do just that. Anything she wanted, so long as she stayed with him, forever.

His valet coughed again.

"What is it, Quimby?" Whit forced himself to say, gaze on Ruby's.

"I regret to interrupt such a momentous moment,"

his valet said. "But you see, there is still the matter of your cousin."

Whit sighed, even as Ruby sobered and nodded.

"Charles is no threat to me," Whit told them both. "You must take my word for it."

"Happily, my lord," Quimby said, "if you can assure me that you also had paste copies made of the rest of the Danning diamonds, and recently."

"Yes, Whit," Ruby added, peering at him from his embrace as if to judge how he might take the news. "Mr. Quimby and I would be greatly relieved to see your cousin in the clear."

At least she was willing to give his cousin the benefit of the doubt. Whit glanced between them. "There was no need to create copies of the other pieces." He grinned at Ruby. "I can hardly wear the tiara fishing."

She did not laugh at his joke. "Then you authorized him to remove them from safekeeping for another reason."

"No," Whit admitted. "Nor do I know that he has done so."

"He has," Quimby said, and the depth in his tone told Whit how little he liked reporting the fact. "I saw him. He later replaced them."

Whit nodded, smiling down at Ruby and not bothering to hide his relief. "There you have it. Very likely he was developing a description of them to send to his sister. She wishes to wear them soon." Doubt pricked at him, and he looked to his valet. "Or was that request also a ruse, Quimby?"

"No indeed," Quimby promised him. "Miss Calder would very much like to appear in the diamonds. And as she talks about them each time she visits, I doubt she needed further description. She made her request in innocence, I am convinced. She would have no way of knowing her brother had already stolen them."

"Enough," Whit snapped. "Charles has been as close to me as a brother. Why would he steal the diamonds?"

"Money?" Ruby suggested quietly, as if hoping to soften the blow.

Stokely-Trent's tale of gambling debts came to mind, but surely that was untrue. While his cousin would play whist at the drop of a hat, Whit had never known him to wager against the results.

"If he needs money," Whit insisted, "he knows he can apply to me."

"Perhaps pride prevented it," Quimby hazarded.

"Perhaps he wanted more than you could give," Ruby added, green gaze probing his. "Perhaps he wanted it all."

Whit shook his head. "Why must you see the darkness in every deed?"

She stiffened. "Why do you see only light?"

He had to make her understand. "Because I know Charles is a gentleman. He would never forsake his honor to steal from me, to shoot at me. You talked of expectations? Every gentleman knows that honor and duty are expected of him."

"Honor?" Ruby pushed away from him, eyes blazing. "You trust your life to a gentleman's honor? Let me tell you about the honor of gentlemen, my lord. You know those stones Lady Wesworth wore the first night? Paste. It seems her husband coveted a new hunter, and he didn't have another way to lay his hands on the finances except to pawn his wife's diamonds."

The bitterness on her face cut into him. Whit reached for her, and she stepped back.

"Then there's Lord Pellford, fine upstanding fellow.

Supported the repudiation of the slave trade, I read in *The Times.* That's because he'd already sold all the gems he beat the natives into mining to a less scrupulous jeweler than my father."

Her pain was his. "Ruby, those are isolated instances. I assure you, not every gentleman distains his honor."

"No?" Tears were falling now, trickling down her pale cheeks like rain on a carriage window. "I'll give you one more example. Phillip, Lord Milton, quite dashing, with aspirations of a Cabinet post. Perhaps you've heard of him?"

Whit nodded, remembering the man from Parliament. Milton took the wind like a navigator on the sea, then always voted for the winning side.

"He courted me." There was no pride in the words. "Such a charming gentleman, such a catch! But he didn't want my heart." She thumped her chest, her reticule bumping against her. "He just wanted a mistress. Couldn't sully his bloodline with marriage to the daughter of a shopkeeper."

Whit wanted to rip out the fellow's heart and throw it at Ruby's feet. "He's a fool."

She raised her chin, tears dripping off it. "Yes, he is. But so, I've come to learn, are most of the aristocracy. I know you want to champion your cousin, Whit. You can't believe he'd be so dastardly. I can. I've seen it. In fact, I am hard-pressed to offer you a good example of an aristocrat who lives with the honor you ascribe."

"I see." Anger and dread poured over him like water from the cascade, leaving him nearly as cold. He'd been wrong. It wasn't concern about expectations that had kept Ruby from giving him her heart. She thought all aristocrats were craven, dishonored.

Even him, it seemed.

* * *

Ruby felt as if every part of her body stung. There—she'd told him all. Surely now he'd take steps to protect himself. She couldn't bear the thought that something might hurt him. Sacrificing her dignity would be worth it to save him from pain.

But she saw pain now in the tightening of his skin across his nose, the way his chin rose as if to deflect a blow.

"I see," he repeated. "I suppose I should be glad we had this conversation."

Ruby nodded, relaxing. At last she'd gotten through to him. He set such high standards for himself he thought others could actually meet them. Now he'd realize how few did.

"I can understand why you refused my proposal the first time," he continued, standing so tall and proud she felt the first blush of misgiving. "How could you possibly want to marry a scheming, wastrel aristocrat like me?"

Ruby felt as if she'd been slapped. "No, Whit! I didn't mean…"

He shook his head once, hard. "But you did. All these events, these horrid things that you've witnessed and that have happened to you, have convinced you to trust no one, especially not an aristocrat. You're angry they couldn't be honest, that they couldn't value you for the fine woman you've become."

Her tears continued to run; she dashed them away with the back of her hand. "That's not important right now. What is important is that you have a care for your life!"

"What is important," he said, "is that I live by my principles. Do not ask me to doubt my cousin, someone who has stood by me my entire life, because you cannot trust. *I* trust him. That should be enough for you."

Perhaps it should. But what if he was wrong? Oh, what if he was wrong?

"Whit, please," she tried again, but he held up his hand.

"No, Ruby. If you care for me, if you want a future together, then I ask you to live by your principles, as well."

Ruby threw up her hands, her reticule swinging. "I am! They dictate that I try to help those I love. Don't ask me to stand by and watch you be hurt."

"I know you care," he said, and she thought he was trying to gentle his tone. "You have been my best advocate, from the day we met. But you ask, no you demand, that others accept you for yourself. Can you not offer me the same courtesy?"

Every part of her trembled. "I accept you."

"Do you? Can you accept that I am an honorable aristocrat?"

She nodded. "Yes! I've seen how you treat others, your kindness. You saved my life when it would have been far easier simply to save your own."

He was watching her. "And can you accept that I know my own cousin?"

That was harder. She could feel the struggle inside her. As if he saw it on her face as well, he sighed and stepped back.

"Think on what I said," he told her. "For now, I should check on my other guests." He inclined his head, then turned to clamber down the stairs.

"Oh!" She stomped her foot. "Of all the prideful, stubborn…"

"Overly optimistic, honorable fellows," Quimby

added, reminding her that he had just witnessed her worst moment.

Her face heated, and she could not look at the valet.

"I didn't mean to imply he had no honor, Mr. Quimby," she said. "He is easily the most honorable man I've ever met. But being so honorable, so bound by duty, he doesn't seem to realize that all men are not cut from the same cloth."

"And you, I think," the valet murmured, "cannot see that many truly are. Forgive me, Miss Hollingsford, for contributing to your conclusions."

Ruby wrapped an arm about her waist, but the motion brought no comfort this time. "I still think Mr. Calder is up to no good. We have to find a way to protect Whit."

She looked at the valet at last, challenging him to disagree with her, too. He inclined his head. "I will not allow Lord Danning to be lax, I promise. I fear there is nothing further we can do."

Ruby nodded, then murmured her excuses and turned for her room.

Her maid must have been downstairs on some errand, for the space stood empty. Ruby shut the door behind her and threw her reticule on the bed. Was she so very wrong to want to protect Whit? She'd never felt this way about any other man. Even her infatuation with Phillip seemed pale, distant, compared to her feelings for Whit. The very thought of something happening to him sent her into panic, made it hard to breathe, to think. Was this love?

When Whit had taken her in his arms and kissed her, she'd thought her heart would burst with joy. At that moment, she was certain she'd found her place at last—at his side, helpmate, wife, beloved. Now she couldn't avoid feeling that she'd disappointed him, and all because she couldn't trust a scoundrel!

She went to the bed, yanked open her reticule and pulled out the pistol. With her hands still shaking, now was no time to be working with lead balls and powder. It reminded her of the way she'd trembled the day a man in a dark cloak had grabbed her outside her father's shop, held a knife to her throat while her father pleaded for her life.

You can have her back, the kidnapper had promised in a gravelly voice, *for a thousand pounds sterling.*

He'd started to drag her away, when a shot had rung out, and she'd found herself free. Davis, her father's coachman, had used the rifle he kept on the box. The would-be kidnapper had been uninjured, but he had fled all the same, never to darken their door again, frightened of the power of the gun. After she'd stopped shaking, she'd told her father she wouldn't rest until she could fire one, as well.

And what good had it done? She set the pistol on the table by the bed. She hadn't had it with her when someone had fired on Whit, couldn't have shot back even if she'd had it without knowing the villain's location. All she could do was take Whit at his word and trust him to protect himself.

Trust.

The word made her shudder, and she gasped, stiffening. She could trust. Surely she could trust. She trusted her father...well, until he'd lied to her about coming to Derbyshire. She'd have to keep a closer eye on him if she and Whit could not find a way back to each other. Who knew what he'd try next in his plans to marry her off!

She shook herself. She could trust. She trusted herself. She'd never let herself down. Except just now, when she'd hurt Whit so badly. She'd talked too soon, moved too quickly. She should learn to stop and think.

Was he right? Had she lost the ability to trust?

Sorrow swept over her, pushed her down upon the bed. *Oh, Lord, what have I become? I thought I was just taking care of myself, protecting myself. You know I had cause. If people who said they cared about me— the girls from school, Phillip—could not be bothered to take care of me, if You could not be bothered with Ruby Hollingsford, why shouldn't I take over the job?*

From somewhere, a verse echoed in her mind:

The rock of my strength, and my refuge, is in God. Trust in Him at all times; ye people, pour out your heart before Him: God is a refuge for us.

Ruby raised her head, sniffing back a sob. What a thought. Even God, it seemed, expected her to trust.

And that was the hardest thing for her to do. People let her down, failed to keep their promises of friendship, of love. Trusting meant opening herself to fresh pain, more disappointment.

Yet, she knew, if she wanted to have any hope of marrying Whit, of finding peace within herself, of making peace with God, she had to find the strength to trust.

But, oh, how much easier hoped than done!

Chapter Seventeen

Whit found himself standing by the stream. He wasn't surprised. Something about the water, whether the flash of silver or the cheerful chatter, had ever calmed his spirits. But this time, even bathing in the chill waters would not erase the past few moments.

She thought him a monster.

Given the stories she'd shared, he could understand why she so distrusted the aristocracy in general. He'd simply never thought she saw him in the same light. That Milton had been so cruel to her made his hands fist. But that she thought him capable of the same cruelty cut deeper.

How could he offer for her, how could they make a marriage, if she could not trust? What a wretched life that would be for her, feeling as if she must watch him constantly, expecting perfidy. And what an equally wretched life for him, never knowing what might make her think he'd betrayed her, every least fault seen as a warning of worse to come.

He kept going over his actions from the day he'd met Ruby, wondering how else he might have proved to her that he was trustworthy. His father, his tutors and his

guardians had instilled in him the belief that a true gen-
tleman was known by his actions. He had never lied to
Ruby, never attempted to take advantage. Nor would he.
If she couldn't accept that now, what hope did he have?

And if she couldn't trust him, she'd never believe she
could trust Charles, no matter how many times Whit
promised he had no reason to believe his cousin was a
danger. If Charles had removed the Danning diamonds
from the safe, he must have had good reason. Whit
would ask him, but after this house party was over and
everyone was in a more congenial state of mind.

The King of Trout leaped from the stream, flicking
his tail as if to make sure Whit had seen him.

"Swim, my lad," Whit told him. "I've no heart to
chase you today."

Indeed, his heart had been captured by Ruby, and he
didn't know whether he'd ever get it back.

Inside the Lodge, Ruby hurried down the stairs. She
had to find Whit and apologize. If they never spoke another word beyond this, he deserved to know that she
held him in the highest esteem. She still feared what his
cousin might do, but she knew she had to trust Whit to
see to the matter. She owed him that at the very least.

She tried the library and narrowly avoided a conversation with Charles, who seemed to be hunched in one
of the armchairs. Ruby could only hope his morose look
came from an attack of conscience. One of the hardest things about the rest of this house party would be
to spend time around Charles and keep herself from
spitting in his eye or kicking him in the shins or any
number of other actions that flashed through her mind
when she thought about his evil intentions toward Whit.

She next tried the withdrawing room, but Whit was

not with his other guests. Henrietta and her parents were also missing. Ruby stepped back into the corridor and glanced up and down length. He couldn't have left! He was far too upright to desert his guests.

In desperation, she tried the door to his fishing closet. The rods and books of flies were all in their places, and Henrietta stood gazing at them.

"What are you doing here?" Ruby couldn't help asking.

The bluestocking rubbed a hand along the sleeve of her sprigged muslin gown. "In truth, I simply wanted a little privacy."

Ruby opened her mouth to apologize, then noticed the red rims on Henrietta's eyes, the puffiness on her soft cheeks. Ruby shut the door behind her and ventured closer. "What's happened?"

Henrietta swallowed before answering, as if trying to master her emotions. "My father refused Mr. Calder's suit because he thinks Charles isn't good enough for me."

"Oh, no!" Mixed with her sympathy for Henrietta's sadness was a bolt of fear at the thought of Charles's possible reaction. Faced with losing the woman he loved, would he become even more desperate to gain a title? She'd promised the Lord she would learn to trust, but surely Whit deserved to know. Yet, even if she told him, would he act on her concerns or wave her off once more? Or worse yet, see her actions as proof Ruby could never trust, even him?

Henrietta nodded, wiping away a tear with her fingers. "I don't have it in me to disobey my father, Ruby. I know he wants the best for me."

In other circumstances, Ruby would have argued. Now she had to admit to relief that Henrietta would not be marrying a man willing to attempt murder. Still the bluestocking could hardly know the fate she had avoided, and it was plain to see she was sincerely attached to the man.

"I'm very sorry," was all Ruby could think to say.

Henrietta sighed. "Unfortunately, I cannot see myself marrying Danning, meeting Charles at every family gathering, wondering what might have been. Nor would I torture Charles in that way."

"Then what will you do?" Ruby asked with a frown.

"I must think," Henrietta murmured, gaze returning to the fishing gear stacked neatly on the shelves, as if she wished her life was as easily arranged.

Ruby felt for her. She knew how it had hurt to lose Phillip, even after realizing he was a dastard. Henrietta didn't know that Charles was evil. His loss could only hurt deeper.

She was highly tempted to tell Henrietta her suspicions, if only to cushion the blow of loss. But she was determined to leave the matter to Whit. Wasn't that what trust meant?

She laid a hand on Henrietta's arm. "I will give you the privacy you crave, but know that I am happy to listen if you feel the need to share your thoughts."

Henrietta regarded her. "Thank you, Ruby. I believe company would be very welcome right now. Why don't we locate Lady Amelia and have a chat?"

Ruby wanted to demur. She yearned to find Whit. But she'd run out of places to look inside the house short of knocking on his bedchamber door, and it wasn't often a lady showed interest in her company.

She linked arms with Henrietta. "Lady Amelia was in the withdrawing room last time I saw her. I'm sure she'd welcome company, too."

The beauty was at the spinet, playing a mournful air. Ruby glanced about, but Whit still wasn't to be seen. She resigned herself to a ladylike discussion of the weather, the latest fashions and the usual impersonal topics the aristocracy seemed to enjoy sharing.

Henrietta, however, clearly had other ideas.

"It is evident to me, Lady Amelia," she said, casting a quick glance to where the two mothers were on the sofa discussing the management of servants, "that you are not enamored of Lord Danning."

Lady Amelia drew her fingers away from the keys and folded her hands in the lap of her muslin gown. Ruby was proud of her for not blushing. "That is quite true."

"Neither am I," Henrietta confided. "However, it is equally evident that Miss Hollingsford has caught his eye. I suggest we help that along."

Ruby blinked. "Oh, I say!"

Lady Amelia hopped to her feet, face brightening. "What a lovely idea! You may count on my support!"

"This isn't necessary," Ruby said, feeling a bubble of panic rising inside her at the thought of them actually helping her. "Lord Danning is quite capable of finding the proper bride without any assistance. Besides, I'm certain you'd both agree that he needs a wife who will do him credit in Society. You cannot believe I am that woman."

"In my experience," Henrietta said with arched brow, "the title countess in front of a name solves a host of problems."

Lady Amelia nodded. "There may be a few high sticklers, like my mother, who will never warm to you, but very likely you will be happier for not knowing them."

Ruby glanced between them. Henrietta Stokely-Trent was regarding her solemnly, and Lady Amelia now had her graceful hands clasped earnestly.

"I can't believe you," Ruby said. "You were both so determined to become his countess. Now you're willing to cede that place, to me of all people?"

Lady Amelia resorted to blushing again as she dropped her gaze. "I suppose we have both learned the meaning of love and are unwilling to settle for less. And we have you to thank for that, Miss Hollingsford."

Henrietta gave Ruby a tight-lipped smile. "Then we are agreed. Lady Amelia will keep Mr. Calder occupied, and I will chaperone Ruby and Danning when needed. That way, we all achieve our goals."

Lady Amelia looked up to frown at her. "But I thought you and Mr. Calder…"

Henrietta held up a hand. "My father will not settle for less than a title."

Her face fell. "Oh. Well, I'm very sorry."

"Nor more sorry than I am, I assure you." She turned to Ruby. "Now, let's just make sure one of us ends up a bride from all this."

Just like that, Ruby had allies. The change in their attitudes was as amazing as it was gratifying. Unfortunately, she wasn't so sure spending more time with Whit would make her a bride. He wanted a trusting wife, one who passively waited while he solved the problem. She still wasn't sure she could do that. But she knew she wouldn't be easy until she spoke with him and at least apologized for seeming to question his honor.

Her opportunity did not come until after dinner. Whit appeared in the doorway and looked ready to offer to escort in Lady Amelia, but the blonde deftly managed to avoid him. Ruby found herself walking beside

Whit, but with people right behind him she didn't dare begin her apology. His gaze, steadfastly forward, did not encourage her either.

Henrietta had apparently spoken to Mr. Hennessy about rearranging the seating, because when Ruby entered the dining room, she located her name at the seat to Whit's right, with Lady Amelia opposite her and Henrietta beside her. That Ruby had been given the place of honor was lost on no one, and both Lady Wesworth and the Stokely-Trents cast her dark looks as if they thought it her doing.

As if to forestall complaints, Henrietta monopolized the conversation, keeping everyone entertained with her interesting facts and observations. If Charles moped a bit through the meal, only Ruby and the bluestocking seemed to notice.

What Ruby noticed more was the change in Whit. He remained the charming host, helping Lady Amelia and Ruby to the quail in apricot sauce that had been served, adding to the conversation when expected. However, she seldom saw him smile, and he held himself still, poised. She wondered whether he feared any movement might betray his innermost thoughts. His gaze rarely collided with Ruby's, and when it did, she thought she saw something sad behind the purple-blue.

She'd hurt him. The very thought sent an ache through her. She wanted to make things right between them, but how could she be the woman he seemed to expect?

The other two women continued to put Henrietta's plan into effect after dinner. When the gentlemen came to join the ladies in the withdrawing room, Lady Amelia requested Charles's help in selecting music to play on the spinet, which earned her a scowl from her mother.

Henrietta engaged Whit in a game of chess, earning her a smile from hers. She kept looking up and nodding to Ruby, trying to encourage her closer. Perhaps she thought Ruby might play the next set.

Ruby felt as if her feet were once more dragging in the mud of the hills. She knew she must approach Whit, request a moment of his time and apologize for what he saw as her lack of faith in him, but she dreaded seeing more disappointment on his handsome face. Perhaps when he'd finished playing, she thought, wandering up to the two players. Very likely Henrietta would give him a good game.

A game that was remarkably short-lived.

"Checkmate," the bluestocking said after only a few moves.

Whit rose and offered her a bow. "Well played, my dear."

"I suspect," she replied, setting the pieces back in their starting places, "your mind is on other matters, my lord." She looked pointedly at Ruby, standing at her shoulder.

Ruby swallowed. Here was her chance. She should step forward, claim his arm for a promenade about the room, whisk him out the doors to the veranda. Yet her feet seemed planted on the soft brown of the carpet, and her tongue stuck to the roof of her mouth.

What's wrong with me, Lord? Have I finally become one of those wilting Society women? My teachers at the Barnsley School would be so proud. Yet how can I live this way? Is this what You want?

As if he sensed the struggle in her, Whit stepped closer and held out his arm. "Favor me with a promenade, Miss Hollingsford."

It was a command, not a request. Ruby raised her

brow, but put her hand on his arm nonetheless. Like his demeanor, it was stiff and formal.

He avoided the doors to the veranda on their left and began to walk with her about the little room, headed toward the card table where her father and Mr. Stokely-Trent were playing.

"I am a little surprised you haven't left for London," he murmured. Ruby's father raised one thumb in support as they passed. Ruby ignored him.

"I would never leave while you are in danger," she replied.

She could feel the sigh rippling through his body. "Can you not accept my word that Charles is harmless?"

The way his cousin was dutifully turning the pages for Lady Amelia made him appear so, but Ruby knew a fair facade could mask a dark heart.

"I regret that I cannot," she replied. "I also regret that the way I voiced my suspicions seemed to imply I included you in them. Please know that I hold you in the highest esteem, my lord. You have proved to me that some gentlemen are truly honorable."

His arm relaxed a little, and his smile to Ruby made her breath hitch and Lady Wesworth grimace as they passed. "Then you concede that it is possible to be both an aristocrat and honorable," he said.

Ruby felt a smile playing about her lips, as well. "I concede that you are the exception to the rule."

He chuckled. "I suppose that is a start. When we return to London, I'll have to introduce you to other honorable aristocrats. I'm sure I can find a few."

Her smile broadened. "Oh, I wouldn't make you work so hard."

"I assure you, it would be my pleasure."

Before he could say more, Henrietta moved to intercept them. Though Ruby knew the bluestocking's role was to play chaperone, she felt a distinct annoyance that she had to share Whit so soon.

"I have read," Henrietta said as they stopped beside her, "that sailors have a way of predicting the weather at sea. 'Red sky at night, sailor's delight.' There is a lovely sunset, my lord. I hope for good weather tomorrow."

It was but a few steps to the doors leading to the veranda to see. To the right, rosy light outlined the trees, setting the very air to glowing. Doves cooed from the river. A sigh escaped her, and Whit's arm stole about her waist. For a moment, she thought he meant to hold her close, and her heart started beating faster. She glanced over at him, caught the tender look in his eyes and sucked in a breath.

He still cared. He still cared!

As if she were oblivious to the emotions sizzling in the air, Henrietta continued talking from the other side of Whit.

"I never saw your cascade up close," she reminded him, gaze on the sunset. "Perhaps you and Miss Hollingsford would be so good as to show it to me tomorrow."

"Would you like that, Ruby?" Whit murmured.

Ruby nodded, unable to tear her gaze from his face. The soft light bathed every angle, his golden brows, his perfect nose, his firm lips. He smiled, so warmly, so sweetly, and she leaned closer, ready to press her lips to his despite her chaperone and the rest of his guests. But he turned to Henrietta.

"I'd be delighted," he assured the bluestocking. "I've been meaning to inspect the slide in any event. It is possible, however, that the path to the falls is still blocked."

Henrietta smiled around Whit to Ruby. "Oh, I'm certain we can find a way. Aren't you, Ruby?"

"Isn't she what?" Charles asked, joining them. "Charming? Beautiful? Witty?"

Lady Amelia came hurrying to his side. Her panicked look told Ruby she'd tried to dissuade him from joining them.

"You are too kind, Mr. Calder," Ruby said, knowing the reply was neither particularly charming nor witty.

"Henrietta wishes to see the cascade," Whit informed his cousin. "Care to join us, Charles?"

Oh no! This trip could be the perfect opportunity for Whit's cousin to get him away from the others and do him harm!

Lady Amelia was obviously more concerned about protecting Ruby's time with Whit, for she met Ruby's gaze, then raised her head. "Oh, but, Mr. Calder, I was counting on your help tomorrow."

Charles stilled. Ruby could see the struggle in him. He wanted to go with Whit and Henrietta, perhaps to harm his cousin or perhaps to plead his case with the woman he loved. Unfortunately, he would raise questions as to his character as a gentleman if he refused Lady Amelia outright.

"Surely so lovely a woman has no need for my humble assistance," he tried.

Lady Amelia nodded earnestly. "But I do! Lord Danning attempted to teach me to fish today, and I was an utter failure." She put a hand on his arm and trained her big blue eyes on his. "I thought surely an angler of your stature could help me improve."

Lady Amelia might never land a fish, but she had clearly hooked her man. Charles's smile visibly grew, going from polite to downright pleased. "I would be delighted to teach you to fish, Lady Amelia. The others can dine on our success when they return."

Ruby puffed out a sigh of relief. Her feelings must have been evident, for Whit frowned at her.

She offered him a bright smile. "That's settled then. Tomorrow, we attempt the cascade."

He did not argue with her, and when Lady Wesworth demanded his attention a few moments later, he inclined his head to Ruby and the others and went to speak with the marchioness.

But though he played the dutiful host the rest of the evening, Ruby kept remembering the tenderness in his eyes when he'd looked at her. That was the love she'd once dreamed of, that was the future she could claim, if only she could be the woman for him!

Somehow, she made it through the evening and retired with the other guests for bed. She felt certain Quimby would make sure Whit was safe that night. But just in case, she offered a prayer before closing her eyes.

Lord, please protect him. You've taught me so much on this trip, but please be patient with me. I simply don't have the knack for this trust thing.

Then she smiled, realizing that the Lord had just given her an opportunity to practice, for even praying took trust!

So did going with Whit and Henrietta the next day. She kept glancing about, half-afraid to see Charles lurking behind a shrub. She was actually relieved when Henrietta's father insisted on coming with them. Surely the three of them could keep Whit safely away from his cousin. And she couldn't help smiling when she thought of how Lady Amelia would have to learn how to sew a worm.

Just as the sunset had promised, the day was bright,

and Ruby's green-striped walking dress, now cleaned and refurbished from her previous adventure, felt a little warm as she and Henrietta, in a blue-striped walking dress, accompanied Whit and Mr. Stokely-Trent up the hill. Henrietta's father chatted with Whit at first as they walked, asking about his estate in Suffolk, the number of horses in his stables, his various financial interests. Ruby listened, watching the way the sunlight played across Whit's features under his broad-brimmed felt hat when he lifted his head to make a point.

Henrietta, however, was clearly grieving. Her face inside her straw gypsy hat was pale, and she contributed little to the conversation. She didn't once lift her Claude glass, which hung from a chain around her neck, as if she thought there nothing picturesque left to admire.

They'd passed Bellweather Hall and had started the climb toward the Edge when Whit loped ahead to check on the path. Henrietta paused beside Ruby.

"Does he know you care?" she asked.

Now there was plain speaking. For once Ruby found it difficult to answer.

"I hope so," she said, watching as he stood near the crest and surveyed the area like a king considering conquest. "But I haven't told him I love him."

"You should," Henrietta advised, gaze on the path ahead. "We never know what the future brings."

No doubt she wished she'd told Charles her feelings before her father had refused him. But these were different circumstances.

In truth, Ruby longed to talk with Whit as she had when they'd made the walk the first time. But she kept remembering that adventure, the way he'd helped her up and down rocks, the way he'd encouraged her when she'd been afraid, the way he'd kissed her under the cascade. With her mind so full, small wonder her mouth was blocked!

Whit came back along the path toward them, stride confident, head high. In his tweed jacket and chamois trousers, he was the angler who'd first charmed her. When he smiled at her, she felt as if the world had settled just as it should.

Yet she knew it for a lie. He had asked her to trust, and she wasn't trusting. She was within an inch of declaring her fears to Henrietta, of taking her story to the local magistrate, of having Charles arrested. Anything to keep Whit safe! Panic seemed to be building inside her again.

She felt as if the day had dimmed, the breeze chilled. Whit had a vision of the woman he planned to marry, just as she had had a dream for her future husband once. She could not bear to look at him knowing she'd betrayed him by failing to live up to that ideal as surely as Philip had betrayed her.

She excused herself from Henrietta, who went to stand by her father, and moved to meet Whit partway up the hill.

"Whit," she started, "I must tell you something."

He held up a hand. "You know I would ordinarily listen, Ruby. But can you feel that?" He stomped his feet in the mud of the path, and Ruby did feel it, a subtle shifting.

She gasped, and he caught her elbow as if to steady her.

"It's all right," he assured her as Henrietta and her father came up level with them. "It's still unstable," he explained to the group. "I'm afraid I cannot risk taking you to the cascade."

"A shame," Henrietta's father said, drawing a pistol from his coat. "I was hoping to get farther from the house. But this is as good a spot as any to be rid of you, Danning."

He aimed the pistol at Whit's heart.

Chapter Eighteen

Whit stared at the gun, held so firmly in Stokely-Trent's gloved grasp. This couldn't be happening. Just when he'd thought Ruby might be coming around to believe in the good in people, here was someone else proving the bad. Had the entire world gone mad?

"You!" Ruby cried, clearly as shocked, body stiffening beside his. "You caused those accidents!"

"No, he didn't," Henrietta protested, as if that somehow made the current betrayal better. A bead of perspiration ran down her cheek from under her straw hat. "They truly were accidents in the beginning."

"But they gave me the idea," her father said. "Who would question one more accident?"

"So you shot his fishing rod!" Ruby accused, as if that were the worst sin.

"What?" Henrietta demanded.

Whit edged closer to her father. If he could just push the man's hand away, cause him to shoot wildly, Ruby would be safe. The pistol could only hold a single shot. But the thought of that ball striking Ruby nearly stopped Whit's heart.

"I was merely practicing," Stokely-Trent assured

his daughter. He waved the pistol at Whit, who froze. "That's close enough, Lord Danning."

Whit held his ground but spread his hands. "You needn't do this, sir."

"Easy for you to say." His bulldog face was lined with disgust. "You refuse a fine daughter from an excellent family, for what? Coppery curls and an impertinent mouth. Without you, Mr. Calder can have the title and my girl will be a countess as she deserves."

Whit scanned down the man's body, looking for any weakness in the thrusting gut, the sturdy legs. Henrietta stepped closer to her father, as well.

"That's your plan?" she cried. "You promised me you'd reconsider Charles if I did as you asked and arranged this trip. You can't just murder Lord Danning! You have a witness for one, and where would you put the body for another? It just isn't logical!"

"Not particularly moral either," Ruby pointed out as Whit stared at her.

The gun swiveled toward Ruby, and Whit's muscles tightened.

"Oh, Miss Hollingsford is going, too," Henrietta's father promised. "And as for the bodies, I'll simply push them off the cliff and into the mud. We'll claim they fell and were washed down the stream. It will be years before anyone comes upon them." He gestured to the cliff ahead. "Now walk."

Whit felt cold all over. He took a step back, blocking Ruby with his body. If he went down, at least she might have a chance to run before Stokely-Trent could reload.

Ruby pressed her hands against his shoulders, and he felt her breath on the back of his neck. "Act when you can, Whit," she whispered. "I trust you."

The words brought a brief spurt of joy, then determination tamped it down. Before he could act, however, Ruby raised her voice again. "Even the condemned are allowed to speak before they are hung. And all I can say, Lord Danning, is I TOLD YOU SOMEONE WAS TRYING TO KILL YOU! HA!"

Stokely-Trent jerked back in surprise, foot catching on the soft edge of the ground. He wavered, eyes widening, pistol pointing upward. Whit leaped to reach him, clutched the hard barrel in his fingers.

"Father!" Henrietta darted forward, and the path crumbled beneath her feet. She slid away, fingers scrabbling at the dirt.

Her father yanked the pistol from Whit's hand and ran to where she'd disappeared. Out of the corners of his eyes, Whit saw Ruby start forward, as well.

"Back!" he cried. "Stay back, or it will swallow you, too."

Of course, being Ruby, she didn't listen.

Whit's only thought was for her safety. Gathering himself, he shoved back in a loosening shower of dirt. Ruby collided with him, but he turned, nearly falling anew. Blood roaring in his ears, he grasped her about the waist and caught her up in his arms. She gasped, but he didn't allow her a moment to protest. He scrambled up the slope, boots slipping, ribs complaining, found a boulder and shoved Ruby up onto it.

She scrambled to her feet and glared down at him. "Why won't you let me help?"

Chest heaving, he leaned against the rock and glared back. "You said you'd trust me."

Her face crumbled, and she sank onto the rock. The look nearly broke Whit's heart, but he knew he couldn't spare the time to soften his words.

"If anything should happen to me," he called up to

her, "remember what I told you. Stay on rock. You know the way back to the Lodge."

Tears were flowing down her cheeks. "But, Whit…"

He turned back for Henrietta.

Just beyond where they'd stood a few moments ago, the slope had sheared off steeply, tumbling down to the stream. Stokely-Trent stood at the edge as if frozen with fear. Whit approached cautiously, feeling his way. Mud sucked at his boots, pulled at his legs. He stopped just short of Henrietta's father. "Put down the gun and help me save her."

Stokely-Trent swung toward him, gun once more pointed at Whit. This time his hand shook.

"No!" Ruby cried from her vantage point, and he heard her feet scratching at the rock.

"Stay there!" Whit ordered, knowing the rest of the hillside could come down any moment. He kept his gaze on the man before him.

"Your daughter is in danger, sir," Whit said, keeping his voice level. "If you kill me, you lose the chance to save her."

Stokely-Trent blinked as if he'd lost his way. Then he tossed the pistol aside. "Anything you want," he begged. "Just save her."

Whit tugged him back, away from the edge, then knelt to peer over.

Just below the level of the path, the bluestocking clung with one hand to a jutting rock, skirts half buried in mud.

Balancing himself, Whit reached for her. "Give me your hand."

"Why?" she said, sucking back a sob. "There's no reason to live. My father will be hung for attempted murder, my family's reputation will be ruined and I'll never be able to marry the man I love."

He could see the despair on her face. "Listen to me. Take my hands, and let me pull you up. I'll talk to your father. We can forget this ever happened."

For a moment, she vacillated, face twisted as if she feared to hope. Then she reached up her free hand.

Whit lay flat, stretched as far as he could to get both arms under hers. But even as he pulled, he felt the slope beneath him giving. Instead of pulling her up, he was being sucked down. The panic on her face told him she knew it, too.

"Stokely-Trent!" he shouted. "Help us!"

Behind him, nothing moved. Was the man too afraid to help his own daughter?

Whit dug in his knees, his elbows. Still he slipped. He would never marry Ruby, or catch the King of Trout. It seemed Charles would be Lord Danning after all, but Henrietta would not live to see it.

Lord, please, help us!

Something pressed against his boots, tugged him toward safety.

"Easy," Charles said. "We have you."

Glancing back, he saw Ruby clinging to one of his ankles and his cousin the other. Her face was white, her body straining. What was to keep her from being pulled over, too?

He looked to the front again. Terror lined Henrietta's face, and she clung to Whit. His arms strained to hold her, pain building.

He refused to give in to it. All his life he'd lived by duty. If he was to die, he'd die by it, as well.

"Pull!" he shouted to Ruby and Charles.

Slowly, his body came back up the cliff, until he

could find purchase again. Henrietta scrambled over him to collapse in Charles's arms. Her father stood aside, looking as if he'd fallen in on himself.

Breath coming in pants, Whit sat on the cold ground. Though his limbs felt as heavy as the mud around them, that didn't stop them from shaking like leaves on a gusty day.

Ruby slumped beside him, threw her arms around him and hung on as if she'd never let go. Somewhere along the line her bonnet had fallen behind her, so that her glorious hair tumbled free down her back. He leaned into her warmth, buried his face in the cinnamon-scented tresses. Thanksgiving rose up inside him, brought his arms around her, held her close.

Thank You, Lord, for Your mercy.

They were both alive, and now he just had to find a way to convince her to marry him.

Even Ruby's bones seemed to be shaking. She'd thought she'd known terror yesterday when the shot had rung out by the stream. But when she'd seen Whit start to slide, she'd felt as if she were the gold her father melted in his crucible, coming apart and on fire at the same time. All she'd known was that she had to save him.

"I'm so sorry, so sorry," she said, breath catching in a hiccup. "I wanted to do as you'd asked, but…you could have been killed."

Whit patted her hands where she had them wrapped around his chest. "I'm all right, Ruby."

Next to them, Charles had cradled Henrietta in his arms and was murmuring assurances while her father looked on, face drawn and pale.

"He wouldn't have done it," Henrietta said, meeting Whit's and Ruby's gazes in turn. "He couldn't."

Ruby pulled back to stare at her. "You can say that after what he tried? For all I know, you both encouraged him!"

Charles flinched, but Henrietta struggled to sit upright, mud-streaked face ashen. "We didn't. I didn't know what Father had planned when he insisted I arrange this trip today."

"She's telling the truth," her father put in, lifting his head. "I never explained my plans. Couldn't say them aloud. I doubt I would have pulled the trigger, in the end. I shook for an hour after practicing yesterday. But you just wouldn't see reason, Danning. You were so sure this girl was better than my own daughter."

Henrietta pressed her hands together, face anguished. "Oh, Father! I didn't feel slighted. I wouldn't want Danning to choose me, not when I love Charles so much I can't bear the idea of living without him."

Ruby felt ill looking at them. "So run away to Gretna Green," she retorted, hugging Whit close once more. "Tell your father to mind his own affairs. Kindly do something to keep your love without depriving me of mine!"

Henrietta hung her head with a sob, and Charles pulled her back into his arms.

"Have you never felt desperate, Miss Hollingsford?" Mr. Stokely-Trent scolded. "You people have no idea what we endure."

Ruby felt a laugh coming up and knew it for pure hysteria. "No, we certainly don't. I expect that's because we're too busy trying to feed our families or put clothes on their backs."

"Easy," Whit murmured beside her. "He doesn't know what he's saying."

"I know desperation," Charles put in. "That's why I left Lady Amelia and followed you. I hoped to convince Henrietta to marry me, despite her family's wishes." He gave his love a squeeze.

"My wishes no longer matter," Henrietta's father said darkly, shifting on his feet. "I suppose you'll call the constable when we return, Danning."

Whit rose and offered Ruby his hand to help her to her feet. Though she didn't need the help, she refused to let go of his hand. Henrietta's father took a step back as if expecting Whit to strike him.

"No one is going to the constable today," Whit said.

Ruby stared at him. "Why not? He tried to kill you!"

"But I didn't!" Mr. Stokely-Trent protested, holding out both hands as if begging for mercy. "And I only considered it in the first place out of love for my daughter!"

Love? Was that the excuse he would use for such a betrayal? Anger made Ruby release Whit.

"You call that love?" she demanded, voice shaking along with the rest of her. "I've heard the vicar speak of it often enough. Love is patient and kind. It doesn't rejoice in wrongs but at the right."

From beside her, Whit spoke up. Though his voice was quiet, it seemed to echo along the hillside just the same. "'Love bears all things, believes all things, hopes all things.'"

He gazed at her, and Ruby felt the look like a blow to her heart. She knew his statement was another part of the verses she had summarized, but still she struggled with it. If she had simply sat on that boulder and hoped for the best instead of acting, would he be alive now?

Her chin was trembling, too, now, and Whit's face

was blurring with her tears. "You asked me to believe in you, Whit, to trust you. I didn't, not to see to your own future. I distrusted your cousin until the end. And I wasn't far off. Do you truly expect me to stand by and do nothing when I believe you to be in danger?"

Even through her tears, she saw his face tighten, as if she'd hurt him again. "And do you ask me not to protect you?" he replied. "I would sooner stop breathing."

So would she. Her chest felt heavy, painful. She dashed a hand across her eyes to clear her vision. But all she could see was the need for distance, from these people, from this place, from Whit, before he broke her heart. Fear was closing in, and she knew only one way to truly escape it.

She raised her chin, widened her stance, let her hands swing freely. "I would not ask that of you. You are a man of honor, of duty. You have always, ever, been true to yourself and what you believe in. But I can't live the way you expect. I'm so sorry."

She turned and fled.

Chapter Nineteen

Whit started after her, but Charles caught his leg. "Stay. She needs time to think."

"From what I can see, thinking only makes matters worse," Whit countered, shaking him off. He had to catch her, had to tell her he understood.

He'd asked her to trust him, but when he'd been unable to act, she'd been there to help save him. She seemed to think he wanted her to trust and wait; knowing her, he could never ask that of her. He was alive right now because she acted.

He'd never thought to question his definition of love, until Ruby. He'd seen only his father's distress at the loss of his wife. But love wasn't one-sided. It was mutual admiration, mutual protection. It was sharing feelings even when it was uncomfortable. He had to tell her he understood that.

Stokely-Trent cleared his throat. "What do you intend to do with me, then?"

Henrietta's head came up, and Charles was watching Whit, too. He wanted nothing more than to chase after Ruby, but he knew his duty.

"You will give your blessing to your daughter's marriage to my cousin, if he still wishes to align himself with your family."

Charles gazed at Henrietta with a tender smile. "Gladly."

"And none of us will ever speak of this again," Whit continued. "I think you know what would happen to your family's reputation if this incident ever became news."

Stokely-Trent visibly swallowed. "You are very generous, my lord."

"See that you remember that," Whit replied. He went to help Charles raise Henrietta to her feet.

She wavered on the path, clutching at his cousin as if she expected to fall again. With a sigh, Whit draped her arm over his shoulders while Charles came along on the other side. Her father lumbered along behind.

The way back was slow and painful, and not only because of their exertions. All Whit could think of was Ruby. She was clearly trying to have faith in him, in others. Indeed, he realized, she had never completely given up. She had tried to trust, confessed her fears to him freely. Somewhere inside, she still hoped that her concerns about the aristocracy were misplaced.

And where hope lived, love could grow.

Mr. Stokely-Trent said little on their walk, and Charles and Henrietta were both quiet, as well. Whit could only think they, too, were assessing their futures. But as they reached the hill overlooking Bellweather Hall, Charles spoke up.

"While we're confessing things," he said, angling his body to help Henrietta over a bump in the path, "I should tell you, Whit, that I knew Hollingsford before he and Ruby arrived."

"Oh?" Whit replied, only half listening. His mind

had already raced ahead to his reunion with Ruby at the Lodge. There had to be something he could say, something he could do to reach her.

Help me, Lord! I can't lose her!

"Yes," Charles said. "I had him appraise the Danning diamonds. I thought to sell them, you see."

Whit nearly stumbled. "What?"

"Ha!" Stokely-Trent crowed. "I knew you gambled."

At a look from Whit, he quieted.

"I was in a bad way," Charles admitted, with a smile to Henrietta as they descended toward the carriage road. "I didn't see any future for myself. But when it came time to do the deed, I couldn't. You've only ever been a friend to me, Danning. Forgive me for even considering the matter."

Whit wished Ruby could have heard his cousin. For one thing, she'd have felt vindicated to find this theory also validated. But more importantly, perhaps she'd see that while temptations abounded, not all men fell to them.

"There's nothing to forgive," Whit replied. "Just know if you ever find yourself in financial difficulty, come to me, and we'll meet it together."

"That's why you were willing to give up on the idea of marrying me when Father refused to give you his blessing," Henrietta murmured, head once more hanging. "You needed my dowry, which he could withhold if we married without his consent."

Stokely-Trent's eyes narrowed.

"No, love," Charles replied, and Whit saw his grip on her tightening. "I didn't want to pull you into the mess I'd made. I love you too much."

Henrietta's head came up, smile growing. Whit released his hold on her and allowed them a few moments of privacy. Her father squirmed but held his tongue.

Whit hoped to give Henrietta a chance to escape upstairs and change before seeing her mother, so he brought them in through his fishing closet. For once the sight of his rods and flies didn't encourage him to head for the stream. All he wanted was to find Ruby.

Unfortunately, the firing squad called them into the withdrawing room before they could pass.

"Lord Danning," Lady Wesworth declared, rising from the sofa, "your cousin abandoned Amelia on the riverbank." She raised her formidable chin as if prepared to defend her daughter from invaders. "She could have been accosted by ruffians!"

"Now, Mother..." Lady Amelia started, offering Whit an apologetic look from beside the marchioness. She had dressed in her riding habit as if intending to go out. Now she took in the state of his and Henrietta's clothes, and her eyes widened.

Henrietta's mother must have seen the mess at the same time, for she came rushing forward.

"Henrietta!" she shrieked. "Look at your gown! It's ruined! What have you and Lord Danning been doing!"

Henrietta touched her hand to the chest of her gown, and mud fell in a clump to the carpet.

"Miss Stokely-Trent slipped on the hillside and would have fallen if not for Charles's assistance," Whit said with a warning glance to his cousin. "I suggest we allow her to repair to her room to recuperate."

Henrietta smiled at him gratefully, but her mother would have none of it.

"Henrietta!" she scolded. "We told you we would not countenance an alliance between you and Mr. Calder."

"Perhaps you should reconsider," Lady Wesworth

advised, raising a feathered brow. "It seems that may be the best she can do."

Mr. Stokely-Trent reddened, but his wife puffed up, and Whit prepared himself to wade into the fray. Then Henrietta raised her head from off Charles's shoulder.

"Yes, you told me," she said to her mother, "and I despaired. But no more. I love Charles, and I'd marry him if he was an untitled pauper."

"Which I am," Charles admitted, giving her a squeeze. "But I love your daughter, and I'll do all I can to be worthy of her."

Before Mrs. Stokely-Trent could protest anew, Whit stepped between them and his cousin. "I'm sure you'll all need to discuss the matter, once Henrietta has been made comfortable. Excuse me."

He turned for the corridor, but Lady Wesworth's voice called after him, spite evident in each syllable.

"If you're looking for that Hollingsford chit," she said, "you're too late. She called for her carriage some time ago."

Her carriage? She'd run from him on the slope, but surely she wouldn't run away for good…would she? Doubt set his heart to pounding. With a nod to his guests, Whit strode for the front of the house.

His staff opened the door for him just in time to see the Hollingsford coach make the turn out of the drive.

Whit rushed forward, nearly colliding with Quimby, who stood at the edge of the gravel and watched them go. "You are an idiot," Quimby said.

The world had just crumbled like the slope, and Whit could only stare stupidly at him, no doubt confirming his valet's suspicions about his intelligence. "What?"

Quimby shrugged as he turned to face Whit. "It needed to be said. It was clear from the start that you and Ruby Hollingsford were perfect for each other. And she has such an outstanding sense of style." He sighed. "Ah, well. I suppose I'll have to dig deeper for the house party in Suffolk."

"There will be no house party in Suffolk," Whit ordered, backing away. "There is no need. I've chosen a wife, and I intend to catch her." Turning, he ran for the river.

He slipped once on the grass above the bank and nearly went down on the rocks of the shore, but he beat the coach to the bridge and flagged it. The Hollingsford coachman reined in with a smile, and the two servants in the rumble seat were grinning, but their looks were nothing to the smile on Ruby's father's face as he lowered the window.

"Well met, my lord," he declared. "Do I take it you'd like a word with my daughter?"

"I would indeed," Whit said, sucking in a breath from his run. He glanced in the coach, but the seat opposite Hollingsford was empty.

"Funny thing, that," the older man said. "She was so certain it was time to leave, but she couldn't bear it in the end. Jumped right out of the coach shortly after we left the drive. Davis was taking us to that wide spot below the bridge to turn around and go back for her. Unless I'm mistaken, she ought to have reached the river by now."

Whit whirled. A redheaded beauty was careening down the slope, muddy skirts bunched in her fists.

"I'm going to marry your daughter," he tossed over his shoulder before running to meet her.

Where was he? Ruby could scarcely catch her breath. Her ribs hurt, her feet hurt, her face hurt from crying, but worse was the pain in her chest at the thought of leaving Whit.

She'd been so sure leaving was the right thing to do. She could not be the woman he wanted, could not find this illusive faith he so praised. She'd managed to slip into the house unnoticed and had gone straight upstairs to order her maid to pack only the essentials.

Is something wrong, Miss Hollingsford? Mr. Quimby had asked, pausing before the open door to her room.

I'm leaving, she'd said, as if he could have doubted the purpose of her maid throwing her things into a band-box willy-nilly. *Fetch the coach and my father, in that order.*

He'd opened his mouth as if to protest, then peered closer, bowed and gone to do as she'd bid.

All the while something had pulled at her, whispered that she was making a mistake. She'd felt as if hands tugged at the sodden skirts she'd refused to change as she climbed into the coach.

Are you certain? her father had asked.

Tell Davis to drive, Ruby had said, head high and tears falling.

And she'd no more than settled in her seat before her heart tried to break free of her chest.

This was wrong. She was wrong. Years ago, when the bullies had threatened her, she'd run, and she'd promised herself she would never run again. This time, it wasn't a bully after her but the fear of her own making.

She was afraid Whit would hurt her.

Yet he had never hurt her. He'd been kind and considerate from the very first moment he'd seen her at the river. She'd been annoyed by it, railed against it, but there it was. She'd doubted him, and he'd forged ahead. No other had ever been so loving, so determined. She'd thought she'd mastered fear with her boxing, her shooting. But this was a different fear—a fear of opening her heart, and it was what stood between her and Whit.

Even between her and God.

"Stop the coach," she'd said to her father.

He'd frowned, but reached up to rap on the ceiling. *Don't go getting sick on me now,* he'd warned.

Before the coach had even halted, Ruby had thrown herself out the door.

Now she paused on the riverbank, scanned the area. Mr. Quimby had taken one look at her in the doorway and pointed her toward the river. Whit had to be here. She had to see him. She had to tell him the truth, hope that he would still be willing to give her another chance.

Please, Lord, give me another chance! I see the problem now. I won't run again, from him or from You.

"Ruby!"

She gasped in a breath as she sighted Whit. He was coming down the bank from the bridge, pell mell, muddy boots sliding on the rocks. She never doubted he'd make it safely. She ran to meet him at the river's edge.

"Oh, Whit, I believe in you, I do! I love you. I know I've been stupid and headstrong, but if you could ever find it in your heart to... Oh!"

Her perfectly proper earl pulled her into his arms and kissed her, and every other thought, the sound of the river, the feel of the breeze, the pounding of her heart, faded away. She'd been so blind, expecting things that didn't matter. What mattered was this, the two of them, the love between them, spending the rest of their lives together. In his arms, at his side was where she belonged, forever.

When at last he raised his head, his smile sent a delicious shiver through her.

"Ruby Hollingsford," he said, face once more solemn, "I love you. I love that you aren't afraid to speak your mind. I love how you attack problems head-on. I love that you are never still, always moving forward, always acting to protect those you love. I am honored to be counted among their number. I may be a crafty aristocrat, but I will never do anything intentionally to hurt you. Marry me."

Breath still shaky, Ruby managed a nod of approval. "Well said. I accept."

Whit raised his brows. "Just like that?"

Ruby grinned. "Just like that. You've won your wife campaign, my lord."

"Allow me to demonstrate my gratitude." Whit lowered his head to hers once more. Just before she closed her eyes, Ruby saw a massive trout leap from the river.

Whit didn't even notice.

That's when she knew he really loved her.

Epilogue

P eter Quimby stood at the edge of the woods, watching as Whit tenderly kissed his bride-to-be. A smile curved Quimby's lips. He couldn't have imagined a better partner for his friend and master. Whit would give Ruby the place among society that had been denied to her, and she'd help him remember how to have fun again.

Thank You, Lord, for nudging me to invite her.

Yes, things were looking up in any number of ways. Charles Calder had already begged Quimby's pardon. Now Quimby understood how Whit's cousin had narrowly avoided the temptation to steal from the estate. He thought Charles would be a better man for coming through the fire. And what a relief to know most of the accidents truly were nothing but accidents! He suspected something had happened up among the hills today—he'd never seen so much mud in his life! But all seemed to have resolved itself nicely.

Behind him the veranda doors opened so quickly they slammed against the walls on either side. Surprised, he turned to see Lady Amelia running out, with her mother right behind her.

"Stop this instant!" Lady Wesworth ordered, face set and head high.

Lady Amelia turned to meet her mother's outraged gaze. She was dressed in that plum-colored riding habit Quimby longed to update with at least a scarf.

"Forgive me, Mother," she said, her words coming out stiffly, as if each one was spoken painfully. "I know you want the best for me. But I will not pursue Lord Danning. It's clear to me that he loves Miss Hollingsford."

If Lady Wesworth took a few more steps away from the house, it would be clear to her, as well. Quimby melted back among the trees.

Her mother sniffed. "And why not when she all but threw herself into his arms."

Actually, she'd done that, too, Quimby thought with a quick glance down to the river to confirm that Whit and Ruby were still standing there kissing.

"I can't promote myself to a gentleman in that way," Lady Amelia protested. "It's not in my nature. And I think it only right that the man I marry appreciate me for myself."

Lady Wesworth bore down on her daughter as if she would seize her and carry her back into the house. "The man you marry must be a credit to your family. That is the purpose of marrying."

Quimby raised his brows. Lady Amelia raised her head. "No, Mother. I don't believe that anymore. Marriage, a true marriage, should be about the meeting of hearts and minds, of two becoming one. That's what we should look for in a match."

"Oh, Amelia." Lady Wesworth stopped just short of her daughter with a sigh. "That Hollingsford girl has filled your head with nonsense. Perhaps the lower classes wed on a whim, but we know better. We marry for proper reasons, like advancement and alignment of property."

She took a step back from her mother. "Is that why you married Father? There must be more to life than that cold existence."

Lady Wesworth stiffened. "How dare you! You've no idea what I've endured for your sake, ungrateful child!"

Lady Amelia turned and fled. Her mother clutched her chest a moment, as if her daughter's behavior had truly pained her, then retreated to the house, shutting the doors quietly behind her. A few moments later, and Quimby spotted Lady Amelia riding out of the stables, encouraging her horse to fly.

It seemed Lord Danning wasn't the only one to benefit from an acquaintance with Ruby Hollingsford. Lady Amelia was trying her wings, and Quimby could only applaud her.

Come to think of it, her ladyship had begun acting strangely after the visit to Hollyoak Farm. Her maid had complained of the fact when the servants had gathered to eat. Could Lady Amelia have felt the first pangs of amour at the sight of Lord Hascot? Was that why she was now so set on marrying only for love?

Quimby had known John, Lord Hascot, nearly as long as he'd known Whit. The fellow had all too many reasons to avoid marriage, not the least of which was a first love that had gone horribly wrong. But perhaps if Quimby put a word in the ear of Hascot's veterinarian, Marcus Fletcher, the seed of romance might be planted. After all, if Quimby could mount a successful campaign to find Whit a wife, what was to say that

Fletcher couldn't wage a campaign to make Hascot a proper husband?

All Hascot needed was the good Lord's help and a little nudge from the master matchmakers.

* * * * *

Dear Reader,

I hope you enjoyed the story of the fishing earl and the jeweler's daughter. Whit and Ruby were both truly Originals, as they said in the Regency period, and I quite agree with the wily Quimby that they make a good pair. I'm sure they'll go on to celebrate many anniversaries together at Fern Lodge.

I will admit I'm not much of a fisher, but I am indebted to Izaak Walton, for writing a most enlightening book about the fine art of fishing, and to Earl Sutton, for helping me see why so many still love the sport today.

If you'd like to learn more about fishing in the Regency, please visit my website at www.reginascott.com. You can also find me online at my blog at www.nineteenteen.com or my Facebook page at www.facebook.com/authorreginascott. I look forward to hearing from you.

Blessings!
Regina Scott

Questions for Discussion

1. Ruby has a lifetime of betrayals to prove to her that she should not trust, not even God. How can those who have been hurt learn to trust the Lord?

2. Ruby's fear makes her hesitate to love. How can we learn to trust other people?

3. The other guests treat Ruby with disdain at first. On what should we judge others?

4. Whit believes in honoring the responsibilities placed upon him. When is it appropriate to step away from a responsibility?

5. Ruby realizes that many expectations are placed on those with power and privilege. When should expectations be honored?

6. Lady Amelia and Henrietta struggle to meet their parents' expectations for marriage. When should we refuse the expectations placed upon us?

7. Peter Quimby takes it upon himself to find his master a bride. How should we help others reach their goals?

8. Ruby's father wants her to marry into the aristocracy to improve her future. What kinds of goals should we have for our children?

9. Ruby has taken many steps to protect herself. What steps are appropriate today?

10. Ruby struggles to see God as caring about her personally. How much does the Lord love His children?

11. Ruby fears that faith means waiting patiently for something to happen. When is it appropriate to wait on the Lord?

12. Ruby sometimes acts without thinking. When is it appropriate to take action?

13. Whit confuses his devotion for duty. What duty do we owe the Lord and others?

14. The story had several themes. What was your favorite?

15. How have you seen that theme played out in your own life?

COMING NEXT MONTH FROM
Love Inspired® Historical

Available January 7, 2014

CLAIMING THE COWBOY'S HEART
Cowboys of Eden Valley
Linda Ford

Jayne Gardiner is determined never to be a damsel in distress again. But when her shooting lesson goes awry, she must nurse an injured cowboy back on his feet. Will he walk away with her heart?

LONE WOLF'S LADY
Judy Duarte

Outspoken suffragist Katie O'Malley and guarded bounty hunter Tom McCain couldn't be more different. With a child's life in danger these opposites must find a way to work together—or risk losing each other forever!

THE WYOMING HEIR
Naomi Rawlings

Rancher Luke Hayes wants nothing to do with his estranged grandfather's inheritance—or the floundering local girl's school in need of a donation. But will beautiful Elizabeth Wells teach him the importance of family—and love?

JOURNEY OF HOPE
Debbie Kaufman

Even the perils of the Liberian jungle won't discourage missionary Anna Baldwin from fulfilling her calling. It isn't until Stewart Hastings arrives that she realizes the greater danger may be falling for the wounded veteran.

LIHCNM1213

REQUEST YOUR FREE BOOKS!

2 FREE INSPIRATIONAL NOVELS
PLUS 2
FREE
MYSTERY GIFTS

Love Inspired
HISTORICAL
INSPIRATIONAL HISTORICAL ROMANCE

YES! Please send me 2 FREE Love Inspired® Historical novels and my 2 FREE mystery gifts (gifts are worth about $10). After receiving them, if I don't wish to receive any more books, I can return the shipping statement marked "cancel." If I don't cancel, I will receive 4 brand-new novels every month and be billed just $4.74 per book in the U.S. or $5.24 per book in Canada. That's a saving of at least 21% off the cover price. It's quite a bargain! Shipping and handling is just 50¢ per book in the U.S. and 75¢ per book in Canada.* I understand that accepting the 2 free books and gifts places me under no obligation to buy anything. I can always return a shipment and cancel at any time. Even if I never buy another book, the two free books and gifts are mine to keep forever.

102/302 IDN F5CN

Name _____ (PLEASE PRINT) _____

Address _____ Apt. # _____

City _____ State/Prov. _____ Zip/Postal Code _____

Signature (if under 18, a parent or guardian must sign) _____

Mail to the **Harlequin®** Reader Service:
IN U.S.A.: P.O. Box 1867, Buffalo, NY 14240-1867
IN CANADA: P.O. Box 609, Fort Erie, Ontario L2A 5X3

Want to try two free books from another series?
Call 1-800-873-8635 or visit www.ReaderService.com.

* Terms and prices subject to change without notice. Prices do not include applicable taxes. Sales tax applicable in N.Y. Canadian residents will be charged applicable taxes. Offer not valid in Quebec. This offer is limited to one order per household. Not valid for current subscribers to Love Inspired Historical books. All orders subject to credit approval. Credit or debit balances in a customer's account(s) may be offset by any other outstanding balance owed by or to the customer. Please allow 4 to 6 weeks for delivery. Offer available while quantities last.

Your Privacy—The Harlequin® Reader Service is committed to protecting your privacy. Our Privacy Policy is available online at www.ReaderService.com or upon request from the Harlequin Reader Service.

We make a portion of our mailing list available to reputable third parties that offer products we believe may interest you. If you prefer that we not exchange your name with third parties, or if you wish to clarify or modify your communication preferences, please visit us at www.ReaderService.com/consumerschoice or write to us at Harlequin Reader Service Preference Service, P.O. Box 9062, Buffalo, NY 14269. Include your complete name and address.

LIH13R

Bygones's intrepid reporter is on the trail of the town's mysterious benefactor. Will she succeed in her mission? Read on for a preview of COZY CHRISTMAS by Valerie Hansen, the conclusion to

THE HEART OF MAIN STREET *series.*

Whitney Leigh rolled her eyes. "Romance! It's getting to be an epidemic."

Because she was alone in the car she didn't try to temper her frustration. Fortunately, this time, the editor of the *Bygones Gazette* had assigned her to write a new series about the Save Our Streets project's six-month anniversary. If he had asked her for one more fluff piece on recent engagements, she would have screamed.

Parking in front of the Cozy Cup Café, she shivered and slid out.

As a lifelong citizen of Bygones she was supposed to have been perfect for the job of ferreting out the hidden facts concerning the town's windfall. Too bad she had failed. Instead of an exposé, she'd ended up filling her column with news of people's love lives. But she was not going to quit investigating. No, sir. Not until she'd uncovered the real facts. Especially the name of their secret benefactor.

She stepped inside the Cozy Cup.

"What can I do for you?" Josh Smith asked.

Whitney was tempted to launch right into her real reason for being there. Instead, she merely said, "Fix me something warm?"

"Like what?"

"Surprise me."

She settled herself at one of the tables. There was something unique about this place. And, truth to tell, the same went for the other new businesses on Main. Each one had filled a need and become an integral part of Bygones in a mere five or six months.

Josh Smith was a prime example. He was what she considered young, yet he had quickly won over the older generations as well as the younger ones.

He stepped out from behind the counter with a steaming cup in one hand and a taller, whipped-cream-topped tumbler in the other.

"Your choice," he said pleasantly, placing both drinks on the table and joining her as if he already knew this was not a social call.

"I see you're not too busy this afternoon. Do you have time to talk?"

"I always have time for my favorite reporter," he said.

"How many reporters do you know?"

"Hmm, let's see." A widening grin made his eyes sparkle. "One."

Will Whitney get her story and find love in the process?
Pick up COZY CHRISTMAS to find out.

Available December 2013 wherever
Love Inspired® Books are sold.